THE END BEGINS

by

Braxton DeGarmo

Christen Haus Publishing

COPYRIGHT

DEDICATION

This book is dedicated to all families who have lost children to trafficking and to those dedicated to finding them.

ACKNOWLEDGMENTS

As always, I again want to acknowledge and thank my dear wife, Paula, for her valuable proofreading skills, help, and encouragement. BTW, with the retirement of my other proofreader, I also decided to try *Grammarly* for additional error checking. If you find any errors, it missed them.

Plus, a big thank you to my editor, Patrick LoBrutto. His feedback always makes my stories better.

And finally, my sincerest compliments to Adrijus Guscia for his incredible covers.

ONE

February . . .

"Wha . . .? No, no, you can't be here!"

Adam Afton couldn't believe his eyes as he peered through the peephole of his apartment door and saw his colleague, Sam Renner, standing in the hallway. He quickly opened the door, looked up and down the hallway, and pulled the man by his jacket into the room. His heart raced, and cold sweat appeared on his brow.

"Man, you shouldn't be . . . Why did you come here? W-we had agreed not to come to each other's place."

Sam looked ragged, disheveled as if he hadn't slept for days. But then, Adam hadn't seen much of the back of his eyelids either since the two had met and confided in one another four days earlier. What had started as a simple "How ya doin'?" had devolved into a nightmare neither man wanted nor anticipated.

"You shouldn't have come here."

For the past five years, Adam had made a point of living as much off the grid as he could, outside of work where he was so profoundly part of that grid, he felt like an electron bouncing between nodes on the deep web. Sam's presence brought the grid to *him*.

He had provided no physical address to his employer, other than The UPS Store, where he maintained a postal box. His first Single Scope Background Investigation had been performed upon employment at CCS before his move off-grid. It resulted in his obtaining a Top Secret/SCI—Sensitive Compartmented Information—clearance level. With the onset of the Continuous Clearance program and its use of risk- and event-driven re-evaluations rather than calendar-driven assessments, his security clearance had not been risked by his move. By other things, yes, but not by the move.

His employer had his cell phone number, but out of caution, he made a point of turning that phone off and keeping it in a lead-foil-lined briefcase whenever he left work. On those nights when he was "on-call," he stayed in a motel closer to the office. He used a burner phone to talk with his family and his girlfriend.

Well, ex-girlfriend. She had given him up as a lost cause months earlier. He couldn't blame her. They had met while he was in rehab at the lowest point in his life. She was someone who'd been there, who understood some of what he was going through . . . still slogging through. Yet, there were too many things he couldn't share with her . . . like, what he did for a living.

Despite caring for her, he had made the hard decision not to fight to keep her because he didn't want her to get hurt because of him or what he'd discovered. And the hardest part of *that* had been not being free to tell her *why* he wasn't begging her to stay. The less she knew, the better. Who wants to stay with someone with secrets?

His ex-wife, Rachel, had been an exception. They had

been college sweethearts, the perfect couple, Ken and Barbie. His crunchy peanut butter to her sweet jelly. With one child—their two-year-old son, Arthur—and another on the way, he had been offered the job at CCS with all of its security clearances and work he couldn't share with anyone outside of those with whom he worked. That was okay with her, as long as there were no other secrets between them. There hadn't been.

And then came that tragic day three years later that changed everything. A day that was supposed to be a fun one in the park. A day that destroyed their family. She blamed him. Her family accused him. His family wavered between support and blame. Yet, he blamed himself. A month later, she and Arthur were gone. Maybe it was that hole in his heart he was trying to fill in with the ex-girlfriend. Maybe only Rachel could fill it.

The divorce was not so much acrimonious as it was the wrong stick in a game of Jenga®. She won all custodial rights and left for parts unknown. He began a trip through the bottle and might have lost everything if it hadn't been for his little brother. Where had the kid gotten so much insight and wisdom? So much faith?

"Sorry. I made sure no one followed. I drove around for an hour, stopped at a convenience store to check for anyone following me, doubled around the neighborhood. I even parked two blocks away and walked. I didn't see anyone. No one. Period. Not even that nosy, old lady across the street you always complain and laugh about."

Adam sighed. The old lady was fiction, like all of his stories about his neighbors. He had justified choosing the apartment he now called home for three reasons, of which one was its anonymity. He knew names from mailboxes only. The occasional face he might recognize could belong to any one of those names. Still, he'd never be able to place one with the other.

He had provided Sam with his address in a moment of weakness. He regretted that now.

Adam walked to his fridge and retrieved two beers. He knew he needed something to help calm his nerves. He offered one to Sam, who raised his palm to decline.

"No, thanks. I need more than that, but I don't want to risk getting a foggy brain. We get enough of that from rebreathing the carbon dioxide in our masks at work."

Adam nodded and placed both cans back in the refrigerator. His friend had a good point.

"So, why are you here? We came up with a plan, and we need to stick to it."

Sam began to pace in front of Adam's large-screen television in the front room. "I know, I know. I-I just don't think I can go back to work tomorrow and act as if everything is normal. We know too much. I don't want to get 'Clintoned.' "

At one time, Adam would have chuckled at that comment. The ex-president and his ex-secretary of state wife had been the butt of many jokes and memes about dealing with their "enemies" through questionable suicides and robberies-gone-bad. Upon comparing "notes," he and Sam had discovered proof of who was behind many, if not all, of those mysterious deaths. The Clintons had played their roles well. In return, they were under the protection of powerful men.

President Eisenhower had once warned against letting

the military-industrial complex get too powerful. If he were president now, he might recognize Big Pharma and Big Tech as part of that modern technocracy that pulled politicians' and bureaucrats' strings throughout the government and protected those most useful to them.

"We talked about that. We just need a bit more information to blow the whistle. We can only get that through our computers at work. And once we go public, they won't go after us. It would be too obvious."

"Would it? I wish I was as convinced."

Adam had his doubts, too. Yet, he had worked through the issues, as well as the names they could out. There were U.S. attorneys and an Attorney General at the Department of Justice who would take their proof and run with it. But the timing was critical. The next presidential election could change everything. President Graham was pro-law and order and had promised to clean house. His challenger was a socialist and globalist aligned with the technocracy.

"You know, we could have talked this through again on the phone. We both have secure burners. You didn't need to come here in person."

Sam stopped pacing and stood looking squarely at Adam. He reached behind his back and pulled a disc out from under his jacket. He'd had it stashed in his waistband at the small of his back. Sam also took a flash drive from his left pants pocket and then extended both to Adam.

"I came to give you these. It's all the data I've collected, the stuff I told you about. I want out—"

As Adam took the items, he saw the red dot on Sam's temple, and his mind shut down for a microsecond in disbelief. Recovering from the shock of what he knew was coming, he dove to the floor, trying to take Sam with him, as the window shattered a blink before Sam's head followed suit.

He rose to his hands and knees, his breathing and heart rate again accelerating, and scrambled toward his bedroom. He rolled to his left as a bullet tore through the floor where he'd just been. This time he stood and sprinted from the room. Another shot hit the frame of the doorway to his bedroom as he ran toward his closet. He was out of view from the window, but the killer, or killers, would waste no time coming for him.

His appreciation for this particular apartment grew ten-fold. He grabbed his "go bag" from the closet, stashed Sam's data inside, and ran to the second bedroom, which he used as an office. He had been searching for clues to his daughter's abduction when he first discovered what became his treasure trove of incriminating evidence several months earlier. He needed more than a smoking gun but knew he might one day have to escape and go to ground. He had taken the time and spent the funds required to make that happen.

With Sam's adding several missing pieces to his puzzle, they raced against the clock to blow the whistle. Now, Adam was too late. And yet, he was sure he was closing in on finding her . . . and that was paramount to him. He wouldn't give up. And for her sake, he couldn't let them find him.

Inside the "office," he raced to the bookcase. It appeared to be built in, but that was the point of his craftsmanship. He pushed one specific title on the top shelf, and the case eased away from the wall, opening just wide enough to allow him egress through it. The route took him into a small janitorial closet adjacent to that wall of his apartment, which opened into a rarely used service hallway. He had installed cameras both in the closet and hallway to assess their feasibility as an escape route. After six weeks of review, he felt satisfied that they would work. The building janitor used the area twice a week. The other residents appeared either to not know of the hallway's existence or to need its use.

He quickly pulled the wall shut and latched a separate hidden lock that would prevent the bookcase from opening again from inside the apartment. By the time his pursuers discovered what happened to him, he would be long gone—if they ever figured it out.

He pulled his phone from his pocket and opened an app he had developed. That app had been created to give him access to the small brick computer he used to monitor the cameras focused on the hallway and closet. However, it also allowed him to keep an eye on a camera in his front room and doorway. He checked and confirmed that it had caught the events of moments ago. He directed that computer to forward the video and audio files to an off-site location, his personal version of the cloud, and to continue to do so. Now, he could only hope that they wouldn't find the computer before it uploaded its files showing who would undoubtedly enter his apartment in short order.

"Short order" was the key phrase in his mind. He needed to get out of there. He opened the closet door, checked to make sure the hall was clear, and raced toward the back of the building.

The large service elevator—used by people moving in and out with furniture and boxes—opened both to this service hallway and the main hallway's back end. On the first floor, it opened next to a set of double doors leading to the alley—again used primarily for moving things in and out. He expected those doors to be covered, and he would be fully exposed by using them. Even activating the elevator could clue in the killers to his movement. As such, he made use of the fire stairwell and ran to the basement.

There he would make use of his third and final justification for renting the apartment—a utility tunnel connecting his building with its twin across the alley. He hurried through the tunnel, down a basement hallway past various storage units for the other apartment building's occupants, and up a flight of steps to a fire exit on the opposite side of the building.

After checking the street, he ran across to an alley on the other side. Two blocks later, he slowed down and caught his breath. He then entered a long-term parking facility to his left, where he had rented a space for a six-year-old Chevy Sonic registered to a different name. He tossed his bag into the trunk and climbed behind the wheel. From the glove compartment, he pulled out a cheap costume beard, the kind that hooked to both ears like a mask. In keeping with the times, he had attached a real surgical mask to it so that he would appear to be a bearded man wearing a mask in his car. He topped off the disguise with cheap black glasses, frame only, and a baseball cap. Even a blind man could see past the disguise up close, but he would be driving in traffic and have the additional advantage of slightly tinted windows. Anyone looking for him wouldn't glance twice at the image he presented now.

He had multiple options for getting out of the city. He

reasoned they would expect him to head north into Maryland from his location in the capital's northern neighborhoods, using one of two main arteries—16th Street NW or U.S. 29. Both would be the fastest ways for him to get out of Washington. Both would be covered if they were looking for him hard enough, which he had to assume to be the case.

Instead, he drove south and cut west past the National Zoological Park. From there, Connecticut Ave. NW would take him toward Bethesda. He picked up I-495, the Capital Beltway, and then I-270 to head northwest. Only then did he feel comfortable removing the beard and glasses, having left the traffic cameras behind him. An hour later, he drove down the gravel drive to a small rural cabin he had prepared for such a contingency, his mind weighing heavy with the few options before him.

TWO

March . . .

Lt. Gen. (Ret) Wallace Chamberlain was not a man accustomed to failure. How hard was it to find one man?

He stood at the floor-to-ceiling windows of his top-floor office in the Custodia Circumdant Systems, Inc. building and watched as the sun set over the Washington, DC skyline. The Washington Monument's obelisk reflected the golden glow of that late-day light—the "Golden Hour" photographers called it.

The White House, too, would take on an amber ambiance at this time of day. Although he could not see the West Wing from his current vantage point, he remembered it well from his days of distinguished service as the Director of National Intelligence under the previous administration. While disappointment surrounded that appointment at first—he had been promised the Secretary of State position, only to have it given to *that* woman—he came to relish the job . . . for more reasons than the obvious ones.

Compared to him, J. Edgar Hoover would be deemed an amateur in collecting dirt on those who opposed him, as well as "friends" who might turn on him in the future. Where

Wallace once had rank and the UCMJ to keep those under him in order, he now had "intelligence" to control those in power and authority. 'Dirty little secrets' was an oft-used phrase for such blackmail potential. He preferred dirty *big* secrets, especially those with long-term prison potential.

And yet, one man held such information on him.

Wallace hated orange. It was a garish color not suited to his clothing tastes, whether in a golf polo or a necktie. And certainly not for an ill-fitting, warden-issued jumpsuit.

Yes, one man held the key to Wallace's wearing orange for the rest of his life. That one man had disappeared from the face of the earth a month earlier, and his best operators had yet to find him.

Speaking of which, the soft tones from his desk phone announced the arrival of one of those men, his last appointment of the day, although it was one for which no record would be kept. He pushed a button on his desk console to unlock the door. As the lock buzzed, the heavy, lead-lined door opened with ease, and his subordinate entered the room.

Henry "Buck" Buckner walked across the luxuriously appointed room with a confident swagger and stood opposite the large desk from his boss. His face held no clue as to whether he had good news or bad for Wallace. The older man had once felt the displeasure of playing poker with Buckner. He never made that mistake again.

The two had served together in Iraq and then Afghanistan, where Wallace held his final command before "retiring" to the White House. He had trusted Buckner with his life then, and he trusted him with it still. But then, the sentiment was mutual, and Wallace had twice saved the life of the then-Special Ops Ranger. Literally. They'd been through hell and back. Figuratively.

Wallace motioned to the chair closest to the man, walked around his desk, and sat opposite Buck. The man did not sit until he, his "senior officer," sat down.

"Well?"

"Sir, I wish I had the news you want to hear. We still have no idea where Afton has gone to ground. But, at the same time, nothing incriminating has reared its ugly face to confront you or CCS. The deep web is unusually quiet these days, and our friends at Google, Twitter, and Facebook have ramped up their surveillance. They're clamping down hard on conservative viewpoints and fake news. Between them, if anything at all surfaced regarding CCS or you, we'd know it."

Wallace nodded. He appreciated Buck's use of the term "fake news." Both knew the reality of that concept. Both were postmodern men. One man's truth was another man's folly. Truth was relative. Who could be assured they truly "knew" anything? Facts were what those in power wanted them to be. The heads of Big Tech were on the same wavelength as Wallace and the executive board on that one.

"We even put the latest version of AlterNet on alert for anything Afton might have or wish to expose. Grimes is tweaking those search parameters almost daily, but so far, nothing."

"I'm not optimistic there. Afton knows AlterNet better than anyone, even Grimes. If anyone can figure out how to avoid it, Afton can."

AlterNet was but one component of Wallace's intelligence-gathering operation and government contract work, albeit a potent one. Developed with taxpayer funds for the 4th Psychological Operations Group working in Afghanistan to defeat the Taliban, the private contractors hired to do the work had made sure they kept their intellectual property rights, despite the public funding. In those days, the system was controlled by analysts who collected vast amounts of information on individual Afghani citizens to push the right buttons to defeat the Taliban politically.

Now privately owned as AlterNet, its artificial intelligence collected and analyzed such data much faster, thanks to the world's acceptance of the Internet, cell phones, and social media platforms. The system could focus on a single individual, a group, or even a population-at-large using localization or L-10N technology and learn so much more than what they ate for breakfast that day. They could monitor their travel, daily routines, spending habits, and more while understanding their fears, their biases, their anxieties, their secrets, with whom they associated, with whom they slept, and on and on. With enough information on someone, they could accurately predict how that person would react to anything.

These contractors had also done work for the Department of Defense on developing capabilities for Interactive Internet Activities, or IIA, to support their Computer Network Operations. For this, hacking was an essential skill. The result was CCS's actual influence operations, a form of social media psychological warfare. The behavioral targeting that they could now perform had not even been dreamt of two decades ago. Their influence operations were currently being aimed at the next presidential election using a man-made pandemic to stoke public anxieties. They weren't going to be blindsided by the re-election of President Graham, as they had been by his election four years earlier.

All this "power" and information technology, but they couldn't find one man.

"Any further blowback about Renner?"

"No, sir. As you know, our clean-up crew got to his body and sanitized that apartment before anyone noticed and contacted the police. The family filed a missing persons report two days later, but we covered that with the story of a last-minute overseas assignment. Thanks to the complete dossiers on each family member, we've created realistic emails to communicate with his family. To them, he's still alive, but I believe his death in a tragic accident is scheduled for early next week. No body for recovery."

"Yes, I'm aware of that. Make sure we offer to pay for a memorial service and to assist the family with insurance claims."

Buck nodded. "Already in the works. Obit is written and just waiting for the actual date when the plug is pulled."

"Good. Renner was a good man. Too bad he went outside his boundaries. Compartmentalization is critical, and we need to keep tight control of it."

Unfortunately, they had gotten lax, and Renner and Afton had managed to confer and share what each worked on. Of all the possible combinations for collaboration, these two getting together was the worst. They had enough information to take down Wallace and CCS with it, and that would only be the first in a house of cards.

"Yes, sir. We've implemented new procedures and

increased the frequency of routine surveillance on all employees. I'm just glad Renner came up for an audit when he did. Another week might have been catastrophic."

You have no idea, thought Wallace. Even Buck worked within his own compartment. Only Wallace and the executive board had the privilege to see the broader picture.

Wallace scrutinized his friend, or at least the closest thing he had to a friend. Fifteen years after their last Middle East tour together, the man still looked honed and ready for any action. Wallace kept up his physical training program. Twenty-five years of active-duty service had made that a habit. Yet, he could see differences, changes he could only attribute to age.

"How's your racquetball game these days?"

Buck grinned. "Why? Ready for me to whip you again?"

Wallace smiled. Yes, he was. It was a small price to pay to keep Buck on his side. Someone had once said that loyalty was earned. With their history, both had earned the commitment of the other. And yet, Wallace had learned on his own that sometimes a little give, instead of taking, was best for morale. It made a boss appear more human, someone employees could better relate to, which, in turn, made them more likely to work harder when asked. If things went south, he might have to ask a lot more of Buck.

Late May 2020

THREE

Aric Afton stopped at the curb and glanced back at his family home. The sense of loss he felt seemed a bit overwhelming, certainly more than he had anticipated. Aric had wrestled with the idea of leaving for weeks. Even now, he questioned whether or not he was making the right decision.

He had grown up in a loving, solid Christian home and with a church family he cherished. He thought his faith to be strong. And yet, his prayers for guidance seemed to float out into the cosmos, never to be heard again. Was this a test? He acknowledged that his life was sheltered. His close friends were church kids. His activities centered around their youth group. In school, no one hassled him because he was at the top of his class and a respected athlete. In reality, he'd never faced a real challenge to his beliefs. And, he'd never had to make such an important decision, one that could affect the rest of his life.

Was he doing the right thing? Where was God when he needed an answer?

He loved his family. And he did not question their love for him. He felt that he simply needed to spread his wings, strike out on his own, exert his independence. Whatever the cliche of the day might be.

His sisters relished *their* independence. All older than him, the oldest, Gwyneth, was now married, living an hour away, and pregnant with their first child. She had completed her doctorate in education, which put her on a fast track to become a high school principal. Her personal career map would take her back to teaching at a collegiate level after five years of "real world" experience. Next in line, Eloise just graduated from college and had been accepted into her first choice of MBA programs. Mabel, the sister just above him in the pecking order, would be a junior in college, working toward a nursing degree. All over-achievers, like their parents.

As the youngest of five, he felt as if his folks were clinging to him, afraid of the inevitable empty nest. His mom, in particular, seemed to shadow his every move. His dad harped almost daily on his need to attend college, now that he'd graduated from high school. Having been the valedictorian of his class of nearly 600 students hadn't helped that situation, in Aric's opinion. Aided by numerous calls from his school's guidance counselor, the two double-teamed him. He was too bright to ignore college. He was the smartest of all his siblings. He could really go places. What could they do to help motivate him?

Nothing.

He recognized that his intellect was the largest part of the problem. High school, even his advanced placement classes, had failed to stimulate him. He anticipated college to be much of the same—boring. He needed a year, at least, to explore new options. He hoped to find a field of study that would motivate him and *give* him a goal worthy of working toward. He had argued for taking a gap year to do just that.

His father and counselor saw that as a waste of time. His dad told him he'd have to get a job and help support himself if he did that. He wouldn't let any son of his live in the basement and mooch off them while playing video games. Aric saw that for what it was, a psychological ploy based on a stereotype that Aric didn't come close to filling.

Now? He would call his dad's bluff.

A vehicle screeched to a stop next to him—his buddy, Dan Lewis, in his beat-up old Jeep Wrangler. Dan faced a similar home life, unbearable but for different reasons. Together, they planned to head west to explore their options. Both were 18, adults. No one could stop them.

"Dude, you ready?"

Aric opened the door and threw his backpack into the back seat while keeping close control of the bag with his laptop, cash, and other necessary valuables. He climbed into the passenger seat.

"Yeah, I'm ready."

Was he? Really? His heart raced a bit in guarded excitement. Yes! He was ready, but for one issue.

"Next stop Denver. I've got a cousin who said we can stay with him for a few days there."

"Sweet."

Minutes later, the Jeep pulled onto I-270, the outer beltway around St. Louis, before picking up westbound I-70. Aric felt a twinge of melancholy as he watched familiar suburbs and old haunts pass by. Memories.

As they sped through St. Charles, Missouri, Dan asked, "How'd your folks take it?"

"Huh?"

"How'd they take your leaving to go west?"

Aric took a deep breath. "They don't know yet. They'll find my letter when they get home from work."

Dan shook his head. "Dude, you sure about this? I mean, how they gonna take this? You know, with your brother and all."

That was the one issue. Adam's disappearance three months earlier weighed heavily on all of them. He was the oldest child, almost ten years older than Aric. He still idolized his big brother, the one with the cool job he couldn't tell anyone about, not even Aric.

Fear for his brother's safety had almost overwhelmed Aric that first month. Someone from a company called Custodia Circumdant Systems had come to their home to personally let his parents know that Adam was on a special assignment overseas and would be incommunicado. And yet, it didn't take a brain surgeon to see that some of the questions they asked revealed that they, too, had no idea where Adam was and hoped to gain some insight into his location, hoping he'd been in contact with his family.

What had his brother gotten himself into?

While Aric had once been determined to leave, Adam's disappearance had changed his mind. As Dan had implied, how would his parents respond to "losing" both sons? He couldn't do that to them. Aric honored his parents. That didn't mean he always had to agree with them, but he respected their feelings and needs and didn't wish to hurt them.

Yet, only a week ago, something happened to put Aric back on the path he had first planned, although with a different destination. He hoped his letter would put them at ease, even if it was sparse on details or reasons. Part of him wanted to go back and explain things to them, but then he might never leave. And he *had* to go.

He had received a postcard from Paris. He knew no one in France, nor anyone traveling there. In fact, travel bans existed due to the pandemic. Borders were closed. But that wouldn't stop someone from asking a friend or acquaintance in Paris to help. It wouldn't stop someone creative from buying a postcard, mailing it and some cash in an envelope to the postmaster of the central post office at the Louvre, and requesting him to repost the card to provide, say, a child with a Parisian postal stamp for his "collection." Who would be hard-hearted enough to deny a kid something new for his stamp collection?

Besides the post card's apparent French origin, the nondescript, block letter message was in French, and one number in Aric's home address was faintly underlined. To Aric, only one sender could have reached out to him like this.

While their sisters had taken Spanish in high school, he and Adam spoke both French and Spanish fluently and had a passing ability with Italian. Also, when he was in college, his brother had played a game with Aric—passing along encrypted messages only they could "read." Their gifting with languages had made cryptography a natural extension.

Using the underlined number as the key, the card's message was unmistakable: Portland OR 97204 6-5 gen del Josh Lewis. Aric would find his brother, or another clue to his whereabouts, at that zip code's post office on June 5th under the general delivery name of Josh Lewis. What wasn't clear in the note was Adam's reason for reaching out like that.

Was he in trouble? Why Portland? He could have sent

Aric to a local post office for another secret message. Maybe, if he was in trouble, he couldn't risk being seen in St. Louis. So he went as far away as possible. Maybe. Maybe this. Or maybe that. Aric had racked his brain over all the maybes. For once, his intellect alone wasn't going to solve the problem.

He had to act now. He felt rushed. Denver tomorrow. Portland in one week. Arranging the trip with Dan had taken longer than he expected, but Dan was crucial to the plan. Daniel Joshua Lewis was his means to getting there on time, as well as his means for retrieving the letter.

As he drove into rural Missouri, Dan glanced at his friend in wonder. Two things, no, three popped into his mind at that moment.

First, he remained amazed that they were friends. Aric was the top of their class, the brainiac. He'd been accepted to every university he'd applied to, with offers of full scholarships at all but one. Dan was maybe in the upper part of the lower third of the class and had the local technical college in his future, provided he stuck around.

Aric, with his fancy language skills, had the girls swooning. At least that's what Dan's sister told him, even if the girls denied it. Aric's hamming it up had even won Heather Howard's heart. She was gorgeous, the senior Homecoming Queen, and the focus of sweet dreams for most of the guys at school. Dan hadn't gotten to first base with the class tart, to use a more polite description. Aric was a goody-two-shoes, per Dan's alcoholic stepfather. Dan? Well, he might not have been the class's ultimate bad boy, but he'd been in his share of trouble.

How was it they were friends? Maybe opposites really did attract.

Breaking the silence of the past 20 minutes, Dan said, "I still don't understand why you're leaving. You've got everything going for you. Everything I wish I could have."

Aric squirmed for a second. "I, uh, it's complicated." He continued to wiggle around in his seat. To Dan, he seemed to be searching for an answer.

"Seriously, if I had M.I.T. offering me a full ride, I'd jump at the chance."

Aric now turned and looked at him full on. "And what would you do? What would you major in?"

Dan shrugged. "I dunno. I'd figure it out."

"That's part of my problem. I don't know what I want to do either. My dad keeps pushing me one way. Mr. Kline thinks I should pursue something else. My mom says I'd make a great doctor. My sisters all chime in with their ideas. But not one of them really stops to ask me what *I* want."

"So, what *do* you want?"

"I don't know." Aric offered him a mischievous grin.

Dan might not have been the brightest light at school, but he was pretty good at reading people, and Aric's response seemed like a canned speech, too rote. Something else was going on.

"Dan, look, I'm not saying this to hurt your feelings, but I know you struggled in school. You wanted to drop out, what, when you turned 16? But someone or something convinced you that racing dirt bikes was not the best future, right?"

Dan nodded. "I still race dirt bikes. I'm pretty good at it.

Earned enough to buy this Jeep."

Aric smiled. "Yes, you are, and you did. My point is, you stayed. And you struggled because it didn't interest you, or you just didn't get it; it was too far over your head."

Dan couldn't argue those points.

"Would you believe it didn't interest me, either?"

A questioning look overcame Dan's face. "Huh? But you aced every course you took."

"Sure, it came easy to me. Too easy. It became boring. And I don't want to go to college, spend a ton of money on courses, and find it boring, too. Besides . . ."

"Besides what?"

"Nothing. As I said, it's complicated."

Again, the answers seemed too calculated. Something else was going on; Dan was sure of it. That suspicion had been bolstered by Aric's insistence on going to Portland. Their original plan had been southern California. Why Portland?

The second thing that had crossed Dan's mind was how different their reasons were for leaving home. Aric wanted to "find himself," to use a lame, overused excuse that could mean anything. On the other hand, Dan *had* to leave before he got into real trouble, felonious trouble. For years he had taken the abuse of his stepfather. As Dan grew and became able to defend himself, however, that abuse had diminished . . . for him. He had tried to talk his mom into leaving the scumbag. She wouldn't. Why? he never could understand. He had watched his mother cover the bruises with makeup for years. After learning to drive, he had taken her to the ER on several occasions, only to be told to be quiet about what happened. He knew that should he stay, it might take only one or two incidents before he took a crowbar to the man's skull. He *had* to leave, even if he couldn't convince his mom to do so as well.

Yet, it was the third thought crossing his mind that troubled him the most. Eight years his senior, his cousin Peter talked of helping lead the rebellion. As he spoke about it, he and his comrades, as he called them, needed only one more wrongful death at the hands of police to ignite their "war." Dan had questioned the wisdom of staying with the guy, even for one or two nights, but his bank account was slim, and crashing at Pete's place while heading farther west made sense.

But more than his cousin's crazy ramblings, Pete seemed more than unusually curious about Dan's friend, Aric. As he thought about it, if Dan was reading the guy correctly, Pete appeared to know more about Aric and his brother Adam than should have been possible. Sure, Dan had talked about his unlikely friendship with the class valedictorian at family holiday gatherings, but nothing in detail. And he couldn't remember ever saying Aric's brother's name. Yet, Pete spoke of him by name, implied knowing that Adam had disappeared, and even seemed excited when Dan mentioned Portland when he had called to firm up their plans to stay with Pete. What was that about?

FOUR

"Robert. Welcome. Can I get you a drink?"

Wallace directed his visitor to the casual seating area at the end of the office opposite his large teak desk. Its modern, gray upholstered chairs and adjacent black steel and glass tables offered a sleek, contemporary appearance to the office while providing a comfortable setting for their discussion. The meeting had been requested by his friend, Robert Jennings, CEO of a "sister" company called Lex Fortis Consolidated. They had mutual interests, financing, and concerns.

Jennings waved his hand as a negative reply. "No, thank you, Wallace. Too early in the day for me." The gray-haired, slightly overweight man sat in a chair with a sigh of relief at getting off his feet. "Been standing all morning. Feels good to sit down." He paused. "I heard that Marla got the virus. Is she okay?"

Wallace nodded. "She tested positive. So did the two boys. They had no symptoms at all, and for her, it was like a mild cold. They've all fully recovered. Has anyone in your family contracted it?"

Jennings rapped his knuckles on his head twice. "Knock on wood, no. We've all been healthy. But Janet and I, we're realists. It's in the environment to stay, and masks or no masks, we'll likely get it, or at least be exposed to it before much longer. We're prepared. We've got two hydroxychloroquine cocktails ready, should we need them." He laughed.

Wallace smiled. "I'll pretend I didn't hear that."

"Yeah, yeah. I know. The party line is it doesn't work, but you and I both know it does when started at the right time. I hear you're fighting off COVID by spending more time on the golf course." He grinned.

Wallace nodded. A recent study had shown that vitamin D was crucial in warding off the bug. Wallace took that as a cue to spend more time outdoors, as well as double up on his daily supplements. "Hasn't helped my handicap any, though." He took a sip of his Glenfiddich. "The worst part was the two weeks isolated in quarantine. That didn't help my handicap, either." He crossed his right leg over his left and sat back into the chair. "So, what's the urgent need to meet?"

Jennings laced his fingers together, placed his elbows on the arms of the chair, and leaned forward toward Wallace. "Maybe I should have that drink."

Wallace moved to get up.

"No, no, just a figure of speech. Thanks. Two things. First, I've heard some grumbling from our mutual friends on the executive board. Seems they're concerned that your wayward son has not yet been located and dealt with."

Wallace took a deep breath and nodded once. He, too, had heard such murmurs through the grapevine. "Well, to be honest, I wish we had better news, too. We all have a right to be concerned, considering . . ."

Jennings furrowed his brow and looked Wallace

straight in the eyes. "Considering what?"

"Considering the info we think he has. We can't be sure just what he has, but I'm assuming the worst. However, what he has must be insufficient, or he would have blown the whistle already."

"Okay, I can buy that logic, but it's been three months."

"I know, but the guy knows how we operate, and AlterNet isn't designed to *find* people. It was designed to investigate people and profile them. It monitors social media, credit cards, and such, but unlike TV, we can't tap into and monitor every private security camera system in the country. He knows how we think. He designed better than half the software. And if anyone can successfully go to ground and hide from us, he can."

"Have you made *any* progress? I mean, I need something positive I can say in your defense when one of them approaches me and asks questions. They know we're old friends and worked together in the intelligence community when you were DNI, and I was head of the CIA."

Wallace understood Jennings' position. They were both top dogs in the intelligence community, and this guy made them look stupid, like oxymorons—with an emphasis on the last two syllables.

"Let whoever talks with you know that we're working on it. We're extending our facial recognition capabilities weekly."

Jennings gave him a dubious look. "That was Amazon's bailiwick, but Congress shut them off after much criticism from civil rights and privacy groups."

Wallace nodded. "I know. They were selling their facial rec software to police departments all across the country but had to stop. We've worked around that. We lined up a couple of Hollywood actors, helped them form a non-profit, and now Amazon donates the software to the non-profit, and they, in turn, give it to police departments. They're focused on the bigger cities right now, but it's expanding."

"How does that help?"

"We've modified AlterNet to interface with Amazon's software. It can monitor the feed from thousands of cameras in almost real-time. If he shows up in the range of one of them, we'll have a lead on his location. And, of course, we're still monitoring his family, credit cards, and the other usual things."

Jennings seemed mollified. "Just goes to show we really need 5G up and running nationwide ASAP."

"True."

Both men knew the big push for 5G wireless was that they needed the speed of such a system to improve their surveillance and control of the country when that time came. Which it would. They could sell it to the people by promoting faster download times for their favorite movies and games, but that was just marketing. They could even ignore the health risks that were being proven more month by month. However, without it, when the need came, they wouldn't be able to control the people without real-time surveillance.

"Speaking of which, how's your development progressing?"

Jennings smiled. "Iteration five of the police drone is complete and ready for the market. We just need to create that market. Which brings me to topic two."

Wallace raised his brow and nodded. "That was quick.

Last we talked, you were still on version two, RCPAD-2."

Lex Fortis had called upon pop culture to name its series of drones: Robo-Cop Police Action Drone. Monitoring a business district and dealing with a single criminal was a piece of cake for this thing. It showed its true color in dealing with riots. Not only could it monitor a deteriorating scene, but its AI also allowed it to radio tag up to ten suspects. It could then follow suspect one, and even Taser® said suspect, if necessary, to give human officers time to catch up. With suspect one incapacitated, it would home in on the next radio tag and repeat the process until all tagged suspects were in custody. All without a shot being fired. At least, that was their marketing. Not part of the sales pitch was the drone's ability to use lethal force as well.

"RCPAD-5 has greatly improved AI routines. It scored 96% on its riot tests, which places the greatest demand on it."

"So, this is topic two?"

Jennings shook his head. "Not RCPAD-5 per se. We have a situation in Minneapolis today. Some hooligan on Fentanyl resisting arrest ended up in cardiac arrest and died during the take-down."

Wallace knew where this was going. They—and the executive board—had been waiting for just such an occasion. The peaceful protests would start, but only as a pretext, and then devolve into riots, arson, and general mayhem. Another death or injury at police hands would soon follow—as the odds for such were great—and more cities would come under pressure.

"This gives us a new opening. We've called on our people in Antifa and BLM to agitate for defunding the police.

They'll keep up the pressure until we get one or two major cities to act on that call. From there, the dominoes will fall. First, pull funds from their police departments. Chiefs will resign, followed by their rank-and-file officers fed up with the job. Crime will rise, and the demand for law and order will swell. And into that void, we step in with RCPAD, whichever iteration we're on by that point. Fewer human officers handling the same or higher crime levels with greater efficiency and much lower costs, even when we add in the lucrative, ongoing maintenance contracts we'll require."

Wallace smiled. "Perfect. And as a bonus, the unrest will help us take down this president."

In politics, everyone knew that good times favored the incumbent, while unrest, unemployment, and a falling stock market led to a winning challenger. The Deep State—which many called it and of which Wallace and Jennings were major players—had undergone yet one more rebirth. This president thought he had dealt the Deep State a lethal blow in taking down The Assembly's leadership. However, like a large flock of birds splitting into two as a hawk takes out one bird in the middle, only to reform into a single undulating mass again, the Deep State had regrouped and regained the upper hand. They had added a pandemic to the mix and stoked widespread fear of the virus to guarantee President Graham's fall.

Lynch Cully had awakened early that morning, as he seemed to do more and more frequently of late. The big day had arrived, and he faced it with eagerness and some trepidation. Well, if he was honest with himself, more than *some* apprehension.

He shaved, showered, and slipped back into their bedroom, hoping not to waken Amy. She lay still on her left side in bed, softly snoring. He watched her quietly. She had insisted the night before that he awaken her before he left. He hated the idea of doing so. She needed her sleep. For too many months her nights had been interrupted, although those disruptions had diminished over the past several weeks.

He smiled as he watched her. They had celebrated their second wedding anniversary a bit over a month earlier. Even more amazing to him than they'd already been married that long—it seemed like just yesterday—was the fact that the entire time no one chased after her, no one shot at him, no cars had blown up, and peace had filled their days. No, this time, her sleeplessness was not due to stress but to a normal, physiologic condition.

His trouble magnet no longer attracted danger, and he couldn't be happier that she didn't. He had been able to focus on his studies, and today, all that effort would come to fruition.

He finished dressing and walked to the kitchen. He would allow Amy to sleep as long as possible. He grabbed some vanilla yogurt and granola cereal, combined them in a bowl, and sat it on the table as his coffee perked. The butterflies in his gut wouldn't allow him anything more substantial. Then, with coffee in hand, he sat down to eat, do his daily Bible reading, and pray—a routine he looked forward to each morning.

After emptying his bowl and completing his reading, he bowed his head only to hear footsteps padding his way.

"Hey, thought I asked you to wake me. Mmmm, smells good. Wish I could have some."

He looked up and smiled. He should have known the aroma of brewing coffee might awaken her.

"G'morning . . . to both of you. I was planning to, but I wanted to give you as much time as possible. I can make you some decaf if you want."

She shook her head. "Thanks, but not right now." She sat down next to him. "So, what's the plan again? I thought they were only doing Zoom meetings."

Lynch nodded. "They are, but there are aspects of my defense that require demonstration, so I'll be on campus with George while the others connect virtually."

Amy knew all of the department faculty, so he had no need to explain who George was. George, Celeste—the department chair—and two others would be his examiners as he defended his doctoral thesis in Criminology. And today was the day.

"And I'll have their decision within the week."

Amy smiled. "Well, I know you have this down pat. You will be assured and amazing."

He chuckled. "Not sure about the amazing part, but I love that you think so. He glanced at the clock. He still had half an hour before needing to leave. "Would you pray with me?"

They held hands and bowed their heads as they sought God's favor and that of Lynch's thesis examiners. They asked that He prepare their paths for the day and the needs of friends and family. By the time they ended their time with

the Lord, the butterflies had flown away, and Lynch felt a
renewed confidence in his work.

FIVE

Buck and two of his men sped toward western Maryland. He'd been given a lead, a flimsy one, but it was the first potential break they'd had in finding Afton since his disappearance.

Their first task had been to review public transportation. All of these avenues of escape had video they could run through facial recognition. Although limited by everyone's wearing of masks—which also lengthened the time required to assess everyone—they had ruled out the Metrobus and Metrorail. They even reviewed the MetroAccess calls for paratransit, just to be thorough. Private taxi companies were also contacted, and drivers were interviewed. No luck.

He had then tasked three analysts with reviewing traffic video from a one-mile radius around Afton's apartment from the time of their "intervention" until the next morning. The result was a list of thousands of vehicles, even after the duplicates were culled. Images of commercial vehicles were scrutinized for drivers and passengers. Likewise, private cars and trucks were also checked through the DMV for ownership and addresses. These were then run through AlterNet, and hundreds were quickly eliminated.

Of the hundred or so vehicles that remained in

question, their addresses were monitored until Buck was personally satisfied that there was no connection to Afton. After three months, only three cars remained on his list. At two addresses, the vehicles involved were never spotted, and further investigation discovered the owners were snowbirds stuck in Florida who hadn't realized their cars were stolen in their absence.

Only one car remained. It was registered to a man who appeared not to exist, at an address that did not exist. Why that hadn't flagged this vehicle earlier in their search had not been explained to Buck. And when he learned that the car had been on video just two blocks from Afton's apartment within 15 minutes of the shooting, he wanted to drop someone out of a helicopter.

"So, explain to me again why we're taking this joyride to Nowhere, Maryland," asked his man sitting in the front passenger seat.

Buck didn't want to go through it again, but the Oldies station had gone to static, and all he could find was Country Western. Besides, his passenger, Karl, was his best sniper. He had taken out Sam Renner at 200 yards through a window in suburban Washington. The guy had *cajones*. Buck would humor him.

"Our search led to a car with a fictitious owner and address, and a thorough review of traffic cams followed it out of the city, past Bethesda, and heading toward Germantown. Traffic cams ended at that point, so we started looking into local security videos in the area. We got lucky. The car showed up at a gas station in Poolesville two nights ago. We couldn't get a good look at the driver, but the car and its tags were unmistakable."

Buck heard his back seat passenger—Giorgio, Gio for short—groan. "Soooo, what're we expected to do? Stake out this gas station until it comes back? Ask the police to do that."

"He has a point, Buck. We're not exactly police detectives. If they ran background checks on us, we don't exist either."

Buck couldn't disagree. "Look, you're right, but if the police did the job, they'd be on the alert about the guy. That makes it harder for us to take him out quietly."

"Okay, so I ask again. What're we gonna do?" asked Gio.

"We'll ask about. If Afton's been living out here for the past three months, someone's bound to have seen him and recognized him. With some luck, maybe they'll know where he's living."

The rest of the drive's banter consisted of old war stories, females conquered, and ratings of the latest microbreweries. They grabbed a quick lunch and headed toward the gas station. Buck talked to the young woman behind the counter while his guys approached other workers.

"Excuse me, we're trying to surprise an old buddy. We served in Iraq together. Anyway, all we know is he lives out this way somewhere, but we don't have an address. Do you know this guy?"

Buck showed the gal a photo of Afton. She shook her head. "Nope. Don't know him."

"What about his car? This is his car." He placed a photo of the car on the counter.

She gave him a curious look and again shook her head. "Sorry. I pretty much work behind this counter. I don't pay attention to the cars, and most folks pay at the pump."

Buck thought the chance of Afton using a credit card at the pump to be zip. AlterNet could track card purchases in minutes, and he wouldn't risk it.

"Actually, he doesn't believe in credit cards. He'd pay cash."

She shook her head again. "Sorry. Still nope."

"He might have a beard now." The driver caught by the traffic cams had a beard and mask.

She took another look at the photo and furrowed her brow as she appeared to be trying to visualize the man with a beard. After 30 seconds, she again shook her head.

"Sorry. I see two, three hundred people through here on a typical shift. Faces are a blur unless they're regulars, and this guy isn't a regular."

Buck nodded his head as a slight frown crossed his lips. "Thanks."

He met his two buddies outside. "Any luck?"

Karl smiled. "Maybe." He nodded toward a young man pulling trash bags from the cans near the pumps and replacing them. "Guy over there says he's seen that car here a couple of times and several times out on Whites Ferry Road. One time he saw it pulling out from a gravel drive near Lockhouse 25, whatever that is. As for the driver, our man's photo didn't ring any bells."

Buck pulled up his phone's map app and looked up Lockhouse 25. It was a historic building situated next to an old lock on the defunct Chesapeake & Ohio Canal. The lockkeeper had lived there with his family and handled the water flow, as well as the towpath horses and mules. The place was now a small museum of sorts. Buck attempted to find nearby structures with access by gravel drives. Only one jumped out at him as it led to a remote cabin surrounded by woods. The isolation was completed by the lack of electric or other utility lines going to it. At least, that's what it looked like on the aerial view. The utilities could be buried.

They'd know soon. The place was less than six miles outside of town.

Minutes later, he pulled into the drive and stopped. His two men hopped out and began their approach on foot, one on each side of the gravel road. After giving them a couple of minutes to get into place, he proceeded down the drive. They were going for a frontal assault. His car would block the exit while they covered any escape on foot.

As he neared the cabin, he felt disappointed at not seeing the car parked in the front. The place appeared ancient and unlived in. A sign next to the footpath that led to the front and only door announced "No Trespassing — Property of the C&O Canal Trust."

Clearly, this was another historical building and not the refuge of their man on the lam. They spent the rest of the afternoon pursuing and following new leads in the area—unsuccessfully. Buck was not happy to return to D.C. empty-handed. He would send a couple of men back to the region to continue looking, but he'd only have them on that task for a week—no need to spend more time and money on what was likely another snipe hunt.

Adam stopped working on the software program he hoped could infiltrate and expand upon AlterNet itself. He needed to eat lunch. While feeling pressed for time, he knew his body well enough to recognize that food and sleep were essential. Lack of either would not help him reach his goal.

He was determined to find Carolyn and to make things right with Rachel. Without his family, what was the point of his existence? With few restrictions, he would do whatever was needed to find their daughter. That determination had already unleashed Chamberlain's junkyard dogs against him . . . and, sadly, Sam had paid the price. For the first time, he allowed himself to feel angry over that injustice. Adam would not forget Sam's sacrifice.

His needs while in hiding were simple: real food, not processed, a comfortable place to sleep, clean water, proper sanitation, electricity, and a high-speed Internet connection. He had prepared for them all, and his encrypted VPN setup bounced his Internet connection all around the globe. They could not pinpoint his location that way.

Plus, he had planned for the eventuality that someone might come looking for him. He no longer needed the fake beard. Three months without shaving had made it unnecessary. During that same time interval, his once short hair had grown past his ears. Tinted contact lenses turned his brown eyes blue. He looked nothing like his employment photos. Those changes and the mandated masks helped foil facial recognition software, which he knew he would not be able to avoid much longer.

He drove the Chevy for his sporadic trips to town for food, and he always used the same route purposefully so that any doorbell and security cameras along the way would register it. Doorbell cameras, in particular, were troublesome. CCS had back-door agreements with the major players in that market to allow AlterNet access to those cameras through their Internet connections. Small business security systems still tended to be self-contained without such access.

However, ten miles out of town, in a rented shed, he had an Audi RS3, which he used to travel the additional miles to his cabin across the Potomac River in Virginia. His trips into Poolesville were worth the extra time they required if they provided enough of a diversion to keep him safe. Plus, the Audi was prepped for the cross-country trip he now planned.

The Sonic's gas efficiency was such that he had only needed to fill its tank once since arriving. Yet, it was while at the gas station a couple of nights earlier that he'd come up with the idea that now looked as if it guaranteed his freedom.

He had learned that a 250-year-old cabin—owned by the C&O Canal Trust and awaiting restoration—had a security camera monitoring the building's front. The camera was tied to the Internet for off-site viewing. While getting gas, he made a deal with one of the full-time employees. For $200, the guy was to tell anyone who came looking for Adam's blue Chevy Sonic that he'd seen it along Whites Ferry Road and coming out of the cabin's drive.

Today, as he ate lunch, his motion alert from that camera triggered. Adam chewed his turkey and cheese sandwich as he watched three men inspect the outside of the cabin. He recognized the man who appeared to be in charge—Wallace Chamberlain's right-hand man, Buck somebody.

Adam held no fear that they'd find him that day. The

Chevy was safely hidden away in its shed. It would take a door-to-door, building-to-building search to find the car. And, then they'd have to search that area further, again door-to-door looking for him, only to remain stymied. They'd likely think to ask the folks at White's Ferry, but drivers using that historic ferry across the river stayed in their cars, and the blue Sonic had never used the crossing.

Still, they had finally succeeded in narrowing their search to that part of Maryland. That, in itself, must have taken a lot of manpower and old-fashioned detective work. He smiled at the thought that they considered him worthy of such effort . . . and that he cost them so much time and money.

His time in the area was limited, but by *his* schedule, not because of them. He had been following a lead on Carolyn's abductor. In turn, he had discovered something so disturbing that he felt his only recourse was to check it out personally. However, he would need a wingman with smarts he could trust—Aric. He could only hope that Aric had received the postcard and interpreted its meaning.

SIX

J.B. Gradison drove along two-lane Justice Road surrounded by pines looking for a single-lane road marked only with a sign stating it was private property and no trespassing. This was his first visit to their newest facility in the old, deserted army depot northwest of Madison, Wisconsin. Camp Douglas was a village adjacent to what was now Volk Field, the Air National Guard's premier training facility in the upper Midwest.

Camp Douglas started as a logging village in 1864, and the Wisconsin State Reservation was built there in 1888. The facility functioned as the state's main mobilization center in World War I and as the primary training center for the Wisconsin National Guard into World War II. The Wisconsin Military Academy was also housed there until it moved to Fort McCoy in 1995.

While the airfield continued in operation and the Camp Williams Weapons Firing Range of the Army National Guard took control of the northeast portion of the property, the old facility's wooded areas south of the town had been decommissioned, its buildings mothballed. YFM Corp. had taken recent control of the buildings, just as it had in over a dozen such old military camps in California, Texas, and elsewhere during the past few years.

He pulled up to a tall, chain-link gate, opened his window, and looked squarely into the security panel camera controlling the gate. No words or buttons were needed. Their facial recognition software cleared him within seconds, and a light flashed green while the gate rolled aside. He moved ahead into the small parking lot of the nondescript building and parked, as the automated gate rolled shut behind him, closing off the lot from those who might want to enter unannounced . . . or to leave screaming. At one time, the building had been the headquarters of an engineering battalion that had also been stationed there before moving to Fort McCoy. A twelve-foot-tall, chain-link fence topped with a double strand of razor wire surrounded the property. Security cameras were obvious on poles placed strategically around the lot.

To most observers, such security measures were overkill for a property in the middle of nowhere accessible only by a half-mile-long, single-lane road. For him, his valuable "commodities" couldn't be overly protected.

J.B. had hit upon an upscale product that quickly found favor among A-list celebrities, politicians, and billionaire Big Tech leaders. Most of its consumers had to have deep pockets or a high value to the Deep State's newest controllers, the executive board. All of its consumers would gladly pay more for it. YFM Corp. had been founded to produce this wonder drug.

Adrenochrome—the fountain of youth!

The fountain of youth of J.B.'s childhood consisted of fables and myths. In past times, men of daring sailed the seas on wind-driven, four-masted cutters searching for it. Florida was discovered in such a quest, or so he'd been told. Hot mineral springs attracted people in droves, hoping for cures and longer life in the belief of such a fountain. Science soon dispelled those beliefs.

But recently, science had delivered the key to long life, if not immortality. The science behind genetics had shown that telomeres on the ends of our chromosomes shortened over time, bringing with it cell death. J.B. had stumbled onto a group of researchers who had found a way to delay that process, maybe stop it altogether. Adrenochrome was the key component.

But there were ethical issues involved, none of which bothered J.B. He saw the goldmine represented by their work.

All of their detention centers were heavily secured and isolated. For those existing in decommissioned military posts, like Camp Douglas, their architectural plans remained secret in case the military would require them again. Their underground structures had been built to protect occupants in the unlikely case of a missile strike or air attack. No one casually observing the aboveground buildings would suspect their presence. Now, they suited the needs of YFM Corp. well.

Two men emerged from the building to greet him. J.B. needed no introductions. He'd been part of the hiring team that brought these men on board. In fact, he and the older of the two went back many years in working together. Alaine Tavernier, Ph.D., was in his fifties, slim, and had a receding hairline leading into longish salt-and-pepper hair, which he swept to the back. With tortoise-shell-rimmed glasses, he looked like the scientific type that he was. Brian Skelter was much younger, athletic, and had a military bearing consistent with his special ops background. He was officially the center's warden, holding the rank of O-6 within YFM Corp.'s Special Projects Division.

"Good morning, sir. Welcome. We have looked forward to your first visit," said Skelter. The usual protocol of shaking hands had gone by the wayside with the pandemic. Yet, none of them wore masks. The scientific evidence against mask use was well-known to them. Besides, if they contracted the virus, they had access to top-level therapy.

"Thank you. Good to see you again, too, Alaine."

"You also, *monsieur.*"

J.B. nodded. Tavernier had always been a man of order and efficiency, as well as great intellect. He alone remained of the original European research team and shared J.B.'s ethical standards—significant advances in science and medicine sometimes required great sacrifice. The others? Well, the unexpected loss of funding had led to such despair that two of them took their own lives. One collapsed from a cardiac condition while jogging. The final member was the tragic victim of a hit-and-run accident, which has never been solved.

Those were the official stories anyway. Like others before them, they knew too much and posed too grave a threat.

"This way, sir. Would you like to see the new labs or the housing area first?"

"Just the labs, please. This time. My schedule has had a minor glitch thrown into it, and I can't stay as long as I'd originally planned." If he'd been truthful, he didn't like touring the housing areas of their centers.

"Yes, sir."

Warden Skelter led them into a hallway lined with large glass windows showing brightly lit medical labs on both sides of the passage. Men and women in surgical scrubs and white coats worked in those labs. This part of the facility was tranquil and smelled of mint.

Tavernier described what they were watching as they stood outside each lab. Typically, they would have entered each lab and introduced J.B. to the workers, but again, the pandemic had forced them to alter that practice. The change was mostly for show, should any government inspector show up unannounced. Plus, these labs were all such uninitiated visitors would see.

"I'd like to see your initial production reports. I assume you have them ready for me."

Tavernier nodded. "But of course. This way, my office is at the end of the hall." He ushered J.B. into the room, which was tight on space at the moment. "My apologies. I did not want this equipment left in the hallway. They are due to be installed in Lab 4 later this week." He worked his way around to his desk. "Here are the reports."

Tavernier picked up a thin packet of papers, stapled in the top left corner, and handed them to J.B. He knew the format of the report like the back of his hand and scanned it entirely within seconds. He nodded.

"Good job. Looks like you found a way to increase both quantity and quality. Should I expect these numbers from now on?"

Tavernier waggled his head back and forth in a noncommittal fashion. "Too early to say, *monsieur*. I would ask that we give it two, three more weeks before we can expect any projections on consistency. You no doubt saw that we had to dispose of one production unit, and three more are likely to fail soon. We will need to replace those units."

J.B. nodded. "Will you handle that?"

Skelter answered that question from the doorway. "My team will take care of that. We have everything we need."

J.B. nodded. "Very good."

"Sir, I know you have an affinity for hunting. We have two hunts scheduled soon. Would you like to come back to join in? Perhaps bring a special guest or two."

Both sounded good to J.B.—that they would be able to procure the necessary production units without additional help and the hunt. While he had no qualms in providing corporate assistance, he paid his people *very* well to perform such essential tasks as procurement. As for the hunt, he immediately thought of a few people who would find such an outdoor activity stimulating. His favored role as CEO was that of being the "face" of the company, although his face would never grace the pages of *People Magazine* or the like. He enjoyed schmoozing with celebrities and power brokers—most on a first-name basis—while wining and dining at the most elegant restaurants or attending the finest cultural events. Still, he had no desire to be someone whose name was recognized on the street, so to speak.

And as the first recipient of their adrenochrome compound, his body felt more robust and energetic than he had forty years earlier. His hair had begun filling back in, while his skin seemed more supple and youthful as well. And his libido? Well, well.

"Would you like to see the rest of the facility?" asked

Skelter.

J.B. shook his head. "Perhaps next time, if I'm able to return for your hunting adventure." Skelter looked disappointed. "I am assured that you have done an excellent job with the housing facilities." He pointed to a briefcase on a nearby table.

"Yes, *monsieur*. That is for you to take as well. The vials are labeled as usual. I believe you will find it of exceptional quality."

"Thank you, Alaine."

He picked up the case and left the office. The three men talked as they walked toward the parking lot. He would have his secretary follow up on the hunt's details and see if his schedule would allow his return. He hoped to see the reported quantities become consistent. As for the quality, he would have his samples tested at a private lab. He trusted his managers only so far. Quality assurance was one task he insisted on being given priority. After all, their clients were paying top dollar and deserved certainty that they were getting what they paid for. Of course, the real test was in the results they noticed personally.

Leaving both men at the door, he walked up to his car and carefully placed the briefcase in a padded container in the trunk. They could not afford any accidental breakage of the vials inside. As he closed the lid, a blood-curdling scream pierced the air.

The noise appeared to come from behind the building. J.B. waited for a moment, but no other outcries occurred. A subtle frown crossed his face. *Skelter needs to get a handle on that*, he thought as he climbed into the driver's seat.

SEVEN

After 11 hours of sitting in Dan's Jeep, half of the trip in the dark, and almost all of it in silence, Aric was eager to get out and stretch his legs. He had turned off his cell phone upon leaving St. Louis and dreaded turning it back on. His thoughts focused on his parents, who had read and probably reread his letter by now. His mom would be upset and crying. His dad, too, would be concerned, maybe agitated and angry. Both would be worried. Both likely would have tried calling and texting. Both would want him to return home, especially in these times of the pandemic. At his age, he had a greater risk of dying from falling down a flight of steps. He could also see his sisters getting involved. Would turning on his cell phone deluge him with a tsunami of voicemails and text messages?

And yet, he couldn't tell any of them the main reason he had left. If Adam was in real trouble, all of them could be under surveillance. To let slip to any of them that he was leaving to find and help his big brother would put Adam, and them, further into harm's way.

Surveillance. Another reason for Aric not turning on his phone was that it would make it easier for them—whoever "them" was—to track him. He debated taking the battery out as well, but he figured he should do that without anyone around to witness and question his action.

"Hey, we're almost there."

"Okay. It's almost midnight. Is your cousin expecting us this late?"

Dan smiled. "Pete? He's always been a night owl. Two is more likely his bedtime. By the way, I should warn you. Pete's, well, he's a rebellious sort. Your folks would definitely call him a radical left-winger. So, it might be best not to egg him on. You know, don't bring up politics or religion."

Politics *or* religion? Hadn't they become almost one and the same in many Christian circles in the U.S.? Aric had never confused the two. God was not American, Republican, or Democrat. He was sovereign, and Christ was the King of kings and Lord of lords.

In reflecting on that, Aric again wondered why his prayers for guidance seemed to go unanswered. The Lord had clearly used him in the past, giving him the right words for others seeking answers and putting him into situations where he could help. He recalled two incidents where God gave him premonitions that had prevented friends from being seriously injured. Aric looked to Christ as the author and perfecter of his faith and felt that faith continuing to grow. So, why the sudden confusion, his questioning his faith?

"I hadn't planned on it. I thought we were just crashing there for a night, maybe two."

Dan nodded. "Yeah, that was my plan, too."

Fifteen minutes later, Dan pointed to their right. "I think that's the right apartment building. Can you see a number?"

Aric strained to find the building's address in the dark. What he could see was that the building was older and not well maintained on the outside. Maybe the inside was better kept.

"There." Aric pointed this time. "Looks like 5816."

"Okay, that's not it. Same side of the street, but we're looking for 6048."

Aric sighed inwardly in relief. That first place was a dump. And yet, as they drove the next two blocks, the neighborhood seemed to deteriorate further. When they arrived, Pete's apartment building looked to be in worse condition than the other, but something was happening there.

Lights were on in multiple apartments. A set of construction work lights set up on a six-foot-tall stand lit up part of the parking lot, where a dozen or more people—young men mostly—moved between cars and the building loading boxes into the vehicles. To Aric, it looked as if at least a dozen cars and trucks were being loaded.

Dan worked his Jeep around the guys and found a parking spot on the dark side of the lights. Both of them emerged from the vehicle and stretched. The cool, Colorado spring night air invigorated Aric as he stood watching the preparations being made for whatever was about to happen.

"Hey, there's Pete," said Dan.

He began walking toward a guy who just emerged from the building carrying a medium-sized moving box. Aric hurried from the other side of the Jeep to catch up. Pete lifted the box into the back of a compact pickup truck.

"Pete!"

The young man turned toward them but showed no

sign of recognition at first. Then he nodded, but no smile crossed his mouth. He did not appear pleased to see his cousin. He was dressed in black, had longish, coal-black hair, and a beard.

As they drew closer, he said, "I see you made it after all. Look, lots going on right now. We're leaving for Portland and Seattle in the morning."

"Wow, I thought we'd have a day or two here to check out Denver."

Pete shook his head. "Not gonna happen this time. We have to leave."

Dan turned toward Aric and back to his cousin. "Hey, sorry, this is my friend Aric."

Pete nodded again and gave Aric a curious look. "Yeah, Dan's told me about you. The class brainiac, I think he called you."

Dan rolled his eyes, but Aric took no offense. Dan had called him that to his face on more than one occasion. He held out his hand to shake Pete's, but the man didn't return the gesture. Aric wasn't sure if that was due to the pandemic or just the guy's unfriendly nature.

"So, look, I told you you could crash here, but it's gonna be a while before things quiet down. Might not be able to sleep until they do. But, if you want to help, that'll speed things up."

Dan looked at Aric. After a long day's drive, Aric suspected that Dan was no more eager to work carrying boxes than he was. But then, if they weren't going to be able to sleep until it was done . . .

"My place is 2B, up those stairs and to the right. There's probably some pizza left on the table and some beer in the fridge. Grab a bite to eat and then pitch in. Every box in my place needs to come down here. You can just put them here, by the lights, and we'll put them into the appropriate vehicles. Then, we have half a dozen storage units in the basement, too. They need to be emptied before we call it quits."

To Aric, that didn't sound like a request as much as an order. He glanced about and wondered what it was they were loading into the various pickups and cars. "So, what is all this stuff?"

Pete replied only by stating, "Pizza's upstairs." He turned and walked away to talk with another young man a few yards away.

Aric noted that all of the men held angry scowls. A few wore BLM sweatshirts—all of them white males. Of the two young, also white, women helping, one's tee-shirt said, *No Justice! No Peace!* Were they always angry? Were they working up their emotions for a reason . . . or perhaps a role to play? What had Dan dragged him into? And what was Pete's role in this?

Aric followed Dan up the stairs and into Pete's apartment. The place was a pit and not because of over half a dozen boxes piled up near the door. A Che Guevara poster dominated the wall over a beat-up couch with multiple stains of uncertain origin. That poster was flanked by BLM and Antifa posters. He had heard the name Antifa but didn't know much about it other than it supposedly stood for anti-fascist. A couple of books by William Ayers and one by Saul Alinsky sat under the single end table's lamp. His parents would call this man something more than a left-winger. If they suspected he'd be somehow tied to a radical communist, even if for one night, they'd be appalled.

He and Dan each wolfed down a couple of pieces of pizza, washed down by a beer. That alone would drive his parents over the edge—underage drinking in the apartment of a radical progressive. However, they'd never use the term progressive for someone whose real agenda was regressive. He wondered why he continued to think of his parents and how they would react to his current situation. Didn't he want to spread his wings? Wasn't he trying to figure out who *he* was? One Coors Light wasn't going to lead him into alcoholism any more than one man's left-wing political opinions would change his own way of thinking. Would it?

"This place is a dump. I thought you said your aunt and uncle were well-to-do."

Dan nodded. "They are. Very well-to-do, in fact. My cousins went to top-notch private schools, spent their summers at camp and the country club, got new cars for their 16th birthdays. All of the privileges of wealth that you and me never saw."

"So, why's he living here?"

Dan shrugged. "Got me."

The two spent the next half an hour moving boxes from Pete's apartment. Some weighed more than the others but not so heavy as to require two to move them. Aric carried one in which he could hear something liquid sloshing around in containers inside. It held a faint kerosene odor.

As they carried the last of the boxes from the apartment, Aric heard one man complaining about police brutality. His companion mentioned someone named George Floyd, who died in Minneapolis while the police were arresting him. No specifics were stated. Aric mentioned that to Dan at his first opportunity.

After two loads from the basement storage units, Dan grabbed Aric and took him aside.

"Whoa, we need to be careful and stick with Pete if we're going to go to Portland."

"Why?" Aric had hoped they would be able to leave in the morning and go their merry way, even if the destination coincided with Pete's.

"These guys are nuts. They're talking about the revolution starting in Portland. They're not going there to carry signs and chant slogans. They're going there to loot, burn, and destroy. And they're getting paid to do so."

Aric's fight or flight reaction was to flee right then. "Look, let's just ease our way back to your car and take off. I don't want any part of this. We can get a motel room somewhere."

Dan looked askance as if he didn't want to say what he was about to say.

"Ummmm, not so easy. A couple of the guys were suspicious of us being here and took videos of us helping load the trucks. Pete says if we don't play along, they'll implicate us as being part of the group. I had no idea, honest. But Pete's evidently the head of the local Antifa cell, and they've been tasked with going to Portland and Seattle. He's willing to protect us since I'm family and we just sorta fell into this whole thing, but we gotta stick with him for him to be able to do that."

Looting, arson, and *blackmail. Lovely,* thought Aric. Now he truly regretted leaving home. Yet, Adam needed his help. He wouldn't have contacted Aric as he had otherwise. Aric didn't like how things had developed, but what choice did he have but to play along . . . for the next week.

In his Special Ops days, Buck could work for days on sporadic short periods of sleep. Since taking his current security position with CCS, he'd come to appreciate a full night's sleep. Perhaps it was also his age that played a role. He was now 18 years older than that young gung-ho sergeant first class in Operation Desert Storm.

So, when the phone rang at four a.m., he groaned at first as he rolled over in bed and grabbed his cell phone from the nightstand. When he saw the Caller ID, he became alert and eased out of bed to not disturb his wife. He hurried into the kitchen to take the call in private.

"Sir, sorry to call you so early, but we leave for Portland in a few hours, and this might be my only opportunity for a while."

"That's okay, Lewis. I know you wouldn't call unless it was important." Now that he was up and alert, he debated making a pot of coffee. The odds of getting back to sleep were slim.

"My cousin and his friend showed up as planned. I've got Aric Afton under direct observation now."

Buck smiled. That was good news. When AlterNet had discovered the friendship between Dan Lewis and Aric Afton and connected the dots to Dan and Pete Lewis being related, Buck had reached out to Lewis to find out more.

Antifa received its funding from a certain Hungarian billionaire who sat on the executive board. In turn, Lewis's "salary" came from those funds. As such, Buck knew the man would heed Buck's "advice" to try to learn more about Afton.

After all, there was a bounty on Adam Afton's head, and Lewis could profit significantly from being the one who led Buck to him. Few things motivated a man—whether capitalist or socialist—more than greed.

As much as Buck wished to take credit, Lewis was the one who had come up with the plan to snare Aric Afton. He had learned that his cousin and Afton wanted to travel west after graduation. While some travel limitations applied due to the pandemic, borders weren't closed between states, and the police had no means of enforcing such restrictions. The governors issuing such limits could only hope for the honor system—and peer pressure—to keep people at home. Lewis offered to let them stay at his pad if their travel plans became a reality.

Pure serendipity—or was it karma—kicked in when the boys' plans changed from California to Oregon. Perhaps that change was the result of California's tough stance on travel and quarantine. Buck had his suspicions that something—or someone—else had triggered the change.

"I take it your plan worked."

"Like a charm, as they say. Thanks for getting us tasked to assist in Portland. The timing couldn't have been better. I scheduled our loading to coincide with my cousin's ETA, and we got them to help load the vehicles. Videos and photos now show them helping, and they've taken the bait. If they know what's good for them, they'll stick with me, and I can watch Afton for any suspicious actions."

Buck did not believe in God. If he had, whether as the Judeo-Christian God, Allah, or simply Mother Nature, he might have seen this as a good sign. The Force was with them.

"Perfect. With a little luck, the guy will lead us to big brother."

EIGHT

J.B.'s driver pulled into the lane and stopped behind the car blocking access to the driveway. To their left, the guard house—staffed 24/7 and with sleeping quarters upstairs for the Secret Service agents assigned to the former Vice President—held offices and other living space for those same agents. J.B. was familiar with the drill. He visited monthly, like clockwork.

Charles Davis Sidon, vice president in the previous administration, had the name recognition and credentials needed to defeat President Bradley Graham in his quest for reelection. Yet, he still had the hurdle of claiming the party's nomination following his success throughout the party's six debates the preceding fall. As for his running mate, the party needed someone committed to the party's progressive side, someone dedicated to the executive board's agenda for a global socialist platform—preferably female, a person of color, or both. As the presumptive candidate, his people were working through the options. The VP candidate was of particular importance to the executive board because, at 77 years, Sidon now showed signs of early dementia related to Parkinson's Disease, despite reports by the media and his campaign of his continued vigor and excellent health.

Nicknamed "Po" for his mythically god-like success in

becoming the third youngest person elected to the U.S. Senate—and on his first attempt, without funding—his strengths as a politician throughout his 40-plus years in Washington were marred by only two phobias. He had wanted to become President since childhood, so he feared losing. To lose his senate seat would derail his lifelong goal. Losers did not get nominated for the top job. He stopped at nothing to win. All bets were off. In a couple of instances, he had even called on "physical persuasion" to prevent potential candidates from seeking his office. And everything under the table would be working in his favor for this election—the pandemic, ballot harvesting, vote-buying, last-minute state election law changes, and any other form of voter fraud they could get away with. Along with the full support of the media, of course.

His other phobia? Well, it was a real one stemming from a childhood accident. "Po" Sidon was deathly afraid of water. Drinking it was as far as he went. Even the large pool at the back of his coastal home was for others to enjoy. He ventured no closer to it than the flagstone patio thirty feet away. And the shoreline? That was for even more distant viewing.

Both J.B. and his driver lowered their windows as a masked agent emerged from the guard house and approached the vehicle. The agent smiled in recognition.

"Mr. Gradison, Mr. Hanley, nice to see you again. Credentials, please."

Despite the personal recognition, the drill would be followed religiously. The two men presented their IDs and sat back while the agent scanned them with a handheld device designed to validate their authenticity. The man returned their IDs and pointed to the nearby parking spaces.

"Please pull over there and come inside. Bring any briefcases or bags with you, and masks are required."

That was new. In the past, J.B. provided the agent with his briefcase, which was then scanned outside under the building's portico.

Just inside the building, J.B. handed over his briefcase. His driver had no bags or other paraphernalia to be scanned, just a paperback novel to bide his time while waiting in the car. That passed muster simply by the agent fanning through the pages. The case, too, passed inspection, as he knew it would.

A young woman emerged from a back office. Her nametag identified her as a registered nurse.

"I need to check your temperatures, gentlemen."

She held up a digital thermometer and proceeded to insert it into J.B.'s right ear. "98.4," she said to the agent who recorded it on his sheet. She changed the tip of the device and repeated the process with the driver. "97.8"

She placed the thermometer on the desk and picked up two nasal swabs. The length of the swab surprised J.B. Where was that supposed to go? His nose? Or to the back of his brain? He lowered his mask, and as she inserted it into and up his nose, she convinced him that she had reached the latter. That was not comfortable.

She repeated the process with Mr. Hanley and exited to the back room. Six minutes later, she returned. "Looking good. Both are COVID negative," she said to the agent, who nodded.

"Thank you, gentlemen. You're cleared to go on. Return to your car and drive up to the house. You'll be met by another agent there. Vice President Sidon is expecting you. Masks are required."

J.B. enjoyed the short drive to the house. Although modest in size compared to many politicians' homes, the grounds of the five-acre lot that held the Vice President's 6,200 square-foot home were beautifully landscaped, and spring color popped from every angle. Beds of tulips and daffodils were backdropped by brilliant yellow forsythias in full bloom. Dogwoods showed off their colors as the redbuds' pink flowers waned.

As directed, they parked in a designated area at the front of the beautiful home and were met by another agent, who ushered J.B. into the front foyer. Janet Sidon Tucker, the Vice President's oldest daughter, met him there.

"J.B., it's nice to see you again. And your visit couldn't be timelier. The old man's not doing so well." Her concern etched her face.

J.B. understood that worry. Upon entering the race, Sidon had acknowledged his age and hated the forgetfulness he was experiencing. The strain of the debates had made it worse. And the pandemic added to the stress—to the point that his opponents accused him of hiding in his basement and running a "campaign lite" in fear. Even members of the alternative press began to wonder in print and video whether or not he would be capable of claiming the nomination.

That's where adrenochrome came in, and J.B. was pleased to provide his services personally. Courting the powerful was a task he would never pass on to a subordinate.

"He was doing well until the last dose or two. Can we

up the dose or something?"

He nodded. "We could, but I'd hate to jump to that too quickly if he expects to last a full term. There is a limit."

She nodded her understanding. "Dad's in the back. The nurse is waiting with him to administer the medication." She began to lead the way.

"I'm hopeful that what I have with me today will help. We set up a new lab in the upper Midwest, and the quality of the adrenochrome is far above what we've been able to provide so far. I suspect we'll know within 24 hours, instead of the usual two to three days."

She stopped at a doorway and turned to face him. "I'll keep my fingers crossed and let you know. He's in here." She stepped aside and ushered J.B. into the room with a sweep of her arm.

The presumptive presidential candidate looked wan and distant.

"Mr. Vice President, good to see you again, sir."

The man mumbled a reply that J.B. could only interpret as gibberish. He saw why the man's daughter felt so concerned.

He walked to a nearby table and set down his briefcase. Upon opening it, he removed a small ice pack, checked that it remained cold, and retrieved two vials of the glistening, reddish liquid from their slots in the foam insert that protected them. A second ice pack sat beneath that section, and he noted that it, too, still felt cold. He handed both vials to the nurse.

"One for today, and the second for his next dose. Keep it well refrigerated."

"Yes, sir. As usual." She smiled as she took the small

tubes.

Within five minutes of receiving his dose, the politician smiled. His flat affect seemed to melt away. J.B. wondered, was this little more than a placebo effect? The timing seemed much too soon for the adrenochrome to be having a real impact. He turned to face the daughter, who was staring at her father.

"Let me know how he does. I'll be back in a month."

"Oh, she'll let you have it, she will. No more mola, um, mele, uh, malarkey from her."

She raised her brow. "I've never seen such a quick change. Maybe this is a good sign."

J. B. nodded. He hoped so, too. His own dose was due in a week, and he'd been hesitant to try the new stuff. To think he was using the former Vice President as his personal guinea pig. Only he would know.

Adam scanned the Internet for his tags, the ones he had set up to alert him should anyone be searching for him, or more specifically, his activity, on the net. All remained quiet. And he'd received no more alerts from the security system at the old Canal Trust cabin, not that he expected anyone else to visit the place in the last 24 hours. Had it really been only the day before?

Now that Buck What's-his-name had come to western Maryland searching for him, he could no longer use Poolesville as a diversion. But did he need to do any additional shopping? He scanned his cabinets and fridge. He had enough food for three or four days easy, if he planned on staying. Which he didn't. He had 40-plus hours of driving ahead of him.

He wished he could get hold of Aric, to avoid sending him into that mess, but that was no longer an option. Plus, he couldn't mail his packet to Josh Lewis and be assured that it would get there on time. COVID had slowed down the Postal Service to less than a snail's pace. Snail mail was no longer an appropriate moniker, but he couldn't think of what was slower than a snail that could make a nice sobriquet.

He had boxed himself in by selecting Portland, but that was where his search for her had led him. Portland was implicated in his investigation, although nothing more specific. He knew that his brother had talked of going to the West Coast and that their parents wouldn't get suspicious about Aric heading there with Dan. They wouldn't like it, but they wouldn't wonder why, like they might have had Adam chosen, say, Texas. Because of this, he now had more than one reason to go to Oregon physically.

And after watching the news online, that thought bothered him further. With George Floyd's death due to Fentanyl being used as a cover for more BLM and Antifa protests, Portland had become a central flash point for riots. He had sent his kid brother into the fire.

He had worked long into the night, but the time had come. He couldn't delay his trip any further, and he wouldn't have time along the way to work on his program. He ran one additional test on the software. He could find no flaw, no hidden access that would allow a hacker to corrupt it. He ran another . . . and another. He tried to disrupt its spiders and bots, change its logic flow, and reverse engineer it to spy on its creator. Every test passed.

Yes, the time had come. It was now or never. Should Adam give it a name? He'd have to think about that. A name would have to be remarkable.

His first targets would be Buck What's-his-name and Wallace Chamberlain. He had plenty of dirt on Chamberlain, but it remained a smoking gun, not a flaming missile. Together, the two posed the greatest immediate threat to him and Aric, so they were easy selections to make . . . for two reasons. One, for Sam. Two, searching out data on just two people would give his system a good test run without overwhelming it. He would move out from there . . . back to looking for her.

He surfed to the site he had created on the deep web. From there, the program would deploy its legion of trackers and collect its gigabytes of data for the AI evaluation routines to parse and analyze. His finger hovered over the key to deploy the program. He took a deep breath of resolve and hit the key.

NINE

When Dan had told Aric that his cousin, Pete, was a night owl, he had understated that fact. Even the owls went to bed before Pete and his friends. With Dan and Aric's help, they had finished the loading by one a.m., but Pete and company still hadn't hit the sack by three. Dan seemed to drift off despite the racket made by the others.

When the marijuana and cocaine came out, Aric knew he didn't want to stay there any longer. He had no desire for a Rocky Mountain high, secondhand or otherwise. Besides that, he was pretty sure he saw bugs crawling on the mattress on the floor on which he was expected to crash. He roused Dan enough to take his keys and headed for the Wrangler. Tilting back as far as he could in the passenger's seat, he dozed off quickly.

Sometime later, he was startled awake at the sound of pounding on the window and door and the movement of someone trying to shake the car.

"Aric, wake up in there!"

Aric blinked his eyes several times. Had fog rolled in overnight? He couldn't see through the glass, but he could tell it was light outside. What time was it? He took a deep breath to help wake up and grabbed his phone. Ten-thirty.

"Wake up!"

That was Dan's voice. Aric glanced around and saw someone shadowy at the driver's window. He reached over and unlocked the door. It opened in a flash. Dan stood there with his backpack. Aric saw that it was a bright sunny morning outside.

"Dude, what were you doing in here? You got the windows all fogged up."

Aric, still trying to fully awaken, rubbed his eyes and again took several deep breaths. "Sorry, must just be from moisture in my breath. I was sound asleep. You okay?"

Dan scratched in random areas of his body. "I-I don't think so. Man, that lumpy mattress was loaded with little brown bugs when I woke up. I think they bit me." He showed Aric both forearms and lifted his shirt to display his torso. There were a dozen or more small red welts in each location.

"Could be bed bugs. You need to check your backpack and clothes for hitchhikers. You could infest your Jeep, too."

"Ugh. Not good. Give me a hand, would ya?"

Aric climbed out the passenger door and came around to the other side. Dan began to strip down. "Dude, not out here like that. Someone could see you."

Dan shrugged. "I don't care. I don't want any creepy-crawlies on me. Let's be fast."

Aric checked his friend's neck, back, and the backs of his legs. Dan pulled at the waist of his boxers. "No way," said Aric. "You can check that area yourself. Pits?"

Dan raised his arms before doing a split-second inspection inside his boxers, shaking and checking his pants, and pulling them back on. He did the same with his long-sleeved tee-shirt. Dan then dumped his pack's contents onto the cement and examined every clothing item and the backpack itself. He found a comb in with his toiletries and handed it to Aric.

As Aric used the comb to scrutinize Dan's scalp and hair, as if checking for lice, he asked, "So, what's up with Pete? He said they were leaving in the morning, and it's almost eleven."

"Yeah, so he has another hour." Dan grinned. "Actually, he was stirring already as I tried to sneak out the door."

"Sneak out?"

"Yeah, I got to thinking about it. With my previous possession charge, I don't need to be caught hanging with a bunch of dealers. Did you see how much weed and crack they had? Nope, not for me. I learned my lesson. Plus, I sure don't want to get you involved. You decide to take MIT up on that scholarship offer, then you don't need these guys wrecking that chance."

The thought of getting busted and losing a scholarship offer hadn't even occurred to Aric. Dan was right. But what about Pete's comrades' threats and videos?

"And, as far as their threats about pinning something on us, well, all they have are videos of us carrying some boxes. Nothing to prove we know what's in 'em, which we don't. Besides, they'd have to get caught themselves before they could try to do anything to us. Right?"

Aric smiled. Dan was right. He was impressed. Dan was thinking things through instead of acting on impulse like he usually did. "Hey, that's the kind of critical thinking I keep telling you about. Keep it up."

Dan grinned. "Yeah, my mom always said you were a good influence on me." He tossed his pack into the back seat and climbed in behind the wheel. "C'mon, get in."

Aric headed around the front of the Jeep and stopped just before the door. Staring at the front, passenger-side tire, he shook his head and sighed. They weren't going anywhere quickly. Pointing, he said, "Dan, take a look."

Dan rushed to his side. His jaw dropped as he saw the flat tire. "It was good last night. What the—"

Aric knelt next to the tire and examined it. He was about to say something when Pete and two of his buddies emerged from the building.

"You might need this," Pete proclaimed, holding up something between his fingers as they neared the vehicle.

"Huh?"

Aric looked at Dan. "They took the valve out of the tire stem."

Dan gave his cousin a look mixed with anger and incredulity. "Pete?"

"Sorry, cous. We got to talking last night and decided we didn't need you two sneaking off and alerting anyone to what we got here and where we're headin'."

"We don't *know* what you've got here, so who and what would we alert them to?" replied Aric.

Pete shrugged. "Yeah, well. We jus' wanted a little insurance. You might as well come back in and join me for breakfast. My friends here will get your Jeep fixed up . . . and then, I'll be riding with you. Again, insurance."

Before heading off into the land of slow-speed internet and unreliable motel Wi-Fi, Adam had a bit of housekeeping and packing to do. But first, some snooping. His $200 payment had paid off with a second benefit. He couldn't see the car used by the three men at the old cabin. Using a sub-account email from a seldom-used email account at Comcast, his snitch had provided him with the make, model, and tag number of the car used by Buck What's-his-name. After copying the information, he deleted the email and the sub-account. With that done, he hacked into Comcast and made sure all traces of the email disappeared into electron never-never land.

From there, he surfed to the DMV database and found out that the vehicle was owned by CCS. He had expected as much. Buck, if that, too, was a real name, wouldn't be so careless as to own a car with the registration in his own name. Too easily traceable. Plus, from his time at CCS and a previous run-in with the man, he had discovered that the man's existence had been wiped clean. No birth certificate, no tax records, no real estate records, never went to school. Yet, how thorough had they been?

Adam would have to be careful with his next few actions. Hacking into any government database was fraught with the risk of serious prison time. Hacking into the DoD systems added the chance of never being seen again. Particularly now with the Deep State on edge. They were doing everything they could to manipulate the upcoming election and regain control through ex-VP "Po" Sidon. He had seen firsthand with Sam what he might face should they trace him. He needed to do this while still in Virginia and then boogie out of there as fast as he could.

The first firewall was a no-brainer to break through, but each successive layer of protection required "looking" forward and backward along his trail to make sure he hadn't hit any tripwires that would initiate a trace on him. He had faith in his VPN's ability to cloak his whereabouts, but even so, he'd added his own protections to break any trace that might begin.

To add to that cover, he used credentials once possessed by Sam. His software had discovered that Sam's family believed him to be alive and on special assignment overseas. Adam had witnessed that ploy once before. In a few days, maybe a week, the family would get a visit from CCS security, sadly informing them of Sam's unexpected demise. That worked in his favor. Only Chamberlain and Buck would suspect that *he* was the one using Sam's creds. To everyone else, his friend remained alive. Once his death was revealed, how long would DoD personnel attempt to trace a dead man?

He wasn't looking for Top Secret weapons plans or operational data. He was looking for personnel data, although of the type that very likely *was* Top Secret. Chamberlain and Buck had a past, of that he was sure. And he suspected that history went back to the Middle East and Chamberlain's activities there. With some luck, he would discover the man's real name and, with a *lot* of luck, his personnel file.

He checked his phone for the time. This was taking too long. The longer he lingered there, the greater the chance of being discovered.

Bingo! He had the personnel file for Wallace Chamberlain open in front of him and wasted no time downloading it. As he scanned select pages from the document, he discovered info related to a black ops group commanded by Chamberlain in Iraq. Within the cadre was a Sergeant First Class Henry "Buck" Buckner.

Now that he had a name, he would find the man's

personnel file, but he needed to hurry. One of his trip wires had just been triggered. He had little time. He set up a false flag, hoping to divert whoever was looking for him down a useless rabbit hole.

There! He had the file. Now he hoped he had the time to download the entire thing. He knew the Army would never erase one of its own. Buck Buckner might have no civilian identity, but he would forever be part of the team.

95% . . . 96% . . . A second trip wire alerted him. One more to go before he would have to shut down. 97% . . . 98% . . . Three strikes. He was out. He immediately closed down his operation and instructed his system to clean the path his VPN had used to protect him. They would not be able to back track and find him. Even if they linked their intruder to Sam Renner, the man was dead. True, they could link Sam to CCS, but no investigator in his right mind would dive into Lt. Gen (Ret) Wallace Chamberlain's pool. The drain in the deep end would suck him down into it and not let him up for air.

So . . .98, maybe 99% percent of Buckner's personnel file was his. It would do quite well for what he had in mind.

With the two men's personnel files in his possession, he lowered their rankings within his nameless software —a program best served by remaining anonymous. It would continue its search in the background, but now its top priority was Carolyn and her abductor.

TEN

"Sir, General Hodge on the phone for you. He insists on talking to you now."

Wallace debated taking the call, but getting one, urgent or otherwise, from the commanding general of ARCYBER was unusual. Professionally, they had crossed paths in Wallace's previous position as DNI at the White House. However, the man had only recently taken a position where they might have worked closely together if Wallace was still DNI. The man's assignment as commander of the U.S. Army Cyber Command was about a year old, while Wallace had joined civilian life five years previously. Socially, they were on a first-name basis through a handful of Washington social events that the man and his wife left Fort Gordon to attend.

"By all means, Sue, put him through." Wallace placed his phone on speaker mode.

Lt. General Michael D. Hodge was one of those men Wallace had never been able to dig up much dirt on—if any. He was a "God and Country" sort who took the security of this country seriously. He lived "by the book" and expected that of his subordinates. Wallace respected him for that, as well as for his military credentials: Airborne, Master Parachutist, Air Assault, and Ranger qualified—all achievements one wouldn't expect of a computer nerd. He had risen through the ranks of military intelligence, had served overseas with NATO's Security Assistance Force, and had directed the Joint Intelligence Operations Center in Afghanistan, but after Wallace's tour there. He was a man Wallace would love to have on his team, but he would never tolerate Wallace's "extracurricular" activities. The guy was squeaky clean with nothing Wallace could hold over him to help mold him to Wallace's ways of thinking.

"Mike, to what do I owe the honor of your call?"

"Wallace, are you on a secure line?"

"As secure as they come. I do have you on speaker, but I'm alone in my office."

There was a pause on the other end. The general finally said, "Okay, but you still might want to go off speaker."

This sounded serious. Wallace picked up his phone's handset and took it off speaker.

"All right, I'm off speaker. What's up?"

"What are you doing, having one of your hackers trying to break into DODIN?"

The man's anger was evident in his tone of voice. And to Wallace, he had every right to be. Breaking into the Department of Defense Information Network was a serious crime.

"I don't know what you're talking about. We have no need to hack DODIN or any other DoD system."

In truth, CCS and 75% of its personnel had Top Secret/SCI clearance to work on the government contracts awarded to them. Of course, "need to know" remained a critical component to such access.

"We had a major breach about an hour ago. From what

my people have been able to piece together, the hacker has some serious skills, and his credentials come through CCS."

"Mike, I can assure you we have no reason to break into the Army side of DODIN, any part of the network for that matter. Can you tell me what he was after?"

"Nothing specific. Just that he was inside an area with sensitive personnel data. We don't think he was able to get anything, but we're still working on that. He managed to set some trip wires, which alerted him that we were on to him. He shut down quickly enough that we couldn't trace him."

Wallace was puzzled. His people were highly vetted—they had to be to get such high-level clearance—and their activities, both on and off the job, were closely monitored.

"You keep saying 'he.' Do you have a name?"

"No, but we found an access code that was used, part of a set of codes granted to CCS."

"Give me the code, and I'll check it right now."

As the general spoke the code, Wallace entered it into his computer. He took a deep breath as a name came up. That couldn't be right.

"Who is it, Wallace?" asked Hodge.

"I'll have to get back to you, Mike."

"No way. If you have a name, I need it now. If you refuse, I'll revoke every clearance CCS has to DoD systems."

Wallace sensed the man was serious, and he had the authority to do just what he threatened. CCS couldn't afford to fight such revocations, and the executive board would take a DODIN breach as seriously as Hodge. They wouldn't side with Wallace on this one.

"The name I'm coming up with is impossible. His name's Sam Renner, but he's been overseas on an assignment, and I just got word this morning that he was involved in a serious incident. Shot and killed."

"Well, you can expect a full investigation."

Wallace now heard more concern than anger in the man's voice.

"Wallace, if your man was murdered for his credentials and access, we have a much more serious problem. You need to cut all his access immediately."

"W-we certainly will. I'll get my security guys on this right away, too. We'll cooperate fully."

"I know you will. I'll be in touch."

As the line disconnected, Wallace sat there stunned. His mind raced for a solution. Renner's being overseas was fiction. His alleged death overseas wasn't to become part of the story for several more days. Wallace gave Hodge that line without thinking. It had been part of their cover-up and was the first thing to come to mind. Now, he regretted that. How in the world would they be able to set the stage for their scenario to pass muster under detailed scrutiny?

He picked up his phone and dialed Buck. "We need to pull the plug on Renner today. Don't wait until next week."

ELEVEN

While Dan seemed nonplussed, Aric didn't like having Pete sitting in the back seat of the Jeep watching their every move. At least they weren't forced to listen to any of his leftist drivel. He was as quiet as Dan in the car. Did it run in the family?

After a quick lunch in Laramie, as they headed west on I-80, Aric's curiosity won out, and he decided to find out a bit more about Pete and his ideas. He turned in his seat and faced the back as best he could.

"So, tell me more about this Antifa group."

Pete eyed him suspiciously. "Why do you want to know?"

"Just curious."

"Yeah, well, curiosity killed the cat."

Aric wasn't to be deterred. "I get it. Avoiding an answer is your way of saying you don't know what it's about. You just follow some leader who tells you this and that." Aric saw Dan roll his eyes and offer a subtle shake of his head. "All I know about it is that it stands for anti-fascism. Do you even know what fascism is?" Now Dan furrowed his brow. Was Aric treading dangerously by challenging Pete?

"Yeah, well, fascism is the Graham administration and its racist, misogynistic, xenophobic actions. He's the Hitler of our day, and we're part of the resistance out to stop him and his followers."

Aric mentally debated mentioning that Hitler led Germany's National *Socialist* German Workers Party, known in short as the Nazi Party. Socialists, not fascists. And the President was far from being a socialist.

"So, you think President Graham is a dictator with total control and absolute power, who has squashed the press and those with opposing views by force? If so, how come you're not in prison?"

Pete's brow narrowed as he thought about that one. To Aric, anyone with half a brain would know that no President in the U.S. had such absolute dictatorial power and that the press was out of control *against* President Graham, no matter what he did. As much as some might like to see the media suppressed, it would never happen.

"No, I said he was a fascist."

"But that's the definition of fascism, having a dictator who uses force to control the government, eliminate a free press, and control all industry and commerce."

Pete's demeanor took on a defiant attitude. "Yeah, well, he's always pushing America first and is a racist."

"Well, I agree with his desire to place America first. What country's leader doesn't? We need jobs for our people, and the previous administrations eagerly pushed our industries to outsource to other countries."

"Listen, brainiac, I don't need no lectures. Dan tells me you're a Christian, too, besides being a brain. If you're so smart, why do you believe that make-believe?" A smirk crossed Pete's mouth as if pleased to turn the tables.

This turn in the conversation totally surprised Aric. Until recently, he'd been comfortable in his faith. Was it really just yesterday that he'd acknowledged he'd never been challenged in it? Yet, how should he answer? He wasn't ready for this test, if that's what it was. He needed time to prepare.

"Why do you think it's make-believe?" Answering a question with a question was a good stall.

"C'mon, really?" Pete gave him a look of doubt. "The Bible says God created the earth in six days and that Adam and Eve were the original people. But science shows us the earth is millions, if not billions, of years old and that man evolved from apes. Chimpanzees even share, what, like 98% of our human DNA. Both can't be true."

Aric realized he had a point. He'd always been taught the universe was old and had started with a big bang. Every school taught that life had evolved from random collections of chemicals in the primordial ooze of the early universe forming amino acids and then proteins and on down the line to man. He'd never really taken time to evaluate that against the Bible. He had no immediate answer that could reconcile the discrepancy.

"And what about this God of yours being a God of love. If that's so, why is there so much evil in the world? Systemic racism, xenophobia, hatred, all of it. If God exists, why does he let that happen?"

Aric thought about that for a moment and recognized he had at least a partial answer to that one.

"So, if you're upset about all the evil and hatred in the world, why are you planning things that many people consider evil? Why do you and your friends spew such hatred for President Graham and the people who support him? Why aren't you promoting unity and encouraging people to get along?" More questions. Maybe he could turn this argument around and put Pete on the defensive.

Pete sat back in his seat and didn't have a quick reply.

Aric felt as if he'd scored a point on that one. After a moment, Pete leaned forward again.

"Because Graham and his cronies *are* the evil ones. We need to purge the world of people like him so we can have unity and peace. And sometimes a purge takes more than marching, protest signs, and chanting slogans."

Aric shook his head. "According to the Bible, what you're about to do is evil, not the other way around."

"How do you know what we're about to do?" Pete gave him a level of scrutiny that made Aric uncomfortable.

"Because it's already started . . . in Portland, Seattle, Minneapolis. It's in the news today. I saw it on my phone. Violent protests, looting, burning, attacking police officers. That's what you're going to Portland and Seattle to support, right? The Bible would call that evil."

"Well, the Bible's a bunch of make-believe, so why should I live by its rules? We make our own rules."

At that moment, Aric realized what he was fighting, or at least part of it . . . and that he was ill-prepared for this particular battle. His youth pastor had taught once about postmodernism. There was no absolute truth. Morality was relative. One man's right was another man's wrong, but both could be valid, even when a third man came along with a different opinion. Even the meanings of words could be different to different people. Everything was relative, while the Bible presented *absolute* truths.

Aric had no idea how to contend with that. He was not an apologist for Christianity, but at that moment, he wished he was better prepared to defend his faith. As he thought about it, he realized he was not alone in such a lack of preparation. Prominent leaders in the church, popular

Christian musicians, and other celebrities who once touted their Christianity were making the news by denouncing their faith. Was this part of the great falling away that Christ had forewarned His disciples about?

Aric felt a renewed concern about going to Portland. The actions of Antifa were not something he would ever condone, but they now swept him and Dan into its maelstrom of violence. He said a short silent prayer that they would be able to escape the thorns after arriving in the City of Roses. Yet, beyond that, he began to wonder what lay ahead for the world as a whole. Was the tribulation described in the Book of Revelation just around the corner?

TWELVE

Adam departed his cabin by mid-morning and headed north from Leesburg, Virginia, to Frederick, Maryland, where he picked up I-70 to start his trek west. He decided to avoid all tollways where possible. Buying a pass would require the use of a credit card, and yet, paying cash would put his face squarely on camera at each tollbooth. He might be able to finagle the former without triggering AlterNet's watchful "eyes," but the latter held the potential to place him in the middle of that surveillance system's cross-hairs. Buckner had already come within 16 miles of his location in the cabin despite his best precautions. His drive would take longer with that decision, but he would avoid the Pennsylvania, Ohio, Indiana, and Illinois tollway systems to the north.

Six hours later, he stopped for gas and food outside Columbus, Ohio. He kept his mask on and the brim of his ball cap low to reduce the profile that might be captured by the center's cameras. Yes, the odds were slim to none that AlterNet's tentacles would reach into this chain's security systems, but he preferred zero chance, not that such was genuinely possible.

He picked up his food from the drive-thru window and parked in the lot to eat. That way, he could still make use of the facility's free Wi-Fi if need be. He'd have to be careful doing so, as such a system would be public and offer no security.

As he ate his burger, he decided to review the personnel files he had downloaded. Chamberlain's file revealed little beyond his formal military service … until the last few pages. *Interesting,* thought Adam. The man still had high-level military security credentials, not just the civilian creds they received at CCS. Was that standard practice for retired general staff officers? Maybe it was because of his previous White House position. He'd have to dig into those possibilities and try to find an answer. Because if it wasn't typical, why did he have those creds several years after leaving public service?

"What's this? He spotted a notation to something called adrenochrome. The note was cryptic. What was adrenochrome? It looked like the guy received it regularly during his last year in service, as well as in his DNI position. Was he still using it?

He pulled up Buckner's file and scanned through it quickly. As he did so, an idea came to mind. But more importantly, there was no reference to adrenochrome. What was it, and why would Chamberlain be getting it, but Buckner not?

He finished his burger and wolfed down his fries. After washing that down with a gulp of iced tea, he moved to the internet, only to stop short. Despite his eagerness to learn more about this mysterious substance that sounded like a drug, he would have to be careful. To search for it on the net might trigger an alert. Plus, if it was a drug for the privileged elites, he likely wouldn't find anything on it on the world wide web. He'd have better luck on the Deep Web, and he sure wasn't heading there via a fast-food restaurant's internet link.

He dumped his trash and hurried back to the highway. He needed to get a minimum of 10 hours on the road each day if he wanted to make it to Portland in time. On his current route, he needed to get to Champaign, Illinois, for the night. There, he could set up his satellite link and more securely surf the Deep Web. He hoped this was not some rabbit hole that would snare him and become a detour in his search. Still, something told him that adrenochrome might be crucial to bringing down Chamberlain and a bunch of others who saw themselves ruling the world . . . and that it would bring him one step closer to discovering what happened to his daughter.

Alaine Tavernier was a man of distinguished tastes, brought up in France's upper class, and trained in the life sciences at École normale supérieure - PSL, France's most prestigious university. His areas of study were Genetics and Developmental Biology, and Dynamics of Genetic Information, in which he graduated with the highest honors. His doctorate from the University of Cambridge focused on epigenetic control of genomic expression.

"Alaine, have you seen this?"

Tavernier furrowed his brow in questioning his assistant. "Have I seen what?"

"The chimp in number 10. Take a look."

Tavernier stepped across the hallway to the veterinary section and hurried up to holding cage #10. He knew this animal well, having brought it with him from the West Coast. The male was 35 years old when they first gave it adrenochrome almost six years earlier. With the average age of captive male chimps being around 41 years, it was not expected to live much longer at that time. Instead, adrenochrome had made it as active as a chimp half its age. No signs of noticeable aging had appeared. He reflected on the fact that this animal was one of the subjects that convinced the executive board to progress to human study.

Today, the animal languished in its cage, its food uneaten. Tavernier noticed a slight tremor in the animal's hands. He wanted a closer look but knew caution was in order. A healthy adult male chimp was ten times stronger than the average man, and this one, being ill, could be unpredictable. As Tavernier eased open the latch on the door, it snarled and bared its teeth but made no move toward him. He quickly secured the latch. Not only was the inactivity unusual, this chimp knew Tavernier and had never made an aggressive gesture toward him. Something was terribly wrong.

Tavernier looked at his assistant, who had followed him to the cage. "Has something changed for our friend here? This is not right."

"Nothing that I can tell. The old guy's diet is the same. No one has been ill around him. Certainly, there is no COVID in the lab. He received his second dose of the new extract yesterday, but he tolerated the first dose well and seemed more robust than ever after it."

Tavernier knew that chimps suffered severely when exposed to human respiratory illnesses. COVID could not be expected to affect them otherwise. He hoped this was no more than a passing condition. To consider it a result of a flaw in the new extract was not something Tavernier wanted to think about. Two dozen doses of the new adrenochrome had left the facility with J.B. Gradison. For whom they were destined, he had no idea, but if J.B. was involved, Tavernier had no doubt that those doses would find their way to some very important and powerful men.

"We must retest everyone here for COVID and check again for viral illnesses. Who was the donor of the extract?"

His assistant checked the animal's paperwork. "Looks like 20161025F290."

"Recheck the donor's serum, too. We need to isolate whatever this is."

"Yes, sir. I'm on it."

Being in isolation as they were, viral illnesses among the donors were unlikely, but the presence of such would demand an immediate halt of their work until the virus' spread was stopped. Tavernier could not afford such a delay. He had promised higher quality and productivity, not the opposite.

He looked at the chimp and said, "We'll get you fixed, old friend." He double-checked the latch, locked the cage, and left the area.

He descended to and walked through the facility's underground housing area, looking for 20161025F290 in particular. He glanced about, without shame, at those being detained. True, it had not been their choice to be here, but they were crucial to his work and held the potential key to unlocking immortality for those deserving of such. Did they understand their importance? If he and his fellow scientists succeeded, they would be remembered throughout history.

Their names would be forever revered, even if they were known only by numbers here.

As he had on other walks through the housing area, he noted the difference between this new facility and the three where he had previously worked. The air held a scent of pine, not feces and urine. The floor was clean, not covered with the body fluids of their detainees. The main area was well-lit as well, not like some medieval dungeon.

Warden Skelter was to be praised for these improvements. To Tavernier, they were the prime reason for the improvements in their adrenochrome. They required the highest adrenalin levels possible in their donors when their blood was harvested. In his previous camps, Tavernier had noted that their donors' baseline levels of adrenalin were high, meaning their adrenal glands were overworked and unable to react when elevated levels were needed. These donors also saw their lifespans shortened by adrenal failure.

But with Skelter's changes, the environment gave the donors time to calm down between, well, between the trials and tribulations used to make them produce the adrenalin and adrenochrome needed. Their adrenal glands had a chance to rest before a renewed terror threw them into panic mode.

As he turned a corner in the hallway, he heard whimpering to his right. He walked to the door and glanced through the portal. Clearly, the individual had been through the harvesting process earlier that day. Tavernier looked at the donor's chart hanging next to the door. Yes, 20091103M150 had been tapped again. The graph of the boy's adrenalin levels showed they were falling below the levels needed, as to be expected of an eleven-year-old who had been with them for five years. Tavernier looked again. Yes, his disposal date had been set for two months ahead. *Perhaps he's one of those involved in the hunt,* wondered Tavernier.

He turned and continued down the hall. *Now, where is that four-year-old little girl?*

THIRTEEN

To call the trip from Denver to Portland bittersweet would have been accurate if you emphasized the bitter. Aric found the mountains and scenic vistas incredible and wished he and Dan could have spent more time exploring the region. However, he needed to be in Portland by the fifth, so sightseeing would have been limited in the best of conditions. At least, this way, he didn't have to come up with excuses to Dan for his need to hurry to Portland.

But their conditions were far from ideal. He and Dan had become literal prisoners of Pete's mob, and they were taking their time about getting to Oregon—not because they wished to explore but due to their addictions. They managed only five or six hours a day of road time—with Pete or one of his comrades in the Jeep at all times—and spent time partying, smoking weed, and doing crack well into the early hours of the morning. They slept in as long as possible before checking out minutes before the required time.

While Dan and Aric were afforded the compromise of having a motel room to themselves, Pete forced Dan—under threat of bodily harm—to give up the Jeep's keys when off the road. On the sweet side, the room expense and some meals were somehow covered by Pete, saving the boys considerable cash. Also, they weren't staying in cheap mom

& pop places or even budget digs like Motel 6 or Super 8. The Holiday Inn - Nampa was one of the three most expensive motels in town, and they'd all eaten carry-out from Olive Garden the night before—not super expensive but not fast-food burgers either.

Nampa, Idaho, was just over a six-hour drive to Portland. Aric hoped they would get there that day. He and Dan ate breakfast in the motel's restaurant, which they found open with limited seating. The others were still asleep and had less than an hour to get up, eat, and check out.

Aric looked at Dan after swallowing the food currently in his mouth. "So, did you find out any more? How are they paying for all of this stuff? They're not exactly living like the proletariat, downtrodden workers fighting for the party."

Dan furrowed his brow. "Prolie-what?"

Aric smiled. "Proletariat, the lower-class workers, selling their labor to survive. That's how Karl Marx sold communism to the masses, promising them they could become part of the middle class."

Dan rolled his eyes. "Whatever, brainiac." He took a large bite of pancakes and chewed. After washing that down with juice, he went on. "I overheard Pete talking with one of the others about an executive board and some billionaire back east. They're covering the tab for all the protesters coming in from out of town. I think he said the billionaire's name was Boris or something like that. Anyway, the other guy mentioned that he and a few of the others had gone to a place called Ferguson some years back to protest a police shooting and were put up at a four-star hotel called the Chase Park Place, or Plaza, or something, for the duration of their stay there." He went back to eating.

Aric nodded. "C'mon, Dan, think about it. Ferguson. We live like fifteen minutes away. We were eleven or twelve, I think. Remember? All the protests? And the Chase Park Plaza Hotel is next to Forest Park and the hospitals. That's where two of my sisters had their senior proms. Really ritzy."

The light of recognition lit Dan's face. "Oh, yeah. All that 'hands up, don't shoot,' 'black lives matter,' and 'no justice, no peace' stuff. I remember that. And they proved the hands up thing was a lie."

"Yep." Aric finished the omelet on his plate and sipped his coffee. Recognition hit him, too. Boris . . . Soros. The billionaire's puppets in Ferguson had protested at the man's St. Louis organization a year later for not having been paid.

"Gee, I wonder where we'll be staying in Portland. If Pete's sugar daddy is paying for all this, wouldn't it be sweet to stay in a four-star hotel? Think about it."

Aric shook his head. "Don't count on it."

They both got cups of coffee to go and charged breakfast to the room. Aric was sure this was as far as Pete's hospitality would go. Once in Portland, with Pete and his comrades busy protesting, they'd be able to slip away. Aric would get Dan to retrieve the package from the post office, and then . . .

Then what? He hadn't thought that far ahead. What would he tell Dan at that point? *Hey, sorry, Dan. I was just using you to get here and get the package, but now we need to split up, and I can't tell you why.* How would that go over? Should he tell him the truth? He still might feel like he'd been used. Which he was. Aric had to be honest with himself.

He was six-plus hours from his goal, but he hadn't been

honest with his friend. Of course, with their backseat chaperones over the past few days, he'd had no opportunity to broach the topic in the car. And at night in their room, he honestly hadn't thought about it.

His best bet would be to take Dan with him, or them, if his brother was there. Dan always talked of adventure. Yeah, that's how Aric would approach it—as an adventure. In reality, it was just that, with Adam on the lam from whatever and having to stay in hiding. Dan would see it that way, too. He was sure of it.

Buck sat at his desk reviewing end-of-month security reports for CCS. The pandemic had taken a toll on his workforce, and the decision to allow working from home had created its own set of nightmares for the security team. Setting up secure internet connections, sweeping homes for bugs and other potential security breaches, and monitoring all online activity kept him and his crew busier than usual, with a workload that seemed to increase with each week.

He'd had no time to even worry about their missing man, much less time to take off on other snipe hunts like the one they'd taken to western Maryland a few days earlier. Wallace would have to be satisfied that no whistles had been blown and that no damaging information had surfaced on the net. Of that much, Buck could assure him.

Yet, his mind wandered. He'd learned of the phone call from CG, ARCYBER, although not of its contents. He debated asking Wallace directly but thought better of it. If the phone call in any way affected Buck, Wallace would have told him so. Best to leave that snake to bask in the sun.

His cell phone rang, and he checked the Caller ID before answering. This call would be brief.

"Yes?"

"It's Pete, sir."

"Yes, I know it's you. Do you have something significant to report? Has the boy been contacted?"

"Um, no, sir. I just wanted you to know that we've had him under direct observation since I called you last. And we'll continue to do so, as best we can."

"What do you mean 'as best you can?' "

There was a pause. "Well, um, we'll be in Portland later today, and then we have a job to do. We, uh, I, uh, can't be expected to babysit this guy 24/7 and do what we're being paid to do."

Buck shook his head. The man was a drugged-out twit. He should have sent one of his own men to infiltrate the group to do the job. Too late for that.

"Look, Lewis, part of the job you're being paid to do is watch Aric Afton. If that's too much for you, I can cut off your funds immediately and find someone else."

He heard a groan. "Okay, as long as you understand that it might distract us from the cause there."

"We'll have 200 others just as dedicated as you there to stir things up. I think we can spare you for a while to keep Afton under surveillance."

"Yes, sir. Got it. Will do."

Buck had to give the man some credit. He might be an addict, but he was committed and eager to stir things up for "the cause." He was the kind whom they could easily arouse to riot and create mayhem. As such, the mundane task of babysitting, as he had put it, was not what he had signed on for. Buck had experienced such feelings in Special Ops when he had to sit on an informant.

"Good. Now don't waste my time unless you have something concrete for me."

Buck hung up and noticed his gut grumbling. Not hunger, intuition. Why was the kid in Portland, especially with the riots and other turmoil there? There had to be a reason. Why travel at all with the pandemic forcing businesses and popular attractions to close? His gut told Buck that maybe this wasn't another snipe hunt.

He looked at his personnel roster to see whom he might be able to spare to go to Oregon. On second thought, this was a task he needed to perform personally.

The route from Nampa along the Snake River, north into the Umatilla National Forest and the Blue Mountains, and finally west along the Columbia River might have been a beautiful drive had one of Pete's buddies been in the car as their monitor. Those guys would have been quiet and allowed Dan and Aric the peace to enjoy the scenery.

Instead, Pete was with them and wasted no time before spouting his worldview about everything wrong with the country: systemic racism, white privilege—despite his being white, the lack of women's rights, the criminalization of recreational drugs, climate change, and ultimately, the role of the current President in maintaining the status quo. His rants against capitalism and corporate America with its overpaid executives seemed incredibly hypocritical since his funding came from a wealthy elite that made its money off capitalism. To Aric, his pro-socialist views revealed a total lack of understanding about socialism and communism.

But that was Aric's opinion. Dan seemed to soak in a lot of what his cousin spewed. Besides his concern that his friend might be swayed by Pete, Aric worried that he might risk too much by confiding in him.

Pete saved his worst vitriol for the last 30 minutes of the trip. As they entered the northeastern urban area of Portland, he again began to denounce God and Christianity. If there's a God, why do we see so much pain? Why would a loving God allow that? He repeated his talk about apparent discrepancies in the Bible and science's challenge to what was taught in church. Then, his focus shifted.

"So, tell me, brainiac. If Christians are such good people, why don't they show the love of God to others? Isn't that what the Bible tells 'em to do, love one another?"

Aric had an answer for that one. "That's a common misunderstanding of what the Bible teaches. Yeah, we're to show respect and compassion for everyone. Still, the teachings about loving one another specifically address Christians loving fellow brothers and sisters in Christ, not everyone in a general sense."

"Then, why don't they do that?"

"Huh?" He thought he'd given a good answer, but the guy blew it off. Again, Pete caught him off-guard.

"So why don't they do what you just said? The Christians I've known weren't any different from anyone else—they smoked, they drank, some cheated on their wives, they were judgmental and hateful, especially of gays and women who aborted unwanted children. And they seemed most judgmental of other Christians."

Aric had no immediate rebuttal. He, too, had seen such hypocrisy in people who professed to be followers of Christ.

"All I can say is that accepting Christ as one's Lord and Savior doesn't make you instantly perfect. We're all sinners in need of grace. And many people claim to be Christians but don't have the foggiest idea of what He teaches. They just call themselves Christian because their parents and grandparents were and because they're not Buddhists or Muslims or something else. And the media does its best to portray these stereotypes and not the Christians who are truly following Christ's teachings."

These criticisms of Christians hit Aric the hardest because they were too often true. While most of the believers in their church were honest, hard-working people who tried their best to emulate the Lord, there were those just like Pete had witnessed. Aric wished he had better answers for Pete. And it hit him that maybe, just maybe, Pete had been placed in his path for that very reason—to motivate him to find those answers.

Aric's first view of the downtown skyline came as they merged onto southbound I-5 and traveled along the Willamette River. They crossed on the SE Morrison Bridge and exited onto the SW Naito Parkway.

"The rest of the crew is heading to our staging area to unload. A bus will bring them to the hotel. We're heading directly to the hotel, and I've arranged a room for you two on the same floor as me," said Pete.

A half-mile later, he added, "There. The Marriott. Pull into the drive."

Dan grinned, and his eyes bugged out as he saw the hotel looming over them. "Sweeet."

That Dan was getting his wish to experience staying in a four-star hotel was a two-edged sword for Aric. Yeah, it would be nice to get that experience on someone else's nickel and save cash for their trip, but it was the reason behind it all that was a problem. He didn't want to be associated with these anarchists or even *appear* to be guilty by association. He also hoped it wasn't going to sway Dan, but free stuff had a way of influencing people. However, there was one strong plus for Aric. The post office he needed to go to was just two blocks away.

FOURTEEN

Adam had put in a 12-hour drive the day before to get to Portland early in the afternoon. As he crossed the Willamette River and headed into the downtown area, he wondered two things: whether or not Aric had made it and what kind of police presence he might encounter.

He needed to get to the post office on SW Madison to post his package that day so that Aric could retrieve it the next day. He had cut it short on timing, maybe too short, which was why he needed to post the package at the very branch he had instructed Aric to go to.

At the time he had sent Aric the postcard, no protests or riots were going on. Now, nearly a week of daily protests and nightly riots had placed Portland among the news cycle's top stories. He followed those stories closely because Aric was heading into the fray, and he had no way of diverting him.

He drove along Naito Parkway, looking for his turn. Between one-way streets and access lanes to the Hawthorne Bridge, he couldn't turn directly onto Madison. *Thank you, Google maps*, he thought. He prepared to turn right onto SW Taylor Street and then left onto 1st Avenue. As he came to that intersection, a police barricade stopped traffic from going any farther along Taylor. An officer flagged him to stop and walked up to his window, his hand on his gun. Adam powered down his window.

"Yes, sir?"

"Where you headin'?"

"Uh, I was heading to the post office on SW Madison to post a parcel."

The officer shook his head. "Sorry, that branch is closed, and you can't go down Taylor. We've had to close off this portion of downtown. Your best bet's going to be the branch on 5th Ave, at Pine. Do you know where that is?"

"Um, no, sir."

The officer gave him directions that took him in the opposite direction he needed to go. But then, if the branch he'd selected was closed, what was he going to do? Even if he got close enough to park and walk, what good would that do?

He turned and headed along the directions given him. He would find a place to park and then strategize his next moves. First, he needed to find a place for the night that would afford him easier access to that part of the city. While looking for a parking spot, he realized he only had one option when it came to Aric. He would have to stake out the postal branch until he spotted Aric. There were two problems with that. One, he had no idea when Aric might show up, assuming he was going to. What if he hadn't gotten the message or had been forced to stay at home? Two, whether he sat there for an hour or several days, he was in the open. And with the city on edge and the police on alert, being exposed was much more problematic than if it was a beautiful day in the neighborhood.

Wallace tidied up his desk at the end of his day, preparing for a night out with his wife despite lockdowns being issued at increasing rates across the country. The information they released through the media was designed to create confusion and uncertainty as a means of causing fear in the people. Likewise, the medical advice being given to the current President came from contradictory sources in the ongoing effort to make him look wrong and ill-informed. The executive board had a PsyOps team that excelled at the game. All stops were being pulled out to remove this administration and make way for global governance.

He picked up a stack of secure papers and placed them in the cabinet safe inside the credenza nearby. As he returned to his desk to close down his computer, the intercom buzzed.

"Mr. Buckner, sir."

"Of course. Show him in."

Wallace glanced up as the door to his office opened and Buck walked in.

"Sir, glad I caught you before you left."

"So am I. What's up?" He always appreciated not being disturbed at home.

Buck walked up to the front of the desk, opposite Wallace.

"I'll be brief. I'd like your authorization to use the company jet to go to Portland. Preferably tonight."

"Portland? Why there? The board has good people on the ground directing the situation and media there."

"I'm aware of that. I have an Antifa group leader watching Afton's kid brother, and they've just arrived in Portland." He went on to explain the younger Afton's intention to go west with a friend and how they changed their plan from Southern California to Portland at the last minute, apparently at the insistence of Aric Afton. He mentioned the coincidence of the boy's friend being a cousin to the Antifa leader and the leader's plan to trap the boys into staying with the cell so he would have direct surveillance at all times. "My gut's telling me the kid's somehow been contacted by his brother, and that's the reason behind the change. I might just find a clue to getting to Afton, or even the man himself, by going there."

Wallace had seen that gut instinct at work. He came to trust it on the battlefield, and he would entrust it now.

"If that's what your gut is telling you, by all means, you have my authorization to use whatever resources you need to rid us of this wayward son."

Buck gave a single nod of his head. "Thank you, sir."

Wallace made a call to have the jet readied and waiting and then pointed to the door. "Walk with me."

"Yes, sir."

Wallace picked up his briefcase, and together they walked to Buckner's office, where he, too, gathered what he needed. They talked business on the way to the executive parking garage. Before parting ways, Wallace decided to incentivize the man's "gut" and offered him a nice six-figure bonus should he succeed in eliminating their problem in Portland.

With earlier lockdowns slowly easing and some restaurants re-opening for limited inside dining, finding places to eat along the way had not been difficult. Portland, however, was another story. The Governor's stay-at-home order of March seemed draconian and remained in effect. Restaurants could not open for on-site dining, so only those capable of offering carry-out food remained in business. The number of restaurants unable to provide such service surprised Aric. And that included the hotel's main eatery.

More shocking was the mask mandate for the outdoors. Aric felt confident that no one would catch a virus, COVID or otherwise, while outside. At least, that's what his doctor once told him. Air currents—whether just a breeze, a strong wind, or the draft from a passing vehicle—were enough to dissipate any virus-containing aerosol such that the amount of virus needed to cause infection never accumulated.

With their ever-present "jailer" tagging along, Dan and Aric hurried outside to find food. Pete acted as though he didn't want to be seen with them and remained a socially distant six feet behind them. Aric led them north, not because of a specific food source but because the post office he needed was two blocks north and one block west of the hotel. He wanted to scope it out in the hope of creating a plan for getting there. The fifth was tomorrow.

"C'mon, you two. We have food being catered in. All you see out here are sandwich joints and Starbucks, just like it shows on Google maps," Pete complained as he held up his phone for display.

"He has a point, Aric. How can you pass up a good meal, a *free* meal, for the stuff we're seeing?" Dan slowed his pace.

Aric leaned toward his friend and, in a low voice, said, "Humor me. One more block, and if there isn't something really enticing, we'll head back."

Dan nodded. "Okay." He turned back to address his

cousin. "One more block. If we don't find something, we'll head back."

Aric saw the post office across the street to his right. The windows and doors were boarded up, barricades blocked the entrance, and a big sign directed people to use the main post office on SW Main Street.

Aric's mind whirled. *Closed? What do I do now?* Would a general delivery package be forwarded to that one post office? Was he going to tell Pete he needed stamps? Yeah, right. This was a disaster. He'd come this far only to be left in limbo.

Every fiber in his body told him his brother was here, in Portland. The parcel, or letter, or whatever was to be delivered was just a tool to connect them. Adam wouldn't have led him this far only to pick up a letter telling him to go someplace else. So, how in the world would he find his brother in this mess?

And calling it a mess was an understatement. In fact, every building they passed was covered with plywood. A block later, they faced a park ahead of them with the county justice center and police headquarters to their right. The area looked like a war zone.

"Oh, wow!" Dan's eyes widened.

Neither of them had ever seen such a scene back home in St. Louis. At least, Aric hadn't, and Dan had never mentioned seeing anything like it to him.

"Look at that, that burned-out police car. I think it's still smoldering. And I've never seen so much plywood. They must have bought out every Home Depot in the city."

All of the buildings facing the park along its entire three-block span were boarded up. Those that didn't get plywood up fast enough no longer had windows. Graffiti covered all of the wood with messages supportive of BLM and Antifa and, to put it politely, not at all supportive of police or any other branch of law enforcement. To Aric, removing or defunding the police would be counterproductive. He'd lay odds that if one of those people had something stolen from his car, he'd demand that the law take action.

As he looked to his right, toward the justice center, he saw a group of maybe 50 people protesting with signs and chants. It appeared peaceful, although the placards spewed the same kind of message as the graffiti. Only maybe half of the protesters wore masks, but no one seemed concerned about that infraction of the Governor's mandate.

"Ah, I see they're getting warmed up," said Pete, smiling.

As the protesters pumped their signs up and down in the air, Pete copied them with his right fist. He noticed Dan glancing back and forth between the protesters and his cousin and halfheartedly mimicking the action a couple of times before looking at Aric and stopping. Was Dan beginning to accept Pete's brainwashing?

Concerned, Aric spoke to his friend. "Dan, don't get swept up by this stuff. Remember the critical thinking skills we've talked about. Think about what they're pushing and what could happen if they get their way."

Dan appeared a bit sheepish, but Aric wasn't sure he got through.

"C'mon, enough. We need to get back to the hotel, eat, get briefed, and grab a short nap. We have a long night ahead."

"We?" asked Aric. He had no plans on joining them. The last thing he wanted to get involved in were the riots in Portland or any other city.

"That's right, brainiac. I'm—"

"Stop calling me brainiac . . ." He was about to call Pete a profane, derogatory name but caught his tongue in time. After the guy's comments about Christians acting like everyone else, he felt embarrassed that he almost proved the man right.

Pete scowled. "Well, well, looks like you've got some spine after all. As I started to say, I'm not letting you out of my sight to bring trouble our way." Pete stepped forward and challenged Aric's personal space.

Dan stepped in-between them. "He won't cause any trouble, Pete. You have my word on that."

Pete backed away. "He'd better not, or blood relative or not, cousin, you'll pay for it."

Aric saw more than malice in Pete's face. He appeared as if there was a demonic presence controlling him . . . which Aric did not doubt.

FIFTEEN

Buck settled into the leather seats of the Gulfstream 650 and prepared for the flight to Portland. While a commercial airliner flying at 500 mph could be expected to make the trip in a little over five hours, the 650 was a transonic aircraft with a max speed of Mach 0.925. They would cruise at Mach .9 and cut off almost an hour from the flight time. By adding in the facts that he had no waiting time at a gate with other passengers and boarding sequences, nor a baggage claim wait on the other end, his actual time savings was closer to three and a half hours. Plus, a private car would be waiting for him on the tarmac upon arrival. With the four-hour time difference, he'd be in Portland not long after his departure time.

Thinking of which, he glanced at his phone for the time. They should have taken off by now. As he prepared to approach the flight deck and ask the pilot about the delay, he noticed two cars speeding toward the plane. After coming to a halt less than 20 feet away, the vehicles' doors opened and discharged their passengers.

Three men emerged from one car. These men he recognized—Oregon's two senators and its congressman from Portland. Wallace must have offered them rides home after departing from Buck at the office. These three boarded without acknowledging Buck with so much as a head nod. They sat as a group closest to the galley, which served mainly as the bar at this time of day. The senior senator wasted no time finding the bottle of Glenfiddich 21-year-old single malt—Wallace's favorite spirit.

The other vehicle held only a single passenger, who took his time retrieving a briefcase and a carry-on piece of luggage. At the base of the steps, the co-pilot relieved him of the carry-on but was rebuffed at his offer to take the case as well. The man took great care of that case. As he entered the cabin, the senior senator greeted him as if old friends and introduced him to the others. They spoke in soft tones, and Buck could only make out the names of the politicians. The man's name escaped him, but the face was familiar.

He had seen this man before, on multiple occasions. He met with Wallace regularly, often with a female assistant in attendance. The meetings never registered on the security logs, and that had puzzled Buck at first. After a while, he shrugged it off as either a personal matter with Wallace or above his pay grade. He understood the latter quite well.

The man's joining the flight piqued Buck's curiosity, but the tender loving care he showed toward that briefcase held more interest. He knew better than to pry, but they now faced four hours together on the flight, and Buck knew they would ultimately engage in conversation. As the man sat down opposite him near the window, Buck greeted him with a nod and "Good evening." Nothing more.

The man held tightly onto the briefcase during take-off and then seemed to relax, placing it on the seat next to him. Upon the pilot's announcement that they could move about the cabin, he arose and walked to the bar. He, too, seemed to know his way around it and fixed a drink that Buck couldn't make out from his seat. The man returned to his place, took a sip, and smiled at Buck. Buck returned the gesture but decided to let the man make the first contact.

Adam found an Econo Lodge near Portland State University just half a mile or so south of the post office. For his situation, the old two-floor, park-outside-your-door style motel, with fast access to the interstate, was perfect for a quick getaway, should it come to that. His other nearby options involved high-rise buildings and relying on elevators to get to and from a room, plus parking garages with exits that could be blocked.

Having spent days in the car, he needed to stretch his legs, and that would allow him to scope out the area. He first checked his map app and saw that two of the four shortest routes took him right into the thick of Chapman Square's protests opposite the justice center. That left two paths, one along 1st Avenue past the back end of the Marriott and another along 2nd Avenue one block west. With the latter, the one-way car traffic would be coming from behind him, providing better anonymity with drivers unable to see his face. For the same reason, the first route might be best for returning to the motel.

With his route decided, he took off for the post office. Choosing to use a hurried pace to get there, he arrived in front of the postal branch less than ten minutes later. As he was told, the office was closed, and signs directed patrons to a branch on Main Street, wherever that was. He glanced about and found he was in luck.

Or is it God's favor? Why had that thought come into his mind? Aric had always been the more zealous of the two for Christ. He recently read that 80% of Christian kids who went to public school and on to college left the faith by the time they graduated. He could understand that. He was one of them.

However, recent events had forced Adam to reflect on his upbringing. After Carolyn's kidnapping and his rescue from the bottle, he found himself on his knees in prayer, sporadically at first but almost daily now. In hindsight, he thought that maybe he could also see God's hand on his discoveries, both the disturbing actions of CCS and Wallace Chamberlain and the mention of adrenochrome.

But why had God allowed the kidnapping of his daughter and the breakup of his marriage and family? Aric had tried to answer that question for him. Something about God having a higher purpose and working all things for the good of His people. And some stuff about God grieving over such tragedies, but that man had free will, and mankind thought it knew better than God how to run society. His brother's comments seemed blurred from the alcohol at the time. Something of those words seemed to ring true in his brain. Still, he had his doubts.

To his advantage, he found that a parking garage occupied the block opposite the post office to the south and a construction storage lot across the street to its east. He could rotate between the two without arousing suspicion and keep an eye on the corner throughout its usual operating hours.

He took his time returning to the motel and found his walking time to be only a few minutes slower. As it ended up, the critical factor was the timing of the stoplights and waiting for crossing lights at the intersections.

His stomach had been growling since his arrival in town, and, as he returned, he stopped into a place called Pizza Schmizza, a block away from the motel. Although he had planned on getting a small pizza, once inside, he impulsively ordered something called the Bac-a-Roni— bacon and pepperoni in a two-cheese macaroni dish. How could that not be a winning dish? With that and a large soda in hand, he returned to his first-floor room.

He set up his laptop on the table with his food and got back down to business as he ate. With information on Buckner from his personnel file, he had been able to use his software to develop a profile on the man. His background information might have been erased to make him a ghost, but his habits hadn't. Three nights earlier, his program alerted him to someone who fit the proposed profile. Two nights earlier, after refinements in the search criteria, he had narrowed his search and obtained marital info, a home address, and more based on the wife's name. Using IP addresses, he had been able to find her social media accounts under a fictitious name. He confirmed Buckner to be her husband via one family photo that probably was not meant for posting. If you looked hard enough under a ghost's sheet, you were bound to find some earthly presence.

Then, the previous evening, while surfing for more dirt on Chamberlain, he had come across adrenochrome again. He still hadn't had the opportunity to dig into the drug itself or its producer. However, he found a reference to others using it: several key senators of both parties as well as senior Democrat leaders of the House of Representatives, the ex-VP now running for President, Big Tech and Big Pharma leaders—but only those over the age of 50, and a dozen or more Hollywood celebs—also those over that age.

That gave him another idea. Buckner had just turned 51, but there was no indication he had been offered the drug. Maybe that could be used to drive a wedge between Chamberlain and Buckner.

He stood and paced the room. *Yeah, that might help*, he thought. But first, he needed to shine a light on the spectral persona known as Henry Buckner—a light that wouldn't pass right through him. For that, Aric would come in very handy.

J.B. sipped his tonic water and lime and eyed the fellow across the aisle on the plane. He knew he worked for Wallace Chamberlain, but not in what capacity. Since the three politicos were hitchhikers like himself, he figured the man was the reason for this last-minute trip to Oregon. And with the three up near the bar discussing various bills before Congress, this was going to be a long four hours if spent in silence.

He smiled at the man again. "I guess you're the one I should thank for letting me tag along, so thank you."

The man smiled back. "Thank Wallace Chamberlain. He's the one who authorized the trip for me."

"I will indeed. I'm J.B. Gradison. Mind if I join you?"

The man pointed to the chair facing him on the other side of the aisle. "Feel free. I'm Henry Buckner. Buck for short."

As J.B. switched seats, he extended his hand to Buck. "Nice to meet you. So, I'll make a wild guess here and assume you work for Wallace. Yes?"

Buck nodded. "Guilty as charged. One of his heads of security. And I'll be upfront and admit that I've seen you at his office on a few occasions."

J.B. thought it odd that he said 'one of' Wallace's security heads. Wallace was a man of many secrets, but how many chiefs does a security team need?

"One of? I've met George Welch. Isn't he the head of security for CCS?"

Buck gave him a look of scrutiny and appeared unsure as to how to answer. "Yes, um, George *is* head of *corporate* security. You might say I'm head of a special projects security team."

Now it was J.B.'s turn to scrutinize Buck. He knew all about the need for a "special projects team," as Buck had termed it. But now, something rang a bell in J.B.'s brain.

"You must be the guy Wallace told me about. Army special ops. You worked with him in Iraq."

Buck nodded again, slowly this time. "Yep. Wallace and I go way back. I was one of his first hires when he started CCS." He seemed reticent to talk about work.

J.B. lowered his voice and leaned toward Buck. "I vaguely remember his telling me about your team. He called it Special Projects Security, too, I think. If I recall it correctly. You interface with the military on sensitive contracts."

Buck had no tells. J.B.'s comment seemed to hit a brick wall and fall to the floor.

"My company has a special projects division, and he recommended a few people to help me watch over it. That's how you came into the conversation."

The man still did not flinch, bat an eye, or lick his lips—zero reaction.

"Well, anyway, nice to meet you."

Buck offered him a meager smile. "You mentioned your company. What do you do, and what company is it?"

"I'm the CEO of YFM Corp. We're a small specialty pharmaceutical firm. You won't find us on any stock exchange, though. We've been privately funded by two members of the executive board. I'm pretty sure you know which board I mean."

Yes, he was positive Buck knew exactly about whom he was talking. In three guesses, he could probably identify which two members.

"Yes."

J.B. waited for more, but the man said nothing further.

"We have a dozen facilities in California and two in Oregon. We don't yet rate our own corporate jet, so I typically charter my flights. Wallace knew of my plan to tour our West Coast operations, and when this flight opportunity came up, he gave me a call and offered me a seat. It's much appreciated, as is his friendship and counsel."

"I'll pass that along to him when I get back."

J.B. finished off his tonic water. "Excuse me while I freshen up my drink. Can I get you something?"

Buck shook his head. "Thanks. I'm fine with my water." He held up a plastic bottle that J.B. hadn't noticed.

J.B. arose and went to the bar. There, he was cornered by the senators and peppered with questions about the pharmaceutical industry. He answered the best he could but had to be careful with his answers. His was not a typical drug firm. Even the senior senator, a client of YFM Corp., had no idea how and where the adrenochrome he received was produced. Few of their clients possessed such knowledge.

Wallace Chamberlain, however, knew the gritty details. Did Buck? His name had never been forwarded to J.B. by the executive board to become a recipient of adrenochrome. Was that because of Wallace or because of the board? J.B.'s top men received it as a perk of the job. As he thought about it, none of the CCS C-level execs were on his list besides Wallace. He found that curious. Wallace had a significant influence on the executive board. If he asked for adrenochrome for Buck, he would get it. So, why hadn't he?

When he finally returned, he found Buck napping. That was good. It spared him from saying too much or the wrong things. Most of all, it saved him from accidentally making a severe *faux pas* over Buck's being denied their miraculous wonder drug.

SIXTEEN

"Here ya go. Put these on and get ready to go."

They were back in the room assigned to Dan and Aric, across the hall from Pete's room, which he liked to call his "war room." Pete tossed some black clothes and a black gaiter at Aric, hitting him in the chest. Since returning to the hotel, Aric had been under constant surveillance, if not by Pete, then by one of his buddies. This was starting to wear thin. He grew tired of his prison, even if it did rate four stars. He needed to find a way to break loose.

"Look, Pete, I told you I don't want to participate."

Pete scowled. "Participate or not, you're coming with us. I can't spare anyone to sit here with you."

"I don't need babysitting."

Pete's brow furrowed, and Aric noticed him clenching his fists. If a fight narrowed down to weight and height, Aric would be the odds-on favorite. But if it came to downright nastiness and hitting below the belt, Pete would win in the first round. Aric wasn't a fighter in the physical sense. He used his brain to win most times, being a brainiac, to use Pete's pet name for him. So, why hadn't a solution come to that brain of his?

"I-I don't give a rat's you-know-what about you or what you do or don't want to do. I've been instructed to have you under a watchful eye 24/7, and that's what we're gonna do, whether by me or someone I trust."

That revelation startled Aric, but at the same time, it was not unexpected. Connecting the dots, he reasoned that if he and his family were under observation because of Adam, why wouldn't "they" want Aric watched now? But again, who were "they," and how was Pete connected? With sudden clarity, the answer to that hit Aric. Antifa was indeed created to cause disruption and funded by those who wanted disorder. And Adam had to be somehow related to that group, with his disappearance connected to something he'd learned about the group. If he was a threat to their plans, he indeed was in trouble. These were people who didn't mess around.

Aric needed to break free of the constant observation. An idea hit him.

He acted disgusted and said, "Okay then. I don't know who your handlers are, nor do I care, but if I'm heading out, I need some things first, shaving cream mainly, from the small shop in the lobby."

"What? You don't need to shave for where we're going. Forget it."

"Not for tonight. I need it for tomorrow, and the shop'll be closed before we can get back. I'm heading there now, with you or without." He tossed the black gear onto the bed.

Dan jumped up from the couch in the room. "I'll go with him. You have my car keys, so it's not like we can leave. We'll be back in fifteen minutes."

Pete looked contemplative and finally nodded. The two left the room and headed for the elevator.

Aric looked at Dan, concerned still that he was falling

into Pete's sway. "What gives? You doing your cousin's bidding now? We need to get your keys somehow and get the heck out of here."

"Naw, we just need to play along, and he'll tire of us. Or maybe get so wrapped up in his protests that he forgets us."

Aric shook his head. "He's tired of us already. You heard him. Watching *me* is part of his job now. You might be okay with this, but I don't like being his prisoner. *I* need to get out."

"Well, maybe. Let's just play along, like I said. Tonight, we'll be part of the crowd, join in a few chants, maybe light a trash can on fire. You know, go along with Pete, be part of the group. Then he might give us, you, a bit of slack."

Aric didn't like that plan. He had one of his own if the time came to leave. It might damage his friendship with Dan, but if blood was thicker than water, whose side would Dan pick? With the post office closed, he had no idea how Adam would come through, but he felt confident that he would.

He noticed one of Dan's comrades following them, but the guy stayed aloof in the lobby when they entered the shop. Inside, Aric picked up a small travel-size can of shaving cream and, while Dan was focused on the snacks, a packet of Benadryl® Liqui-gels. These he quickly stuffed into his pocket after paying for them.

Dan saw him at the register and walked over. "Ready?"

Aric nodded. "I guess."

The sun remained 20 degrees above the western horizon as Buck's car wove its way into downtown Portland. A short call confirmed that many of the people imported by the executive board to protest were housed in a block of rooms at the Marriott. The crew from Denver was part of that block.

He felt that he shouldn't be seen with them in the hotel. Yet, he needed to be close by. Another call got him a room at the Kimpton RiverPlace Hotel. With four-star amenities like the Marriott, it was smaller and more luxuriously appointed. He'd stayed there once before and found the staff quite attentive. Although there was no sit-in dining, their food services remained in business for room service, carry-out, and delivery. More importantly, via the waterfront park, it was a three-minute walk to the Marriott. The place was perfectly suited for his needs.

After signing in, he settled into his room and ordered room service from the hotel's excellent seafood restaurant, the King Tide Fish & Shell—oysters on the half shell, Dungeness crab cakes, lobster tortellini, and iced tea. No alcohol tonight. He needed to be alert if he hoped to spot his quarry in the crowds. Not that he expected him to be there. The time waiting for its delivery would give him a chance to collect his thoughts and check back with his people in D.C.

A while later, with his stomach full, he glanced at the bedside clock. With sunset at 2055 hours and twilight ending roughly half an hour later, he had just a short time before total dark engulfed the city. Well, complete darkness as far as nature's providing the light. Man's lights made the city visible from space.

He took a moment and texted Pete Lewis. He knew he asked a lot of the man to keep a steady watch over Aric Afton while expecting him to fulfill his primary purpose for being in the city. The kid was smart, had the grades and university acceptance letters to prove it, and no doubt resented being monitored. If he was that intelligent, the guy had to know that he was being watched because of his brother. If he was indeed in Portland because of his brother, he would be hyper-alert and suspicious. He hoped Lewis was up to the task.

Within a minute, he received a reply. They would be heading to the protests outside the justice center in 15 to 20 minutes. Afton would be with him.

Gotta go, thought Buck. He quickly changed clothes, grabbed his gear, and headed toward the Marriott. Lewis had no clue what he looked like, although he knew what Lewis and Afton looked like. His dilemma was those blasted masks. He hoped he would be able to spot them coming out of the hotel because once they blended into the crowd, his chances were slim.

A few minutes later, he stood outside the Marriott's main entrance on the parkway. He kept to the shadows to prevent the hotel security people—on high alert because of the protests—from spotting him and moving him along.

Several smaller groups of young men and women emerged from the hotel, dressed in the protester's standard "uniform" of black whatever. At the base of the driveway, a van sat parked with its side door open. Several of the groups veered directly to the vehicle, where they picked up signs. A few of the men also donned backpacks that appeared heavy. Buck assumed them to hold bricks or the makings of Molotov cocktails.

A short while later, a group of about a dozen men and two women exited the doors and headed for the small truck. At the van, the women and three men in the group grabbed signs while two men picked up packs. The man who appeared to be the leader took off his mask briefly to address them. It was Lewis. He replaced the mask with a black gaiter and picked up a backpack, which he pushed toward another younger man. That guy appeared to resist until two others joined Lewis in threatening him. *Must be Afton*, thought Buck. He'd be the only one not eager to join in. Buck noted the backpack had been marked with a red tape 'X' on the exposed surface. *Curious*, he thought.

Adam sat in his room, surprised to find that adrenochrome was not the secret drug he suspected it to be, although he'd never heard of it. Produced inexpensively by the oxidation of adrenaline, it was implicated in some psychiatric disorders. Mainly, a theory once floated about that schizophrenia was the result of adrenochrome accumulation in the brain. Research into that area never really panned out.

He was also shocked to find that adrenochrome had been around for a while. Aldous Huxley mentioned it in his 1954 essay, "The Doors of Perception," in which he likened its effect to that of mescaline. In 1962, Anthony Burgess mentioned it at the beginning of *A Clockwork Orange,* calling it "drencrom." Even Hunter S. Thompson, the counterculture, "gonzo" journalist, referred to it as a psychotropic drug in two of his books in the 1970s. Thompson's character in *Fear and Loathing in Las Vegas* said, "There's only one source for this stuff... the adrenaline glands from a living human body. It's no good if you get it out of a corpse." Supposedly, at the time, Thompson said it was pure fiction.

Supposedly fiction? Then, why was Chamberlain taking it?

This was a job for his software. He entered in various parameters, reviewed and refined them, and launched his program to search the worldwide and deep webs for any and everything on adrenochrome.

With that in motion, he stood and went to the window. Barely moving the curtain, he noted that it was almost dark—time for the crazies to come out.

He mentally debated his next steps. With the post office closed, he had but the one choice, staking it out in hopes of spotting his brother. But what if Aric was already in town and had also discovered that the branch was closed? Would he take the time to go there just to hang out in the hope of connecting somehow? What would he do?

Adam wanted to curse the blasted virus and the people responsible for it, but that would be a wasted effort. COVID was here. It was in the environment, just like influenza. Anyone who thought they could combat and eliminate it was living a fantasy. The proposed fast-tracking of a vaccine was likely to be a disaster, as all previous RNA vaccines to date had been. The hype being created was right out of a PsyOps manual, the stuff which CCS used AlterNet to create.

He paced the floor in front of the beds. He felt jittery, and the idea of staying cooped up in his room with only cable TV to keep him company made him more restless. He wondered what Aric would be doing tonight if indeed he was in town. That's when he realized his kid brother would find the protests and riots fascinating to observe. Of course, he wouldn't participate, but his curiosity would lead him to be a witness from the sidelines. What if they were to connect there? Would that be serendipity or what? No, Aric would say that it was God's doing.

Besides, I think I'd find it interesting to watch, too, thought Adam.

He needed to blend in. The jeans and shoes he had on would work, but he needed something else on top. He rummaged through his clothes until he found a gray hoodie. That and his mask would work. He'd give the protests another 30 minutes to simmer, and then he'd head over to watch the fireworks.

SEVENTEEN

J.B. arrived at Portland Underground's office in time for their five p.m. tour of Old Town, China Town, and the famous Shanghai Tunnels. The tunnels from the 19th century were once used to haul goods from the Willamette River wharves to the hotels, restaurants, and Old Town bars. During Prohibition, the tunnels were allegedly used by bootleggers. A story about men being shanghaied—made drunk, knocked out, and sold to sea captains in search of crew members—through the tunnels eventually gave them the name.

Today, the tunnels were popular with those looking for a paranormal experience through the Haunted Portland or Beyond Bizarre Ghost Tours. Today's ghost hunters hoped to locate a 19th-century murdered prostitute, Nina, at the 1885 Merchant Hotel. Many reported occurrences of moaning, crying, and occasional screams on their tours.

YFM Corp. recognized this as an opportunity to see to it that such seekers were rewarded. Their detention center under construction under the streets of Old Town would soon provide real "audio" for which the tours offered the perfect cover.

J.B. joined the last tour of the day as it began its underground phase of the trip. The guide pointed to a door, closed to the public, which led to other tunnels and rooms. Folks were invited to peer through the iron grate in the heavy wooden door to get a glimpse of what the tunnels had been like a hundred years earlier, but the door was locked. Laying back from the group until they were out of sight, he faced a security camera above the door, which opened for him a moment later. Like any good apparition, he disappeared.

He walked down the poorly lit corridor to the next door, which also opened for him. Upon turning a corner, he entered a brightly lit area under construction. Upon completion, the new detention center would have its primary access through a restaurant—also being remodeled for post-COVID use—that sat across the street from the tour's headquarters. He had entered through what would become an emergency exit.

"J.B., you're here early. I wasn't expecting you until next week," said Sean Parker, the project manager for new construction.

J.B. held out his hand to greet the man. "Hi, Sean. Sorry for the surprise visit. I've never needed to do that for projects you're overseeing. I had a gracious invitation from our friend Gen. Chamberlain to hitch a ride on their corporate jet this afternoon. I came straight here, hoping you'd still be on the job."

Parker frowned. "Yeah, wish I wasn't. I'm ready for a cold one. We're still having water issues, as per my written brief a few days ago. We think we've isolated where it's originating, and we're opening up another old wall to check that possibility."

"Where?"

"It's affecting staff and lab areas, not the main housing section. This way." The supervisor led his boss through a warren of hallways that looked nothing like the old tunnels. They ended up in the lab. "This is the worst area. We can't bring any lab equipment in here with it like this. Right now, this looks dry, but by tomorrow morning, we could have half an inch of water on the floor."

J.B. glanced around. It looked ready to go, but he had to take his man's word for it.

"Source?"

"It's not sewage or river water, so possibly an old water main behind that wall there." He pointed to the spot. "Water department has no record of an active main there, and we can't exactly go digging into their archives since they don't know we're here. We're going to have to open up that wall and excavate to find it and fix it."

J.B. nodded. They held no building permits and discussed the work with no one. The construction team itself was YFM Corp.'s private crew, highly vetted and richly paid for their work and discretion. However, the restaurant remodel was strictly by the book so that its noise could cover that of the underground work.

"Any chance we'll be up and running by the end of the month as first projected?"

Parker shook his head. "No, sir. This problem, plus the virus, has put us back a month, maybe longer depending on what we find."

J.B. acknowledged his comment. The virus had led to a temporary halt in the aboveground construction, which required slowing down the work beneath. This inner-city facility was a test, as well as a replacement for their center at the base of Mt. Hood. It would provide multiple advantages over the isolated, rural centers they currently maintained. If it succeeded, several cities with abandoned subway stations and others, like St. Louis, with caves underneath, all held the potential for the same use.

J.B. frowned. That was not what he wanted to hear, but he understood. They would roll with the punch and reallocate resources planned for this place.

"Okay, Sean, thanks. I know you're doing the best you can under unusual circumstances. We'll move the youngest residents from Mt. Hood to the new Wisconsin facility and the older ones to California. So, no pressure on you. We need to do this right. Once we're nearing completion, we'll find the occupants we need."

"Yes, sir. Appreciate that. Good thing we don't have strict deadlines to meet and shareholders to please."

J.B. nodded. However, he recognized that their "shareholder"—the executive board—could be more demanding than any board or group of shareholders in a publicly-traded corporation. Fortunately, YFM Corp.'s positive cash flow kept them happy, not to mention their anticipation of incredible profits from all upcoming vaccines for the coronavirus. He smiled at the thought that there was nothing like creating a problem and then profiting from its solution.

Upon returning to his rental car, he placed a call to arrange for all level seven and under residents to go to Wisconsin and the others to be dispersed where vacancies existed in the California centers. As he finished his call, he noted several messages awaiting in his voicemail. A level of mild concern rose within as he recognized that all of the phone calls were from the same number—that of Vice-President Sidon's daughter, Janet.

He tapped his phone to dial back. She answered immediately.

"J.B., thanks for calling back. I'm concerned. It's been just over four days since dad's last dose, and within a day, he was back to his usual sharp, demanding self. That was amazing to watch, the transformation. But now, his Parkinson's seems worse. He can barely hold his coffee mug because of the tremor."

That *was* a concern. Sidon and his handlers went to great lengths to conceal his illness. The mainstream media, too, made every effort to avoid showing his rest tremors, shuffling gate and postural instability, the beginnings of dementia, and his handlers helping him from place to place. He fulfilled every condition of the TRAP requirements for the diagnosis of Parkinson's Disease, but to publicly reveal that would end his hope of attaining the office he had striven for his entire career. Many saw him as the Democrat's best chance for regaining the White House, and the executive board would not let his critical illness deter them.

"Janet, I'm going to have to get back with you on that one. I need to run that by my top scientist because we've had no issues with such a thing before. Could it be something else?"

"His doctors are checking into that, but I need to cover the bases. They don't know about the adrenochrome, and I'm pretty sure you don't want them to."

Her tone seemed almost threatening, but he dismissed it as worry about her father.

"Very true. Look, it might take a while to have an

answer. My people may not have that answer off the top of their heads and might have to look into the problem. I promise to get back to you ASAP. Please, keep me posted, so I can keep them up to date, too."

"Thank you, J.B. We will."

He placed a call immediately to Alaine Tavernier, only to get his voicemail.

EIGHTEEN

Wallace sat on their flagstone patio, just off the dining room, overlooking the Potomac River, sipping his favorite single-malt Glenfiddich and mulling the turn of events. Their 8,700 square-foot home—with six spacious bedrooms and nine baths, a large gourmet kitchen, a private gym, a wine cellar, a game room, and two outdoor terraces on two levels among its exquisite features—sat on a one-acre lot located on a cul-de-sac above the river and the old Chesapeake and Ohio Canal Towpath in southwestern Montgomery County, Maryland. And yet, it was a mid-range home for their area, where the vacant three-quarter-acre lot next door was on the market for $1.3 million.

Despite his wealth and deep, influential connections, not everything went his way. The evening's plans had been nixed on two counts. The county leaders had decided to keep their county under the state's Phase One recovery level, even though the governor had taken the commonwealth to Phase Two of the plan. That meant their dining plans to celebrate the reopening of one of their favorite places, Matisse, a classic French restaurant in Chevy Chase, would need to be postponed . . . again.

When he had suggested their other favorite French place, L'Auberge Chez Francois, his wife had begged off.

Although its farmhouse setting was only a mile away as the birds fly, directly across the river in northern Virginia, the drive was a forty-minute trek. That state's Phase One recovery plan went into effect on May 15 and allowed restaurants to reopen outdoor seating at 50% capacity.

However, Marla didn't feel up to the drive. She hadn't fully recovered her senses of taste and smell, and her migraines had become more frequent. About the time he'd returned home, she had taken to her bed in an attempt to relieve the pain. Before pouring his scotch, he had checked on her only to find her fast asleep. Based on previous experience, she would sleep through the night.

Halfway through his drink, he pulled his cell from his pocket and made a call.

"Yes."

"It's Odin2. I'd like some entertainment for the evening."

"Yes, sir. The usual place?"

"That would be fine. Thirty minutes?"

"She'll be ready."

Wallace finished his scotch in one gulp, stood, and returned inside, where he grabbed his keys. Half an hour later, he found himself at a familiar farmhouse. Its secure facial recognition system unlocked the front door for him. Inside, he took off his jacket and hung it on a peg near the entrance. To his right, a simple but charming, country-style parlor with dim lighting awaited him. His entertainment would be either there or upstairs. However, his next glass of scotch was sitting on the small end table next to the antique settee.

He entered the room and looked about. She wasn't

there, so he picked up his glass and headed up the stairway. At the top of the stair, he turned into his usual bedroom only to find it, too, empty.

"Come out, come out, wherever you are. Are we playing hide-n-seek tonight?" Wallace said in a loud voice as he returned to the hallway.

He checked the bedroom across the hall. Empty. Likewise for the third bedroom. The door to the attic area would be locked, so he paid no attention to that area. At the end of the hall, he opened the door to the bathroom. The lights were out, and a plastic shower curtain enclosed the old clawfoot tub. He eased back the curtain and found her there, her knees to her chest, cowering. Her eyes reflected fear and sadness, but no tears flowed.

He extended his hand. "C'mon, sweetie. Be a good girl and show Uncle Wally how nice you can be."

NINETEEN

Aric had little chance of escaping the group as they surrounded him upon leaving the hotel. As they gathered outside a van at the end of the drive, Pete thrust a backpack toward him, motioning for him to put it on.

"I'm not your pack mule. *You* carry whatever it is."

Pete shook his head, and three of the other guys surrounded Aric in a show of intimidation.

"Nope, you're gonna carry it, brainiac, and it's marked so I can watch you closely."

Pete emphasized the 'brainiac' moniker, no doubt to irritate Aric, but he refused to take the bait. However, he did note that only that pack had an "X" taped across the back with red tape. Under duress, Aric took the backpack and found it heavier than expected. He heard some metal cans click together as he slid into its straps and positioned it on his back.

He felt as if he was in the middle of a rugby scrum as they walked toward Chapman Square across from the Justice Center. Within a block, the atmosphere surrounding the group seemed to change. By the time they reached the park across from the Justice Center, the group had dispersed, some chanting, some waving signs. Pete—and whoever pulled his strings—orchestrated their movements so that no observer would see that they had arrived as a group. Pete and two of the other men, however, stuck by Aric. Even should he try to run, he'd have to outrun three of them with a heavy pack encumbering him, at least at first.

"No justice, no peace!"

"Black lives matter!"

"No lives matter 'til black lives matter!"

Small pockets of protesters chanted these and other slogans, many with profanities aimed at the police. Barriers blocked access to the public buildings, and a small army of police officers stood behind the barricades to deal with anyone who succeeded in breaching one. When a nearby trash can began to blaze, no one made an effort to extinguish the flames. Likewise, no effort was made to break up the protest.

Aric saw three guys he didn't know rush toward him after he'd been pointed out by someone from Pete's group. One of them opened the pack and pulled out canisters of spray paint. They took off toward various buildings to tag them with graffiti and slogans.

Great, thought Aric. *Call me Sherwin Williams.* He realized that sarcasm had no place there that evening. He was not comfortable with his role in events, even if forced upon him. He wanted to remain as incognito as possible, but the combination of hood and gaiter as a mask seemed to strangle him if he tried to use both. He opted for the gaiter alone, as the hood also made him uncomfortably hot.

As they ebbed and flowed with the crowds, he noted small pockets of counter-protesters—Proud Boys and Patriot Prayer members, and two apparent differences hit him. The Antifa and BLM crowd spewed hate, pushed violence as the means to their end, and held professionally designed and printed signs. The conservative clusters had American flags and homemade signs, pushed for law and order, and many stood silently in prayer.

Yet, it didn't take long for the Antifa crowds, acting like the fascists they decried, to attack the others. Aric knew that tomorrow's headlines would blame the Patriot Prayer folks for the violence, but he saw the real perpetrators. He knew he had to make a break for it and get out. This was the wrong place for him to be. He scanned the area for a path to freedom, but the protest groups' chaotic movements made that problematic. His best option would be a track directly toward the hotel. While he'd made a point to keep his cash and credit card on his person, and he could always buy new clothes, he couldn't leave behind his laptop. He might ultimately need it to communicate with Adam.

As others removed things from his pack, he noted it getting lighter and lighter. Soon, it would no longer slow him down, but he needed a diversion.

If they continued along their current trajectory, they would soon pass another contingent of President Graham supporters. Maybe he could get their help. Yet, before he and Pete's posse came near, two Antifa thugs decided to take things into their own hands and attacked the group. Big mistake. These Proud Boys were equipped, and bats started swinging at the two assailants.

Aric saw his opportunity. "Pete, those PBs are about to take down your buddies!" He pointed to the scuffle.

Pete and his two comrades—already worked up and eager for a fight—screamed and ran into the fray. More members from both sides quickly joined in. Out of the corner of his eye, Aric saw the police home in on the fracas as well. This was his chance.

He doffed the backpack and began to sprint toward the hotel. If he could get there and grab his things, he hoped to be able to get a taxi to take him somewhere away from Pete. He hated to leave Dan behind but reckoned he'd be safe. His cousin had already made it clear that his interest was in Aric, for whatever reason.

He pulled down his gaiter and gulped in the air as he ran. As he rushed across the plaza in front of City Hall, a long-haired, bearded man with dark-framed glasses stepped into his way and grabbed him. They wrestled a bit as Aric tried to get past him, and then the man just as suddenly stepped aside. As he did so, he yelled something at him, but Aric, so focused on getting to the hotel, paid no attention.

Two blocks to go. One block. The entrance to the Marriott was in sight. Once inside, he had no interest in waiting for an elevator. He took to the nearest emergency stairs and ran up to the fifth floor. Out of breath, he cracked open the door to the hallway, glanced both ways to discover the area empty, and ran to his room. Two minutes, maybe three, was all he needed to get his gear and leave.

Buck followed the Denver cell group at a distance. He had no desire or need to make himself known. Yet, his gut was on high alert. The Afton kid was going to pull something; he was sure of it. Just as he was convinced that the guy was in Portland because of his brother.

He stayed in the shadows as Pete and his entourage, which kept Aric Afton close at hand, joined the other Antifa and BLM protesters. After a while, he saw that the pack carried by Afton carried cans of spray paint. He was being used as a central dispensary of the canisters. *Good thinking, Lewis,* he thought. *Keep the kid weighed down and close by.*

Buck moved to avoid the small congregations of conservative protesters as they passed by. In many ways, being retired military, he could more closely identify with their beliefs. Still, his job was a simple one—working for Wallace Chamberlain and an executive board enforcer. He knew Chamberlain and the exec board well enough to realize they were the only side to join. In reality, they considered themselves apolitical. The membership comprised of both Democrats and Republicans, with one common goal—global power and authority. By putting America first, President Graham had dealt a blow to both and could not be controlled by them, and they wanted to regain their station.

Still, he avoided these pockets of "patriots" because he didn't want to get wrapped up in either side. To be misidentified as one of either faction could lead to trouble from the other group. His only goal was to monitor the Afton kid and hope that he led Buck to his brother.

About an hour into the night, Pete and his gang were about to pass by another collection of Proud Boys when two Antifa members decided to attack the Proud Boys, who were simply standing there with their American flags in a silent counter-protest. The boys were ready, and bats came out of nowhere, pummeling the Antifa guys. That unfortunate encounter led to members of both sides rushing to the aid of their men. Soon, an all-out skirmish was in progress, and the police took notice.

So, too, did Aric Afton. Buck watched as the kid took advantage of the chaos, ditched the pack, and took off running. However, had the kid been smart, he would have abandoned his belongings and taken off for parts unknown. Instead, Buck watched him head toward the hotel.

Shaking his head, he knew he had to pull Lewis out of the way before the police arrived. He waded into the fray, grabbed the man, and fended off his feeble blows.

"Lewis, you're supposed to be watching the Afton kid. He played you and is en route to the hotel. Go! Now! Or forever regret it."

A look of surprise crossed the man's face. Buck had no doubt that he'd recognized a voice that he'd heard only on the phone up until now.

Buck let go, and the man darted from the area. He watched as Lewis, alone, rushed toward the hotel. He could only hope that he'd be in time to stop Afton.

TWENTY

The hour was late, and Tavernier remained at the lab. The serum from 20161025F290, which had been used to extract the questionable batch of adrenochrome, had shown no unexpected qualities on their retests. Was it something they weren't testing for? Was it something they didn't have a test for? He didn't want to entertain that possibility. He could not assure any level of quality if unknown compounds were contaminating their samples.

He returned to the chimp's cage with a chair and parked it next to the enclosure. For the next 30 minutes, he sat and observed the animal. Yes, there was a distinct resting tremor. Although this guy loved bananas as much as the next stereotypical ape, cantaloupe was its favorite. He offered the chimp a slice of the cherished fruit, in which it showed no interest at first. After several minutes, it moved across the pen to take the melon. The tremor disappeared as it reached for the delicacy. Just as important, its gait appeared stiff and off-balance.

Parkinson's Disease first came to mind, but chimps didn't develop that neurological disorder. Tavernier vaguely recalled reading of marmosets that were genetically modified in 2016 to develop Parkinson's, but he'd need to research that more.

He hated the thought of euthanizing this chimp. The old guy had been with him for over six years now. The idea of sacrificing it seemed almost akin to offering up a relative. Yet, the animal remained a *test* animal. Whatever was necessary to isolate the cause would be done.

Tavernier placed the remainder of the cantaloupe within the animal's reach. "Enjoy it, old man."

He left the veterinary wing and returned to his office. He would observe the chimp for another day or two before deciding upon the need for a necropsy. After all, the issue might not be related to adrenochrome at all. Perhaps their tests would reveal a viral illness or that the animal's age was indeed catching up with it. That latter idea would be a disappointment, as it would appear to indicate that their adrenochrome didn't extend life after all, that aging involved more than shortening telomeres in one's DNA.

He needed to get to bed. Sleep deprivation would not help him solve the puzzle. However, as he prepared to leave, he knew he wouldn't be able to sleep until answering a few questions floating around in his head.

He initiated an internet search on Parkinson's Disease. He already knew that a deficiency of dopamine produced many of the symptoms. Within minutes, he refreshed his recall of the disorder's signs and symptoms. He scanned through some of the more current research papers on it— the latest work on alpha-synuclein and the deposits that destroyed the brain cells that produced the dopamine, the genetics of the mutated gene SNCA, and more. With those answers in mind, he ordered dopamine levels to be performed on the chimp's blood, along with all the other tests already ordered by his assistant. Normal levels would indicate that a Parkinson-like problem was not the issue.

Finally, satisfied with their approach to working up the anomaly that he hoped this all to be, he picked up his things and headed home. Getting to sleep, though, would be more difficult than he'd expected. His mind still raced as he tossed and turned in bed.

Thirty minutes later, he knew he needed something to aid his falling to sleep. He had a prescription for a mild sleep aid, but he preferred a more old-fashioned method. He plodded into his study, poured a snifter of brandy, and sat in his den, looking out the window.

The night was clear and the sky starry, although the bright, full moon made those stars hard to see. Unlike his previous home where the light pollution interfered with stargazing, his new home bordered two state natural areas known for their meadows, peat bogs, and conifer swamps. Deep within those areas, one could encounter a completely dark sky that one had to go several miles offshore or high into the Sierras to witness on the West Coast.

His head began to bob as sleep found him. He pushed himself up and walked into his bedroom. His mental switch turned off as his head hit the pillow.

In what seemed like minutes, he startled awake. His phone? He noted that he had managed an hour of sleep. Who would be calling him at two a.m.?

He became fully alert when he saw the Caller ID announcing J.B. Gradison. Something must be wrong, and that batch of adrenochrome he'd given J.B. was the first thought that came to mind.

TWENTY-ONE

Adam watched his younger brother bolt past after he attempted to stop him. He didn't expect Aric to recognize him on sight but had hoped he would remember his voice. Had it been that long? But as he thought about it, if the running shoes were on his feet, would a stranger's voice register when he was focused on getting away?

Adam didn't know what was going on, but the fact that his brother was somehow being restrained by several men became clear after just fifteen minutes or so of observation. He had recognized his brother even with the mask and almost walked up to Aric to make himself known. However, another man was telling Aric where to stand, and two other men stood by to make sure he did as told. Adam had no idea who those men were, but something was off.

After watching Aric disappear, he turned back to where Aric had been. The fight had drawn the law's attention, but before they could get there, Adam saw someone whose presence there explained what might be happening. Buck Buckner!

Buckner approached the man who had been controlling Aric and pulled him away from the ruckus before the police arrived. Seconds later, that man began to chase after Aric. It seemed clear that Buckner was the ultimate puppet master.

How Aric had been snared by them was a story yet to be heard, but Adam knew he was the real target.

Buckner followed the other man but at a subdued pace as if he knew where they were headed and was in no rush to get there. Adam stayed in the shadows some distance away and followed him. Two blocks later, the Marriott emerged as the apparent target. Curiously, Buckner stationed himself in a darkened area outside where he had a clear view of the main doors.

A few minutes later, the man pulled what appeared to be a phone from his pocket and had a short conversation with whoever had called him. At that, he emerged from the shadows and headed south along Naito Parkway, past the hotel. The pace and ease with which he moved pointed to a man who felt that everything was under control.

And that bothered Adam. At least Adam now knew that Aric was in town, but what had happened to him? And just what could Adam do?

He had no idea what floor they were on, much less which room. Even if he did, did he dare to intervene? If Buckner had seen him outside, he would not have hesitated to take Adam out. Would his men do the same? The riots provided a perfect cover for them to do whatever violence they had been ordered to do.

Adam felt assured that Aric would be okay. They couldn't afford to hurt him if they expected him to flush out his big brother for them.

As with the riots, this was a complication he had not foreseen. And each situation not only delayed his search for Carolyn but distracted his focus. He had had the forethought to prepare a brief note for Aric and had managed to slip it into his brother's pocket while trying to restrain him. Would he find it soon, and would it help? At least Aric would know he was there.

He had two choices, sticking to the shadows to help Aric escape, if he managed to do so, or heading back to his motel and reasoning out a plan. Perhaps he could hack into the hotel's computer system, find Aric's room number, and use that info to extract him from the building. Maybe he could trigger the fire alarms and force a hotel-wide evacuation. That would get Aric outside but not free from his guardians. No, he needed to figure out what to do . . . and how to implement his plan without endangering both of them. He would be better able to do so back in his room with the aid of his computer.

Yet, Buckner was also a priority. Even though Adam looked little like he did when employed by CCS, Buckner was a well-trained special force operative whose observation skills were honed. He might not recognize Adam in a brief passing on the street, at least not at first. But the recognition would kick in at some point and put him on alert. Adam needed to be the alert one.

He remained in the shadows and watched as Buckner disappeared into the park along the river. He then pulled out his phone and opened up his map app. Was he heading toward his car? There was a parking lot a block or so away off the parkway, but the expedient route to it would have been to keep walking along the parkway. Also, Adam didn't see Buckner as one who would lodge someplace away from the action.

That left one option. There was another 4-star hotel next to the river. The path through the park would take

Buckner straight to it. That had to be where he was staying. It fit his profile and CCS's pocketbook.

Adam made a point to avoid that area of town. He walked in the opposite direction toward SW 4th Avenue, which would take him back to his motel.

Winded by his climb to their floor, Aric gulped in air as he hurried down the hallway toward their room. Pete had taken his room key upon leaving earlier, but Dan, as if encouraging Aric to flee, had slipped his key card to Aric as they walked toward the protests. That act had assured him that Dan would not be upset by Aric's abrupt disappearance.

He opened the door and didn't bother to close it behind him. In the hope of having an opportunity to leave, he had left his gear packed and ready for a quick grab-n-go departure. Pete had his cell phone, so he would have to abandon that. His iPad, however, had been hidden under the mattress. He retrieved it, stashed it inside his pack, and stepped back into the hallway in under two minutes.

Having previously reviewed the hotel's floor plan and emergency exits, he rushed to the stairs farthest from the room. He reasoned that if anyone had followed him to prevent him from fleeing, they would cover the elevators and first set of stairs by merely parking themselves in the lobby where both emptied onto the first floor. Bypassing the main floor and heading to the basement earned him no benefit, as he knew of no easy route to depart the hotel that way. His best chance was the distant stairs and their fire door to the outside. Even if it was rigged with an alarm, he didn't care whether or not he set it off. He had to get out.

Aric eased open the fire door, not wanting to alert anyone of its being used. He stepped onto the landing and closed the door as quietly as he could for the same reason. Then he moved away from the door, out of view through its window, and listened for any noise within the stairwell that might indicate someone there. Feeling safe, he began his descent while remaining on high alert for anyone else.

Two flights down, he heard a door open from below him, and footsteps began racing up the stairs. With caution, he peered over the railing hoping for a glimpse of the person. He could see a forearm and hand grasping the rail as the person climbed closer to him. One flight below, the footfall stopped, the door opened, and the person exited the stairwell.

His heart racing, he felt he had no option but to get out of there as fast as possible. He began taking the stairs as quickly as he thought he could. Should he run into Pete or one of his posse, he would barrel past, knocking him down if need be.

One flight to go. The exit door was visible, and it *was* armed with an alarm. As Aric had already determined, he shoved open the door, the alarm began to beep, and a moment later, he was outside, free of the building.

It took him a few seconds to get his bearings. To his right, 1st Avenue would take him back toward the protests, closer to Pete and his thugs and the chance they might spot him. He turned to the left to head away. He would get two or three blocks away and then hide somewhere to take a breather and figure out where to go.

He didn't want to run and make himself conspicuous, but he hurried away from the fire exit at a pace he thought reasonable. As he came within ten feet of the first intersection, three men rounded the corner.

"Goin' somewhere?"

Pete! How?

He turned to run the other direction, but two more of Pete's gang hurried toward him along that path. A chain-link fence down the middle of the road protected pedestrians and vehicles from construction across the street. It channeled cars into one lane and prevented him from darting across the street in an attempt to outrun them. He was cornered.

Pete grabbed him by his upper arm. "C'mon, brainiac. That wasn't very smart, 'cause now I'm gonna have to sit on you 24/7. I have instructions to keep you safe. Otherwise, we'd beat some street smarts into you for this stunt. Let's go."

They headed back toward the hotel's front doors but discovered another entrance with keycard access as they rounded the corner. A minute later, they boarded an elevator and rose toward the fifth floor.

Aric looked at Pete. "You said you have instructions to keep me safe. Whose instructions?"

Pete gave him a look as if he'd asked a stupid question. "Makes no difference. They don't care about you. It's your brother they want, and you're the bait."

"M-my brother? He's been missing for months. I-I don't know where he is!"

Pete shook his head. "Don't act stupid, brainiac. Maybe you don't know exactly where he is, but I'm pretty sure you've already figured this out, and I'm not telling you anything you didn't already guess."

That was true. Aric had surmised that his brother was the reason he was being kept an effectual prisoner. But he had spoken the truth; he had no idea where Adam was. Then a thought hit him. The homeless bum! He had addressed Aric in French. What was it he'd said? Something about his pocket? He casually placed his hands in his pockets and tried not to act surprised when he felt a piece of paper in his left pant pocket. He hadn't put it there.

The bum was Adam. His brother had used the contact to put the note or whatever it was in his pocket. He dared not retrieve it in the company of the others, so he tried to act and look as nonchalant as possible.

That discovery seemed to be a two-edged sword. Yes, Adam was in town, and that knowledge excited Aric. And yet, Adam being in town meant he was in greater danger. Still, Aric now knew what he faced, and he could plan accordingly. He felt confident he would be able to get away—when the time was right—but escaping Pete and his buddies was one thing. Getting past unknown and unseen observers was another. Aric didn't have to be clairvoyant to realize that Pete wasn't alone in watching Aric.

Pete used the keycard he'd taken from Aric earlier to open the door and pushed Aric inside. "Make yourself at home. Again."

He whispered something to the two guys with him and left the room. Moments later, he returned with some of his own gear.

"Looks like I'll be babysitting you one-on-one from here on in." He turned and addressed his friends. "You two head on back to the protests and do what you do best. And find my cousin and tell him to hightail his butt back here."

Aric scooted the chair away from the desk and placed it where he could look out the window. Having taken off his pack and put it on the dresser, he sat down and gazed outside. The room faced the area of town where the Justice Center sat, and he could see smoke rising from that area. Sirens echoed through the city canyons and filled the night.

And yet, Aric's thoughts focused on his brother. Their fates were now intertwined more than by blood alone.

TWENTY-TWO

Aric awoke the next morning to find Pete sleeping on the floor in front of the door. After getting caught the night before, Aric found himself under a tight guard by Pete and his goons. He found it difficult to act as if nothing significant had happened, and yet, it had. Adam had made contact. That had made him all the more anxious to leave.

He waited until he required the bathroom and then produced the note from his pocket in the privacy of the john. It had read "*Lodge d'Econo, salle cent quatorze.*" His first thought was to give Adam grief about the "*Lodge d'Econo*" bit, as a proper name would be the same in either English or French, Econo Lodge. But, hey, it sounded good and got the point across even if his French wasn't perfect. Room 114. With that info, he flushed the note along with his business.

Before leaving the bathroom, he closed his eyes and quietly prayed, giving God glory despite his circumstances. He was startled by a clear voice that said, "*By this time next year, the great earthquake of the sixth seal will occur.*"

Where did that come from? He hadn't been even thinking about the Book of Revelation, much less studying it. His thoughts had been focused on Adam and on escaping. His prayer had been one for deliverance and reunification with Adam. He had felt subtle nudges, as well as premonitions, in the past that he had accredited to the Holy Spirit leading him. He was comfortable with the "gifts" of the Holy Spirit as outlined in the Bible. They were just as active today as they had been over the millennia.

Yet, to say that this was a *big* prophetic revelation would be understating things. He had never experienced such an audibly clear voice like that. And for it to detail something as catastrophic as the sixth seal's judgment was both fearful and awesome. And why him? Aric had no national standing and had never aspired to the Biblical office of a prophet. He was simply a recent high school graduate. Then again, Daniel and other prophets were teens when called by God. He puzzled over why he had been given this word.

He looked heavenward and whispered, "Lord, thank you that your people will not be caught off-guard as your plans unfold, but I'm not . . . well, I'm not used to hearing your voice so clearly. Like Gideon, I think I need a fleece to throw out there to know that I heard you correctly. Please show me what I need to know and that I'm hearing you correctly."

He waited a few moments, but he heard nothing further. His mind returned to the immediate. He had a plan, but he needed to execute it at the right time. That meant as few people watching him as possible.

Finding Pete in position across the door did not help matters unless he felt like waking an angry bear. The man was most cantankerous before ten a.m. Actually, he remained testy after ten, too. Still, Aric was hungry, and the group's catering service served breakfast only from nine to eleven. The time was nine-fifteen.

Dan began to arouse, so Aric decided to make coffee in the room's small Keurig. The smell would waken Dan for sure. He hoped it might do the same with Pete, with less backlash than waking him directly.

"Mornin'," said Dan, followed by a yawn. He glanced at his cousin to see if he still slept. "Sorry to find you still here when I got back last night."

"Yeah, thanks for the keycard. I tried."

"Yeah, he did. And failed."

Both were startled to see Pete sitting up, his back against the door.

"And you, cousin, you sorry piece of . . . giving him your keycard. I'll be taking *both* of your cards now. Cross me again, Danny boy, and family or not, you'll regret it."

The man stood and knocked once on the door. He was answered by two knocks. At that, Aric realized that had he managed to slip past Pete, the guy had stationed a second guard outside the door. He would have to account for that and adjust his plan.

Knowing that Buckner was in town, Adam rushed across the street to a small espresso bar that sold sandwiches and picked up food for breakfast. He didn't want to be out and exposed any more than he had to, even if he was a mile away from the man's hotel. Adam doubted Buckner would be in town alone. He wouldn't recognize any of Buckner's men, would he?

Back in his room, he paced as he ate. Burning off his nervous energy would require more than that, however. Had Aric found the note? Did he realize that it was him,

Adam, who had bumped into him and planted it in his pocket? Would he be able to get away? Should he stay put in his room all day on the chance that Aric would show up? Would Aric be followed if he did manage to escape?

The questions popping into his head increased logarithmically, but the number of answers remained at zero. Even his software would prove useless in providing solutions.

Adam's only choice was to sit tight and wait. *When* Aric showed up, he needed to be prepared to move. The car had plenty of gas to get them out of town, and he had kept his things in the room to a minimum. He had used cash to prepay the room for three days, so he had that night plus one more covered. If they needed to leave in the middle of the night, they would not be delayed by the need to settle the room charges.

The big question was what direction to take when they did leave. Adam had suggested Portland for a reason. His search had led him to the Mt. Hood area, although not to a precise address or location. He needed to narrow down the options. Doing so would be a perfect distraction from his questions about Aric, as well as put him back on track for his main quest.

Being in the university's neighborhood had another perk—lots of hi-speed internet access points through which he could hitchhike onto the web. The motel's router was too slow and too public. He spent a few minutes exploring nearby Wi-Fi signals and found a strong one with appropriate security—safeguards meant to keep him and others out. Keeping *others* out was his key consideration because few networks could keep *him* out. Like an expert with a lock pick, he had cracked the best "locks" the internet offered, not maliciously but as a cyber-defense consultant showing companies and governments how to protect their networks.

That skill had been what had drawn CCS to him in the first place . . . in happier times, a time he could never replace. He remained as determined as ever to find her.

Within an hour, another of his software creations had uncovered the passkey to the Wi-Fi account, and he was online at his dark web portal. He checked his logs for new data on Buckner and Chamberlain, only to find a new name pop up, a James Bradford Gradison. The man was the CEO of a company called YFM Corp., which Adam added to his varied searches. He would get the scoop on the company and its holdings in short order, as well as ferret out their connections with Chamberlain.

But first, he needed to work on finding her.

Throughout the day, Aric looked for an opportunity to set his plan in motion. However, that chance never materialized. If Pete and two of his posse weren't guarding him, three or more of the others in his group were. At one point, after Pete left him in the care of others, Aric happened to look out the window and saw the guy talking with a man in his late forties or fifties on the sidewalk below their windows. They repeatedly glanced up toward the window of Aric's room as if talking specifically about him.

As night fell and the protest group prepared to return to the Justice Center, Pete relieved his guys in Aric's room so that they could get ready.

"You'll be coming with us again tonight," announced Pete. "Both of you. And I want those key cards as we leave."

"I'm not giving you squat," replied Aric.

Pete reacted with a strong punch to Aric's gut, taking him by surprise and taking his breath away. He'd been in some scuffles with classmates in school, but never in a real fight. He felt his anger flare, but a need for caution stopped him from responding in kind.

Dan jumped up in protest, though. Together they could take Pete down, but they wouldn't get very far, so Aric shook his head to stop Dan.

"We're paying for this room and feeding you both. If you prefer, we can tie you up and lock you in one of the vans—your choice. Personally, I'd like to do the latter. Save me a bunch of trouble."

"I'm sure your *master* would have something to say about that." Aric was tired of taking guff from the guy, but his options at the moment were limited, and he risked trouble by confronting Pete so blatantly. "I saw you talking with him."

From the man's facial contortions, he knew he'd hit a nerve. That also confirmed to Aric that the man indeed pulled Pete's strings, although others might be controlling *him*. He would watch out for the man at the protests.

"Yeah, maybe," replied Pete. "The boss has his reasons for keeping you safe, and I've been told to toe the line. But that doesn't mean I like it, or that—"

A knock on the door interrupted Pete, who opened the door and let two more men into the room. One of them whispered something into Pete's ear. He glanced toward Aric and gave him a malicious grin.

"Well, well, looks like you get off easy tonight. We've been told to tone things down, so no vandalism, graffiti, or fires tonight. No backpack of spray cans needed. That also means my guys will be able to stay with you."

Aric groaned inwardly, but then a thought came—maybe cooperation would work better than resistance. What was the old saying about catching flies with honey? No, the old song about a spoonful of sugar was better. He smiled inwardly at that latter thought as he hoped it would become apropos sooner, not later. He grabbed his hoodie and a bottle of water and headed toward the door.

"Guess we better get going. It's going to be a long night."

Pete cocked his head at an angle and gave him a curious look. Without saying what was going through his head, he pushed Aric aside and preceded them all out the door. Aric held up his keycard and, with a nod of his head toward Dan, encouraged him to do the same. Pete snatched them both, but the look on his face told a story. He was skeptical and questioned Aric's sudden compliance. That was okay. Aric hoped to keep him off-balance by doing the unpredictable.

Adam wolfed down another sandwich from across the street as he pondered what to do. Night engulfed the area, and even though he stood eight blocks away, he could make out the faint sound of bullhorns in use by protest leaders. Sirens only disrupted the sounds on occasion, unlike the previous night.

Again, he puzzled over how to approach things. He hated to leave the room in case his brother would show up. Yet, almost 24 hours had passed since their anonymous encounter. Adam came to believe one of two things had happened. One, his brother had not made the connection that Adam had jostled him and had not found the note. He knew that the French would be a dead giveaway to Aric as to who had slipped the note into his pocket.

However, there was another option, one that Adam gave better odds to. Buckner would be in town for one reason and one reason only—him. Somehow, he and Chamberlain had discovered Aric's change of plans to come to Portland and deduced only one purpose for the trip—to meet up with Adam. Adam was the big fish they hoped to catch, and Aric was an appetizing minnow. For Adam, it wouldn't be catch and release. They wanted to cull the waters of an invasive species.

Who and how they controlled Aric was a story that would have to wait. For now, Adam needed to focus on avoiding Buckner at all costs. Staying in his room would accomplish that goal.

Still, the thought that Aric hadn't yet discovered the note ate at him. He also needed to know that Aric was still okay. Buckner played for keeps and had no trouble playing rough.

Hesitantly, he donned his hooded jacket and mask and began to walk toward the sound of the bullhorns. The trek took him a while. At every intersection, he stopped and scrutinized the block ahead. If there was anyplace covered in shadow, any sort of alcove to hide in, or the slightest suspicious feature ahead, he detoured a block to miss it. True, although Buckner had no idea where he was staying or whether or not he would appear at the protests, he wanted to give Buckner—or his bruisers—no opportunity to lie in wait. He zigzagged his way toward Chapman Square and blended into those people just there to observe, along the edge, in the shadows.

He found a spot where his back was protected, and the dark helped hide him. He parked himself there and watched. The crowd seemed smaller than the previous evening and more subdued. He saw no fires being set, no windows being broken—although there were few left intact and they were covered with plywood—and no graffiti being sprayed on walls. The occasional water bottles full of urine, bricks, and rocks were hurled toward the police lines. And fireworks and mortars lit up the dark as they were fired toward those same police officers. He had to admire the restraint those men and women in blue used to avoid escalating the confrontation. Yet, he wondered how many of those officers would still be on the job three months from now.

After ninety minutes or so, he prepared to walk back to his room. He had seen no sign of Aric. On a more positive note, he'd also seen nothing of Buckner, which seemed to confirm his suspicions. If Buckner was fishing for Adam, using Aric as bait, he would tend to stick around his bait bucket.

He saw a new group of protesters chanting and marching along SW 3rd Avenue from the far end of the plaza. Shocked, he saw Aric at the front of the group, pumping an Antifa sign up and down in the air and chanting with the rest of them. What the . . .?

Within minutes he saw another silhouette following that group at a distance. As that figure passed under a street lamp, he saw that it was Buckner, wearing no mask and making no attempt at hiding himself other than keeping a short distance between himself and Aric. Did the man expect Adam to just walk up to Aric and make contact?

Adam decided to see what might happen had he been that stupid. He noticed a young man about his size and build holding a BLM sign a few feet away and walked up to him.

"Hey, want to make a quick $20?"

The kid gave him a quizzical look. "Um, maybe. What do I have to do?"

Adam pointed out the group and Aric, as well as Buckner. "I think the guy following the group is an undercover fed. My friends in that group told me he's been shadowing them since they arrived in town. They want to see if they're right. All you have to do is put up your hood to hide your face, run up into the group, approach the tall guy I pointed out—the one with the Antifa sign, say something, anything, to him, and run off the other way."

"Why don't you do it?"

" 'Cause I need to see the man's response and if anyone else is with him. I can't do that if I'm running away."

"For $20, sure."

Adam handed him a Jackson and stood back. The guy played his part perfectly, and sure enough, Buckner gave pursuit. Adam chuckled. Boy, was he going to be pissed when he found out the man wasn't Adam.

Aric still appeared to be under guard, so Adam couldn't use that diversion to approach him. He also needed to leave the area, pronto. Once Buckner caught up to the kid, he would insist on knowing who had put him up to it. Adam didn't want to be around to be identified.

TWENTY-THREE

Tavernier knew better than to keep another late night at the lab. His wife would have a fit, and soon he'd be sleeping at the lab and not by his choice. He set up another test to run, and knowing it would take a couple of hours to complete, he could get home to his family, have dinner, and return later.

As he pulled up the long drive, he noticed the grassy areas bordering the lane were looking tall and weedy. He had never been much of a groundskeeper, and in their other locations, he had had a plethora of neighborhood teens or small landscaping firms eager for his business. Here, he had yet to find anyone—at any price—to do it and had been forced to take on the job. The shaggy yard was yet one more indication that he was spending too much time at work.

He walked through the back door and into the kitchen to a tantalizing aroma of fine French cooking, his wife Adele's passion. He walked up to her from behind and wrapped his arms around her.

"*Allo, ma cherie. Ça sent merveilleux.*" It did indeed smell wonderful.

She turned her head to give him a kiss on the cheek. "*Merci. C'est votre favori, croque madame au poulet caillard aux asperges.*"

"Yummmmm. *Très bon.*" He salivated at the mention of his favorite fare—butterflied breast of chicken topped with Dijon, sliced ham, asparagus, béchamel sauce, and Gruyère, followed by an egg cooked over-easy on top of it all. That had been his mother's signature dish. He could eat it for any meal at any time of day.

"*Vingt minutes.*"

He nodded. That gave him 15 minutes to play with Grace and five to help with the table and pour the wine. "*Où est notre petite princesse?*"

"*Où d'autre? Dans sa salle de spectacle.*"

He smiled. Where else, of course? Her playhouse. He should have known. Precocious for her age, she had wrapped him around her little finger the moment she entered their lives. The playhouse sat in a spare bedroom that they had set up as a playroom for her. She could play with her toys there to her heart's content. Plus, she had learned early on that those toys were to be contained in that room. Then, when she saw the empty boxes from their move, she had insisted on his building her a playhouse from them. He had no idea where she had come up with that idea. He made the structure, and she colored it with her crayons.

"*Frapper, frapper, princesse.*"

He heard a subtle grunt. "English, daddy. We're having tea like the English do."

He shook his head in wonder. Like the English do? Where had that come from?

"Knock, knock."

"Come in."

Some engineering had been involved, but he managed to combine several boxes to create a space ample enough for an adult to crawl in and join her. As he did so, he found her sitting on the floor with two teddy bears, a doll, and her plush dinosaur arranged in a circle with her around her plastic tea set. Each had its own teacup, except the dino, which had a bowl.

"Hello, daddy. Would you like some tea?"

He nodded. "*Qui, merci.* I mean, yes, thank you."

She took a teddy bear's cup, poured "tea" into it, and handed it to him.

"I hope this won't spoil your dinner, Grace. Mama says it'll be ready in about 15 minutes."

She rolled her eyes, actually rolled her eyes. Where did . . .? How was it he was missing so much of her life?

"Daddeeeee, it's only *pretend* tea. It won't spoil my dinner, and I'm hungry. She's making your favorite food." She whispered the last sentence as if it was a secret.

"I know. I'm looking forward to it."

"Soooo, how was your day, Daddy?" She took a "sip" from her cup.

"A little sad. Do you remember Cheeto?" Of course she would remember. She had given the chimp that name with no prompting and not the slightest idea who Tarzan was.

"I do, Daddy. I love Cheeto. He's my favorite."

Now she pouted, which he guessed was her way of looking concerned.

"Well, Cheeto is sick, and I'm trying to figure out why."

She smiled. "I know you can do it, Daddy. You'll fix Cheeto."

He returned the smile and reached over to tickle her. She giggled and scooted away. She proceeded to tell him about her day, and soon it was time for dinner. After a delicious meal, he and Adele spent time with Grace, reading to her in English and French. The girl was fluent in both, well beyond her age. They put her to bed, and Tavernier noted the time.

"*Cherie*, I need to return to the lab. Some tests I'm running should be completed by now."

She sighed and nodded. "Go. Go fix Cheeto, or our daughter will be heartbroken."

He loved that she could be so understanding. She knew he'd be heartbroken, too, if Cheeto were to die. Not to mention the setback that would cause in his research.

If only she truly knew what was riding on his work.

Back at the lab, he soon became engrossed in his work. Before he knew it, a new day had started. Yet, he would begin the new day with some answers. Their new adrenochrome formulation caused a drop in dopamine levels. He hoped none of Gradison's clients were Parkinson's patients, as that could be devastating to them. *Why* it caused a drop was yet to be determined. That would become the new focus of his research—after a night's sleep.

TWENTY-FOUR

Aric had played the role of a protester with abandon, short of doing anything illegal. He held the sign and chanted along with them but stopped short of hurling anything at the police, an act of assault that could get him arrested. The night had gone well, from the vantage point of Pete's group anyway. They managed to get the attention of the mainstream media and found themselves featured on two late-night newscasts.

That seemed to energize the group. Even Pete smiled, once, for maybe 20 seconds.

Only one odd thing happened, from Aric's perspective. Some guy ran into their group, grabbed him, said a bunch of nonsense, and ran off. Curiously, another man took off after the guy. Aric couldn't swear to it, but he thought the second man was the guy pulling Pete's strings. In the dark, he couldn't be sure. And in hindsight, the first man was about the same size as Adam. He wouldn't be surprised to learn that Pete's "boss" followed them and thought the guy might have been Adam.

But that was history now, as they headed back to the hotel. The group stopped in the room where their meals were catered. Coolers of beer were produced to celebrate their night. Of course, the beer would only be the start for most of the group.

Laughing, Aric joined in the frivolity. "Hey, the beer's on me," he joked. Several in the group acted as if he was one of them now. He grabbed three cold six-packs and headed toward the door. "Party's in our room!"

As he walked toward the elevators, he was taken aback by a thought that entered his mind. *You will know My Word is accurate by this sign: Sidon will steal the election.* While not the unmistakable, almost audible voice he had heard the previous night, Aric recognized the still, small voice of the Lord, the voice he was learning to trust more and more.

But Sidon stealing the election? The Democrat's convention was still weeks away. Without question, the man's growing dementia—which was evident to everyone, wasn't it?—would keep him from getting the nomination. Yet, the message was "stealing" the election, not just winning it. Aric took that word to heart. November 3rd suddenly took on greater importance.

He saw Pete give him a curious look before hurrying to follow him to the elevators. Once inside the lift, he asked, "What gives, brainiac?"

"What do you mean?" Aric had to catch himself. Had he reacted strangely to the message he'd just received from beyond?

"You know what I mean, the change in attitude, being a party boy."

Aric came back to the present and shrugged. "You know the old saying, when in Rome . . ."

Pete sighed. "No, what's Rome got to do with it?"

Aric shook his head. "When in Rome, do as the Romans do. I just decided that I wouldn't let the situation, you specifically, ruin what was supposed to be a fun trip for Dan and me. So, I'm gonna join in and enjoy myself. However ... I won't do anything illegal. Unlike you, I don't see getting arrested as some badge of honor."

Pete had no reply, but his look said he remained skeptical.

The elevator doors opened to their floor, and Aric led the way out. "C'mon, you gonna have a beer or not?"

Within minutes, the room was crowded with Pete's friends. The beer flowed freely, and spirits seemed high, certainly not what would be expected of a woke crowd out to change society, to remove the institutional racism they claimed existed everywhere. Where was the rage? Where was the indignation?

This crowd acted no differently than other co-workers blowing off steam after a day on the job. And that's all this was to them, a job—a job with four-star lodgings, catered meals, and free beer and drugs after hours, all paid for by progressive, globalist billionaires.

Aric nursed his beer, letting the others drink their fill. He jested with them and played the game of appearing to be part of the group. Yet, when the cocaine came out, he quietly suggested they go to their own rooms where they could relax and enjoy the high.

Pete, however, avoided the coke and restrained two others as well. Aric knew why—they had to stay alert to monitor him. Yet, could tonight be the night to implement his plan?

By two a.m., everyone had left the room except Pete, his two friends, and Dan. The beer remained plentiful, and the others continued to imbibe. At one point, one of the others left the room, and as he returned with another six-pack, Aric noted no one guarding the door outside. Pete must have felt confident about controlling Aric while keeping his manpower inside the room at this point.

Yes, the time was right. Aric went to the bathroom and after relieving himself, retrieved the Benadryl® and slipped them into his pockets. He returned to the room, where his spoonful of sugar would be replaced with 12 ounces of lager.

"Who needs another beer?"

He pulled five bottles from the fridge and popped their tops. With his back to the others, he slipped two gel caps into each bottle. He hoped that would be enough and, also, that it wasn't too much. These he carried to the others, holding one back for himself so as not to look suspicious. He set that one on the nightstand between the beds while he continued to nurse his previous bottle.

He joked around . . . and watched and waited. Within about 20 minutes, with the doctored drinks consumed, he witnessed each of the others drift off into what would be a dreamless sleep.

Thank you, Micky Finn, or as close as I could make one anyway, he thought, as he repacked some of his gear. He found his cell phone in Pete's back pocket, reclaimed it, hoisted his backpack onto his back, and eased open the door. The hall was empty. He looked back at Dan and whispered, "Forgive me, friend." He slipped out the door and quietly shut it behind him.

He still couldn't afford the time delay in waiting for an elevator. One of the others from a different room could come into the hallway at any time. He made a beeline to the closest fire stairs and hustled down them. He started toward the lobby when he saw the man he had seen talking with Pete. Before he could be spotted, he ducked back into the stairwell, ran up one flight, and followed the second-floor signs to the back stairwell, the one he had tried to use previously. As he neared the door, he heard running footsteps behind him. He'd been spotted.

He entered the stairwell and had a decision to make. What would the man expect him to do? If it was Aric in pursuit, he'd expect his quarry to head to the building's nearest exit, which was one flight down. So, Aric ran up one more flight and, this time, eased the door closed behind him so it wouldn't be heard. As he ran for the first set of stairs, the elevator opened. A couple, both drunk and holding each other up, exited the car. He entered and dropped back to the first floor.

He heard the back door's emergency alarm sound and knew the man had taken the route Aric had hoped he would take. Checking the hallway and lobby to be sure, he saw that the man was indeed gone, so he walked out the main doors. He resisted running and being noticed by the staff. Once outside, he tore off down the parkway in the direction opposite to where the back stairway exited the building.

Only after he had sprinted three blocks away and found a shadowed area in which to hide did he stop. He pulled his phone out and used his map app to locate the Econo Lodge. He was already part of the way there.

He glanced about and saw no one else. Yet, in the dark, he could only hope he had eluded the man to whom Pete reported. If he had, he sure didn't want to be Pete waking up to that man's ire. Of course, Pete would sow what he reaped. That was out of Aric's hands. On the contrary, if he hadn't eluded the man, he was about to bring trouble on himself . . . and his brother.

Adam glanced at the clock on the nightstand between the beds of his room. One-thirty a.m. He had been on autopilot since returning from the protests. At least Aric was still okay, although seeing him chant and raise a sign in protest was a surreal experience. That was *not* his little brother. Who was that, and what had they done with Aric?

He wanted to continue his work. He felt he was close to finding his daughter. Yet, fatigue had finally elbowed its way in and taken control of his being. He closed down his laptop and secured it. Then, without taking off his shoes or preparing for bed, he simply plopped down on top of the bedspread and fell asleep.

However, his sleep seemed turbulent. He tossed and turned and dreamt of loud noises at his door. Someone was pounding on something outside. There was shouting, or was there? Someone was trying to talk with him. *"Ouvrez la porte, frère. C'est moi!"* The person was speaking French. "Open the door; it's me. Open the door; it's me." More noise. Again, *"Ouvrez la porte, frère. C'est moi!"* Wait. This time he caught the word "brother" in there. More pounding, then, *"Adam, réveille-toi. C'est Aric!"* Aric? Aric had been replaced by an evil twin protester.

Aric! Adam jolted awake. Someone actually was pounding on his door.

"Adam, réveille-toi. C'est Aric!"

Aric was there. Adam bolted to the door and jerked it open. His little brother rushed into the room. Adam slammed the door shut and secured it. The two embraced as if both had returned from the dead.

After a moment, Aric pulled away. "We need to get out of here. I'll fill you in on everything, but some guy's been following me. I think I gave him the slip, but I'm not sure."

Buckner! Aric had been observant enough to notice the man even though he had no name to pin on the man, nor a reason to understand why. Adam doubted that Buckner was that easy to slip away from. Little bro' was right. They needed to clear out pronto.

Adam required only a minute to gather his gear. Aric hadn't taken off his backpack, so he was ready.

"Car's right outside."

Together they emerged from the room, hurried to the car, stowed their stuff, and climbed in. As Adam pulled out of the parking lot, he saw Buckner heading their way. He appeared to be alone, which surprised Adam. He glanced about to see if there were others. No one and no cars appeared to be running and prepared to follow someone. Nope, Buckner was on foot and appeared to be using his phone to track something. That fact pointed to one thing.

"Quick, your backpack. Check it. Is there a GPS or tracking device in there?"

Aric turned around in his seat and retrieved his pack from the back seat. After opening it, he pulled out each item from inside and examined them all. Nothing. With a pile of his belongings on the floor between his feet, he checked the pack itself. There! Partially hidden in the bottom was a small electronic device. He pulled it out.

"That yours?" asked Adam.

"Nope. No idea where it came from, and it's not mine."

He lowered the window and tossed it out.

Adam released a sigh of relief. Buckner wouldn't find them now.

Buckner heard a car moving away but had been focused on his tracking app and hadn't seen it. That he'd missed his chance to ID the vehicle didn't occur to him until he found his tracking device on the sidewalk a half block later. The kid had been smart enough to look for one and to ditch it. He had underestimated the guy.

Or had he? If Afton was in Portland, as he expected him to be, the two might have connected, and big brother would be on the alert and was indeed smart enough to be wary of the possibility of a tracker. As he thought about it, that seemed the more likely scenario.

He rushed back to the hotel and went straight to the fifth floor. He started pounding on the door to Pete's hotel room. He kept it up until someone answered, his blood pressure rising with every minute that passed. The time it had taken would have put a less-fit man his age into stroke territory.

"Sorry, dude, Pete's not here. He's babysitting that Afton guy, across the hall in 512."

The guy appeared more hungover than stoned, but Buck expected a combination of the two to be involved. He strode to room 512 and renewed his pounding. After what seemed an eternity, Pete answered the door. Buckner pushed it open and barged into the room.

"Where is he, Lewis?" He already knew where Afton had gone.

Pete replied, "He's right . . ." He glanced around the room. "What the . . .?" Pete threw open the bathroom door to find it unoccupied. He turned back to Buck. "He was right here, drinking with us." He turned to the young man who had come west with Afton. "Dan, where is he?"

The young man shrugged. "Like I would know? I woke up when you did, with the pounding on the door. All I know is he was here with us last night drinking. Last thing I remember is he gave us all a beer."

Buck walked into the bathroom. There, in the wastebasket, was the outer container of a package of Benadryl®. The kid had drugged their beer. Pete had been duped and then drugged. The antihistamine alone would put most adults to sleep. Adding it to alcohol made it much more sedating, better insurance for the guy. He was actually surprised he'd been able to awaken them with his pounding on the door.

Still, Pete hadn't the smarts to have expected something like this. Buck was more irritated at himself for trusting the job to a stoner, revolutionary-wanna-be who liked the pay and perks that came with the job. And he was mad at himself for losing the kid in the hotel when he made his escape. Afton had outsmarted him, too. He'd even discovered the tracking device that Buck had slipped into his pack earlier in the evening while the group walked to the protest area. *His* insurance had failed.

Buck faced Pete nose-to-nose. "You're done here, Lewis. Pack it up and head home, unless you're prepared to pay for all of this yourself. The money stops now."

With that, Buck charged out of the room and headed for his hotel room. His time in Portland had also come to an end.

He had no way to track the Afton kid, who appeared to have linked up with his brother just as they had suspected all along. His last great opportunity to take out Adam Afton had dried up and blown away. He also lost out on that generous bonus Wallace had offered. Yet, it was his failure to complete the mission that bothered him the most.

As he walked back to his hotel to check out, he called the pilot and told him to prepare to fly back to D.C. in the morning. That call was easy. The next phone call was the one he didn't want to make. Did he make it now and get it over with, or wait until he was on the plane and assured of his trip home?

He sat on a bench in the dark park, overlooking the river, and made the call.

"Well, good news, I hope."

Wallace seemed in good spirits.

"No, sir, it didn't pan out. Afton's younger brother is as smart as they say. He figured out that he was under surveillance and slipped Benadryl® into our guys' beers. Knocked 'em out and made good his escape. I had a tracker in his backpack and almost got to him in time, but he discovered that and ditched it, too. Two more minutes, and I would have taken them out."

Silence commanded the other end. After 30 seconds of dead air, Buck asked, "Sir?"

"Just come home, Buck. We'll keep trying."

TWENTY-FIVE

She beamed with pride as she watched the man she loved across the room on a Zoom conference call. Due to the virus, most meetings within the university were now held virtually. This one was no different except for one thing—for her husband, it was possibly the biggest day of his life, short of their wedding and his graduation from the police academy. She would guess that, for him, this day fit in between the two. After all, how could anything top their wedding . . . when the wedding crashers were the President and First Lady, with the King and Queen Consort of England in tow?

Amy Cully's heart felt almost as large as her five-month gestational belly. Almost.

"So, it is my honor to say that the committee has unanimously accepted your dissertation. Personally, I must add that it is one of the finest papers I've had the privilege to review, and I think we were all impressed with your oral defense. I learned a few things."

Amy heard murmurings of agreement from others on the call.

"So, with that, you have met and exceeded the requirements of the University of Missouri-Saint Louis for a doctorate in criminology. Congratulations, Dr. Carson

'Lynch' Cully."

A chorus of 'Congratulations' arose from those on the call.

"Thank you, thank you all. You've been a great group to work with."

Amy had witnessed firsthand the long hours he had put in—60 hours of coursework, two qualifying papers, and his dissertation. And he had completed it all in just over two years. That in itself was something of a miracle.

"You know, Lynch, our offer still stands if you want a position here at UMSL. We'd love to have you on board. You could add a perspective to our program that would help take it to the top of the five."

Amy knew that the University of Missouri at St. Louis's criminology program was already among the country's top five. That, and being in their hometown, had persuaded Lynch to pursue his degree there.

"Thanks, Celeste. I'm truly honored by that offer. I think you know why I'm heading north. I'm looking forward to the challenge of starting a new program from scratch."

For Amy, moving away from St. Louis marked a new beginning . . . as well as removed her from the ever-present reminders of events there, events she preferred to forget. As if she could.

"Well, if you put in the effort there that we saw here, you'll be competing with us for a top-five slot sooner, not later."

"Thanks, George. That might become my next challenge."

Amy heard laughter from the online group.

"Do you think you'll come back for Commencement in

December? Even though the ceremony will be virtual, we're hoping to be allowed to hold a reception for our graduates. "

Due to COVID, the spring, summer, and winter commencement ceremonies were all being wrapped into one larger event, currently slotted to be a virtual one.

"Probably not. Besides the demands of my new job, we're going to have a little one to contend with."

"Well, you'll get an invitation in November anyway if we're allowed to pull it off."

Celeste, the department head, came back on. "Gentlemen, we need to wrap this up. Again, congratulations, Dr. Cully. Please keep in touch."

"Thank you again, and I definitely will."

Amy laughed as Lynch closed his laptop and stood up. She hadn't realized he was wearing swim trunks and sandals under his shirt and tie. Still, had the committee known, they likely would have laughed, too. She had grown fond of the people in the department at UMSL.

She walked over to him and reached for a hug, which was a bit of a stretch in front. He extended himself over her belly and kissed her. As he pulled back, he placed both hands on her abdomen and smiled.

"Well, bump, your daddy's now officially a doctor."

Amy grinned. "My dad would be so proud. I married a doctor."

Tears welled up as she thought of him, and the sadness of knowing her "bump" would never know his, or her, grandfather and that he would never know his grandson, or granddaughter, in this life swept over her. She still missed him terribly but had been able to keep her emotions in check until the pregnancy and its hormonal maelstrom caught her.

Lynch came up behind her and embraced her. He kissed her tenderly on her neck and simply held her. Once upon a time, she had never believed he could be so emotionally supportive.

She shook off the memories and straightened up. "What time is it?"

"Four."

"Gosh, I'd better get busy. Our guests will be here in two hours."

With health authorities advising against large gatherings, they had opted to celebrate his doctorate with a small group for dinner. They had no fear of COVID and found the mask mandates overbearing. Masks were never protective for the healthy and merely encouraged fear of the microscopic, unseen foe. Lynch referred to them as "masks of fear" while stating that he had a "shield of faith." The year, not even half over, had undoubtedly been one for developing their faith in Christ.

"What can I do to help?"

Together they worked in the kitchen, managing not to get in each other's way—too much. By five-fifty, they were dressed and ready. And, as usual, the always prompt Southworths rang the bell right at six. Mike and Mary had become spiritual parents to Lynch and Amy, and their gorgeous historical home in Ferguson was always open to them. Lynch had used it on more than one occasion as a brief refuge between classes, as it was but five minutes from UMSL.

After hugs and greetings, Mike smiled at Lynch and said, "Well, congratulations, *Doctor* Cully."

"We are so proud of you," added Mary.

"Thanks"

The doorbell rang again.

"Jim, Jess, thanks for coming." Jim was their pastor at Destiny Church, and with Jessica, his wife, and their five kids, they had been a great inspiration to Lynch and Amy as they started their family.

Before Lynch could close the door, he saw their final guests walking up the sidewalk. Lynch leaned back into the house. "Amy, Macy's here." She scurried to the door to greet her longtime best friend. For them, the night would be bittersweet. In two days, the movers would be coming, and Amy would be leaving town in three. She would miss Macy and her ever-expanding collection of stories about her cousins' antics.

"Macy! I'm so glad you and Mac could come." Macy Johnson, now Macy Williams, and her new husband Mac had been fortunate to have married and completed their honeymoon just before all of the COVID closures. Two other nurse friends had their venues canceled and plans postponed indefinitely.

"Well, girlfriend, when else was I gonna get to see you before you abandon us for cheese land."

"Our house will always be open to you, you know that."

"Will I have to learn to like Brie, and blue cheese, and some of those other cheeses I can't pronounce? You know I only like Velveeta®."

The group settled in with wine and appetizers before collecting at the table for dinner. Amy had gone all out with homemade, stuffed, baked rigatoni, salads, soft Italian bread, and her dad's favorite tiramisu recipe for dessert. In the end, everyone eased back from the table, as stuffed as the pasta.

The women congregated in the kitchen, talking about pregnancies and childcare. The men moved to the den and talked about . . . pregnancy and children.

"Amy looks like she's doing well, tolerating the pregnancy okay."

Lynch nodded. "She's a trooper. Doing really well, thanks, Mac. It'll be your turn soon."

Mac laughed and shook his head. "Not if Macy gets her way. I won't even repeat some of the things she says about getting pregnant."

"Yeah, well, that'll change. You just watch," replied Mike.

"Speaking of change," said Jim, "your lives are about to change forever."

Lynch offered up a big sigh. "Don't I know it."

"You know these little ones are the original masters of PsyOps, right? The CIA must have taken notes."

"Huh?"

Mike laughed. "Yeah, I can see that. From day one, they use fear to master you. Fear you'll drop 'em on their heads. Fear they'll get sick. Fear you're not feeding them right. Yep, classic PsyOps."

Jim nodded. "Everyone comes along and coos at the baby, 'Oooo, what an angel.' Well, after five of 'em, I can tell you that's no angel. That's a viper in a diaper. God made 'em small, so they can't kill you."

The others all grinned.

"And made 'em so cute, so you wouldn't kill *them*," added Mike.

Jim nodded. "Anyone who doesn't believe in original sin just needs to be around a group of toddlers for a day."

Lynch contemplated that. Original sin was a point of theology that many people today no longer believed. Instead, modern psychology, and even many churches, taught that people were born good. That idea was, of course, diametrically opposite to what the Bible taught. Lynch, having been a police officer, had seen what so many of those "good people" did—the teachers, doctors, lawyers, businessmen, and even police officers, who were involved in drugs, prostitution, child abuse, pedophilia, and more. There were too many things he wished he could unsee. He had never had a problem believing in the concept of original sin.

"Anyway," Jim continued, "tell us what your plans are. I know you're leaving us and moving north."

Lynch nodded. "That's right. The movers show up on Monday, and we leave on Tuesday for Kenosha, Wisconsin. It's just north of the Illinois state line on Lake Michigan. There's a small liberal arts college there. They assess their curriculum regularly and realized they needed a criminology program to stay competitive."

"So, you're going to be part of the program there? Why not stay here? UMSL's top-notch."

Lynch chuckled. "I'm going to *be* the program there. They're looking for me to start it and recruit new people."

Mac's eyes widened. "Wow, no pressure there."

Lynch smiled. "Maybe, but they've assured me that there's no set timetable. They want a good foundation to build on, not something put together hastily. It's a highly respected college in the area."

Mike's face showed concern. Lynch noticed and turned to him.

"Something wrong, Mike?"

He gave a subtle shake of his head. "Um, not with your going there to start a new criminology program. I just . . ." He looked around the circle of men and then directly at Lynch. "I feel like the Lord wants you to be aware. You're going to find yourself involved in something unexpected, presenting as a mystery, but not to worry. The situation there is of His making."

TWENTY-SIX

Tavernier's recent late nights at the lab took a toll on him, and he reported to work about an hour late. He might as well have spent the night there, as his mind had not shut off to let him sleep as well as he'd hoped. Yawning as he entered the lab, his assistant greeted him at the main doors.

"Doctor, Mr. Gradison has called for you twice already this morning. He made it quite clear that you were to call him ASAP."

Tavernier nodded. "Thank you, Edgar. I'll track him down, but my first rule of the lab has priority."

Edgar smiled. "Yes, sir, coffee first. A fresh pot has just finished brewing. Can I get it for you?"

Tavernier shook his head. "I'll get it. We don't pay you to be my gofer. Have you checked on Ten this morning?"

"I was headed that way when I saw you coming in."

"Good. Go check on Ten while I get my caffeine and call Mr. Gradison."

Edgar headed toward the veterinary wing while he walked straight to the coffee maker in their lounge. He took a couple of sips to jump-start his brain again, topped off the mug, and went to his office. He collected his notes from the previous two nights, refreshed his memory, and dialed J.B.

The man picked up and didn't sound happy.

"Sleeping in? I don't pay you to be a slacker."

Slacker? That was a new American slang term for him, but in context, he guessed it meant he wasn't doing his job.

"J.B., I worked past midnight last night and the night before. Without catching up on some sleep, I would not be much use to you at all."

There was no immediate reply. "Okay. So, what do you have?"

Tavernier updated his boss on his findings, emphasizing that they had no idea why the new formulation depleted dopamine in the brain. At that point, Edgar knocked on his door. He looked distraught.

"Give me a moment, J.B."

Without waiting for a response, he put the man on hold and signaled Edgar to come in. His assistant was shaking his head as he entered.

"Sorry, doctor, the chimp is dead."

How would he tell Grace that he had failed to fix Cheeto? Tavernier's heart skipped a beat before his practical nature kicked back in.

"Get it ready for a necropsy. We'll do that straight away."

He resumed his call with J.B. "Sorry, J.B., that was my assistant. Bad news, good news, is how I think you say it."

"What?"

"The chimp has died. The good news is that the necropsy will help us find an answer faster."

"It had better. You have no idea what is riding on this. Keep me up to date. Any time of day."

"Yes, sir."

As he disconnected, Tavernier reflected upon the

tension in the man's voice. Just what *was* riding on this?

Wallace finished his conference call with members of the executive board. They valued his intelligence—both in the sense of the information he gathered as well as his ability to discern what that data meant. With seven weeks until the Democrat National Convention in Milwaukee, they had already determined that "Po" Sidon, with his previous experience as V.P., his business dealings with China, and his name recognition, held the best chance of beating the popular incumbent president.

They needed a candidate for his running mate, preferably one who ticked off several minority checkboxes and could be totally controlled. They didn't want another maverick in the office. Wallace had offered them two names. They would announce their choice . . . rather, Vice-President Sidon would announce their choice in the run-up to the convention.

"Sir, Mr. Gradison on line two for you. He says it's urgent."

Wallace picked up on the line.

"J.B., what can I do for you?"

"Wallace, I don't quite know how to say this. Have you used the latest dose of adrenochrome that I left for you?"

"Actually, no, I haven't. Why?"

"Discard it. I'll get you a new dose."

J.B. went on to explain what was wrong and what they were doing about it. Regarding the latter, he seemed vague on details. Wallace was pleased that they'd discovered the problem before having the drug administered to him, but an annoying thought struck him. Who else had received the new batch? There were a couple of senators he *wished* would take it. Maybe he'd offer them his faulty dose. There was one person, though, that he really, really hoped was not on this distribution list.

"J.B., do we have a larger problem than what you're telling me? Who else has this?"

"Two members of the executive board, but I've already contacted their aides to have them call me. The, uh, person who first alerted me to a possible problem was Janet Sidon Tucker. The vice-president received a dose the same day I brought yours here."

Wallace sank a bit lower in his chair. *That* was the name he didn't want to hear. A marked deterioration in their candidate's health could be disastrous.

"Thank you, J.B., for bringing this to my, to our, attention. Please let us know when you have an update." He hung up before his anger flared and he said something he'd regret. Surely, being hung up on would send a message to J.B. Gradison.

"Sir, it's Director Compton on one. He says it's an emergency."

Wallace sighed. He had no doubt what that emergency would be. Had Gradison called him, or had Janet Tucker? Either way, as a member of the executive board, he was not one to put off, ignore, or refuse.

"Greg, what can I do for you?"

Director Gregory Compton gave him an earful, which Wallace thought a bit unfair as he had no dealings with YFM Corp. other than as a client. Yes, he was acquainted with and on friendly terms with Gradison, but they weren't exactly friends.

"Greg, Gradison assured me they were working overtime on the problem. I'm confident they'll find the cause. In the meantime, we can rely on the older formulation."

"Perhaps. I would appreciate your input on how to handle it should Sidon not do well."

"Well, it's not too late to groom another candidate. The Vice-President is not yet the official candidate."

"True, but that is not ideal either. I've been talking about playing Rob-Your-Neighbor with some others on the board."

The man's code name and allusion to a common party game belied the reality of that option. Wallace had mixed feelings about an all-out coup attempt by stealing the election. While he wanted the current administration out of office as much as any of them, destroying the core of the nation's electoral process still did not sit well with him. Yes, the board had managed to get the Ascendant voting machines into critical swing states, and yes, that software gave them the ability to control the vote, as it had done in Venezuela. But that ploy would be seen through easily. Did they want to live in that glass house?

"Greg, I think the key right now is to have the Vice-President lay low. Use COVID as an excuse for him to avoid public appearances. We can issue statements in his name from his home. That will give us time to see how he fares and whether he recovers from this setback. With some luck, they might even find out why this happened and fix it soon."

There was a short pause on the other end of the line. "Hmmm, that might work. Of course, the opposition will take advantage of that. They'll say Sidon's hiding out in the basement afraid of the virus."

"True, but that damage control is minor, provided this issue gets fixed in a timely fashion."

They ended the conversation with that, but Wallace wondered if they were doing the right thing.

TWENTY-SEVEN

Finding a vacant room in the middle of the night had been a challenge, but Adam and Aric managed to snag a room with two queen-sized beds at a Motel 6 in downtown Gresham. Aric didn't understand why his brother avoided the I-84 corridor just a few miles north. There were scads of motels there with available rooms.

By that point, both of them were so tired that few words were said beyond the usual pleasantries and questions about the family. Aric felt desperate to know what had happened to Adam, and he had no doubt that Adam was just as curious about what had happened to him. Both could wait.

They slept in until the last minute before check-out and headed to the car. The restaurant just outside the motel was closed due to the pandemic, and neither wanted the fare found at the typical fast-food hamburger joint or Starbucks. A half-mile down the road, Adam pulled into a Shari's Cafe and Pies. Aric had no idea what type of food they offered, but the word 'pies' sounded promising.

After coffee had been poured and their orders taken, Aric leaned across the table and, in hushed tones, asked, "What happened to you? Mom and dad are going out of their minds worrying the worst. Our sisters are trying to be stoic for them, but I know they're really upset, too."

Adam sighed and gazed downward as if staring at his shoes through an invisible table. He appeared to be struggling with what to say.

"I-I don't know just how much to tell you."

"Is your life in danger?"

Adam nodded.

"Then you might as well tell me everything because if they find you and I'm with you, they aren't exactly going to spare my life."

Adam furrowed his brow and frowned.

"I'm sorry. I'm aware of that possibility, but I need help, and you're the only one I can trust who also has the smarts to help."

"Then I'm glad we were able to find each other. Honestly, those guys don't scare me."

His brother gave Aric an intense look, but Aric meant it. He would willingly give his life for his brother, for any of his family. He had no fear of death because his Lord had conquered death, and he knew that better things lay ahead of him through Christ. There had been a time when he couldn't say that with complete trust. Now? Well, despite his recent wavering and Pete's challenges, he knew he had the faith to do so.

"How . . . how can you stay so calm? It's one thing for me to fend for myself, but putting you in harm's way really bothers me, no matter how much I need your help."

Aric glanced up and pointed toward heaven. "I know Who my Protector is. The Word says He will take me under His wing if I seek refuge in Him. I've given my whole being to Him and trust Him at His Word."

Adam offered a subtle shake of his head. "Easy for you to say."

Aric weighed his words before answering. "Not really. In the past few days, I've learned I don't have all the answers, but I hope to get at least some of them answered soon, for myself, if not for those who might challenge my beliefs in the future. But giving myself to Him was a simple choice once I realized there was nothing in this world more important to me than Him. Getting to that point of recognition was the hard part. As I continue to live, He's got my back, and if I die, I go to Him. It's a win-win."

Adam remained unusually quiet. Aric hoped he would have the answers he sensed would be coming from his big brother.

After a few moments, Adam nodded and said, "Okay. Here goes." Adam leaned so close to his brother they could almost touch noses over the table. He told Aric of his discoveries about his boss, as well as a dozen major politicians, having ties to the Chinese Communist Party. One of those men was the former vice-president, now running to lead the country. He'd also learned of his boss Wallace Chamberlain's sexual proclivities, interests that coincided with those of many prominent names.

After the food arrived and between bites, Adam filled in his brother about his friend Sam Renner's murder at his apartment, his escape, his hiding in northern Virginia, and his trip to Portland. He then told Aric all about Henry Buckner and his suspicions that Buckner was the man behind Sam's death. He also told Aric that he had seen Buckner following Aric and at the hotel.

Aric soaked this all in. He fully understood why his

brother had to go on the lam. Their parents were still a concern, however.

"Bro, we need to let our folks know you're okay."

"Are they expecting you to check in?"

Aric took a deep breath. "Umm, I kinda left without their knowing about it. Dan and I just took off while they were at work."

Adam groaned. "So, they're gonna be pissed at you if you call home for any reason."

"Yeah, probably. Plus, from what you've told me, our home phone and their cells are probably monitored. We can't risk it."

"Yeah, let's think about that one."

Adam picked up the tab with cash, and they took off. However, instead of heading north toward the interstate, Adam took U.S. Hwy 26 toward Mt. Hood. That question remained for Aric. Why had he wanted to meet in Portland? This added a new facet to that subject. But then it hit Aric.

"Did you find her?"

It was as much an exclamation as a question. As soon as Aric asked it, he knew that Adam had. Or that if he hadn't located Carolyn, he had a significant lead. He knew his brother had never given up. If only Rachel could see him now, see the dedication Adam had in finding their daughter. Carolyn. Wow, after four years, could it really be possible? He felt excited at that prospect.

"I, uh, I don't know. Maybe. So, tell me *your* story."

Aric detailed his travels from St. Louis and how Pete had almost immediately taken control of his life as soon as they arrived in Denver. He finished by telling of his drugging his captors to make his escape and about the man who almost caught him—clearly this Buckner guy. By the time he finished, they had entered the town of Mt. Hood Village, and Adam slowed down.

Aric looked along both sides of the road. Many businesses were closed, and few people milled about those that were. Everyone wore masks despite being outside in the fresh mountain air. The homes and businesses were scattered along the route. What did Adam have in mind?

"So, is this where she is? How do you plan on finding her?"

Adam shook his head. "I honestly don't know. I, uh, took advantage of a classified computer surveillance system at work for personal use. It could have gotten me fired, but I was desperate to find her. That same search led me to all of the other stuff I discovered. Anyway, I found the van that I knew was involved. I saw it speed off. I set up a surveillance ticket on it, which led me to a house just a few miles from our home outside D.C. I got a name and photos of the family's vehicles from that property record, but I could never catch a photo of the family. So, I don't know if the guy is married, has kids, or what, and I couldn't flag the guy in the surveillance system without raising some red flags. Next thing I know, they're gone. I almost lost them but finally traced the vehicles here. No address, just their cars."

Aric thought about that and an idea popped into his head. He wanted to use his cell phone's map app but knew better than to put the battery back in.

"What do you think? A town like this might have what, one, maybe two, gas stations. They would have to have filled up there regularly." He pointed off to their right. "There's a 76 station. Let's check it out."

Adam pulled in, and together they entered the store and approached the clerk.

"Mornin'," said Adam. "Hey, I was wondering if you could help me." He pulled up a photo of one of the cars on his burner phone. "I've been told the owner of this car lives around here, and I'm trying to locate them. I figure they're regulars here."

The clerk, a redheaded woman in her mid to late thirties, gave them a suspicious look.

"You cops? You don't look like cops."

Both of them shook their heads. Aric thought fast about the towns and stores they had passed en route there. "We're trying to return the gal's backpack to her. We were at a grocery in Sandy, and she pulled away from her parking slot with it on top of her car. We couldn't flag her down in time, but she sped off in this direction." Aric didn't like lying, but he prayed God would forgive him for this willful indiscretion.

"Yeah," Adam picked up. "There was a wallet in it, but the only ID was an out-of-state driver's license, so we had no address to go on. We went to turn it in to the store manager, and he recognized it. Said the woman shops there weekly for items she can't get around here and gave us a last name: Hashim. Anyway, he said they live here. He was going to keep the pack, but when we told him we were heading this way, he suggested we come in here and ask about her. Figured we might save her a trip back to Sandy."

Aric resisted rolling his eyes. A "trip back to Sandy" was only 20 minutes.

The woman did not seem convinced. "Look, I don't know what kind of scam you're trying to pull here, but that story of yours is a bunch of bull. They moved from here over a month ago."

Aric and Adam looked at each other. It had been worth a try. Now they'd be unlikely to get any info on the Hashims.

Adam turned back to the woman. "I'm sorry, yes, that was a story. Our boss sent us out here to repossess a large screen TV they stopped paying on six weeks ago. I figured you'd be more receptive to our story than if you knew why we were really here. Most people don't exactly cater to helping us repossess things. My apologies. We went to the address we had on file, and the place was empty. We didn't know they'd moved. The boss is *not* going to be happy."

Now the woman looked sympathetic. And Aric tried to hide his surprise. What a remarkable comeback. He'd always been the storyteller of the family, not Adam. He was impressed.

"Been there, had that boss. I hope he doesn't take it out on you. Not your fault."

Both of them nodded in agreement. Aric sighed and said, "So true."

"Look, they've not been here in, like I said, over a month. Hard not to notice them. She wore her, what's it called, a hijab, I think, and that made her stand out in these parts. The husband worked at some kind of lab that leased the old CCC camp and its buildings up on East Lolo Pass Rd, past French's Dome. It's only about 15 minutes from here. Just look for Zigzag Mountain Cafe and take a left. There are signs for the old camp, so you won't miss it."

A co-worker had walked up as they talked and overheard the last part of the conversation. "You looking for that lab company?"

Adam nodded. "One of its employees."

"Nobody 'round here knew much about what they did there, but I've heard some wild stories. I heard a rumor that some of the lab people were transferred to someplace in central Wisconsin, others to California. Can't vouch for that, but that's what I heard."

"Thanks . . . to both of you."

They hightailed it out of the store before having to dig any deeper holes by embellishing their story.

"Didn't know you were such a good storyteller, big bro."

"Yeah, well, I was sweating it there for a minute."

They found E. Lolo Pass Road without difficulty, and as described, ten minutes later, they came across the old Civilian Conservation Corps camp. The gate at the entry was closed and appeared chained, but as Aric inspected it, he found it wasn't locked. He opened the gate for Adam and closed it behind them. The drive into the camp itself took another five minutes.

They exited the car and began to inspect the nearest building. Whoever had been there appeared to have left in a hurry. Tables, desks, lab glassware, and more still occupied the space—left behind as if unnecessary. None of the papers scattered along the floor offered any hint about who had been there, what they did, or the company's name.

They left that building and moved to a large barn-like structure. The building looked like something used to hold equipment like trucks, tractors, and the like. In its heyday, it might have also stored building supplies. What they found, however, spoke to something else altogether.

Two tiers of cages lined both sides of the structure. But

these weren't animal cages . . . unless the animals were primates or large dogs. Yet, what primates used children's clothing or ate cold cereal? Inside many of the cages, Aric saw signs of *human* habitation. He was startled by wailing coming from his brother.

"Nooooo! No, no, no, no." His brother fell to his knees and began to sob.

Aric had never seen his brother cry, much less lose control and sob as he now did. Aric felt a wave of apprehension creep through him, causing the hair on his arms to stand on end. After a moment of hesitation, he looked in the direction where his brother's eyes were focused. A child's hand emerged from the dirt of a hastily dug grave that someone had tried to disguise by piling old crates on top.

"I-is th-this what happened to her? Nooo. I . . . Dear God, pleease, not this!"

Aric felt the distress his brother showed. While at the park that day with his children, his son Arthur had been snatched by a man. But Adam was torn. His one-year-old daughter, Carolyn, sat next to him, napping in her stroller. He couldn't just leave her to pursue the kidnapper. A woman nearby, whom Adam assumed was watching her own children play, offered to keep an eye on Carolyn and call the police. She urged him to go, get his son. So, Adam pursued the kidnapper and succeeded in getting his son back, only to see the woman loading Carolyn, stroller and all, into a van parked on the street in the opposite direction. Taking Arthur had been a ploy to kidnap Carolyn all along. The police were called but ultimately were of no help. And Adam's marriage fell apart not soon after.

Aric felt tears well up in his own eyes. Carolyn would be four, almost five years old now. Had this been her fate? Living in a cage? A "life" as some kind of test "animal?" A "thing" disposed of in a shallow grave when no longer useful?

TWENTY-EIGHT

Edgar and Tavernier completed the necropsy of the chimp before lunch. He had hoped to find something objective on the gross exam, but that had not happened. The animal's organs looked healthy and, in his opinion, like those of a much younger chimp. That was the ideal situation they expected to see with adrenochrome—restored youthfulness.

"Doctor, I'll get the tissues into formalin right away and begin the fixation process. Then I'd like to grab a bite to eat."

Tavernier shook his head. "No, you go ahead and eat first. I want to do frozen sections on some of the brain and kidney tissue. What I don't use, I'll begin fixating for us to work with tomorrow, along with the other tissues."

As often performed during surgeries where a quick answer was needed, the frozen sections required rapid freezing in a cryostat, after which thin slices were made using a microtome. Tavernier wanted to examine the tissue as soon as possible. Their standard procedure of fixating the tissues in formaldehyde and then infiltrating the tissues with a paraffin-based histological wax to support them for slicing would take time. Yet, that would preserve the bulk of the tissue needed for further study in a way that freezing couldn't.

"Yes, sir. Then I'll begin the toxicological studies after I eat."

Tavernier nodded. "Yes, excellent."

He suspected that their answer, or answers, had a greater chance of coming through the toxicology testing rather than the light microscopy, but both were necessary. Unfortunately, those tests would take time as well, and J.B. could be inpatient. Thus, his desire to do frozen sections. He wanted to tell the man *something*, not just put him off and look as if they weren't working on the problem.

He arranged for another tech to take the chimp's carcass for incineration and headed toward the lab. As he did so, he mulled over test results from the four-year-old donor whose blood had been used to create the new formulation. He recalled nothing in those results that might clue him into a potential cause. He would have the female's DNA sequenced for various markers to make sure there wasn't some genetic variant they would have to be alert to in the future.

Thinking about the donor reminded him that they required new subjects. Skelter had promised J.B. that he would secure four new production units to replace those failing or already disposed of. He used the phone in the lab to call Skelter. The facility warden answered on the second ring.

"Hello, Alaine. What can I do for you?"

"*Bonjour*, Brian. You might already know, but we had to euthanize one of the chimps. I will need to replace it, plus one more. Can you handle that for me?"

"Of course, but it might take a while. Chimps are not easy to procure these days, and COVID has temporarily shut down some of our resources. I will get them ASAP."

"And the replacement production units?"

"That is in the works already. Hashim and his team are in Chicago as we speak, but that process has also slowed down due to the virus. The lockdowns have most people indoors, and they're not finding people outdoors and in the parks as we did before. Particularly with the age requirements you asked for. You still want units between one and five years of age, right? Runaways and throwaways are always easy to find, you know."

Tavernier frowned. He had never liked that the process involved kidnapping, despite its benefits. Too many of the production units procured through government protective services had health issues from drug-addict mothers, fetal alcohol syndrome, and more. The more pristine blood came from healthier units, those found in parks and such places.

But kidnapping tore families apart. Before Grace came into their lives, he hadn't thought about that much. After all, the benefits of his work far outweighed the distress some families would face. Since Grace, however, he had become more sensitive to that plight. What if someone took *his* little girl to become a "production unit?" It would tear him apart. Even the term now soured his mouth when he used it. The sanitized title no longer shielded him from the reality of what they did.

And yet, his work was invaluable. Until he could develop a process for synthesizing their adrenochrome formulation without needing to extract it from blood, his work had to continue. The new formulation had been a step in the right direction . . . until this setback.

"*Oui*, we still have that age requirement. The older ones

fail too quickly or become too resistant."

Yes, the runaways and throwaways, as Skelter called them, were all too easy to find. But they also often came with drug and alcohol issues of their own. Elevated adrenochrome levels required fear, and the techniques used to induce that terror provoked little response in too many of the older "units." They had lived through worse on the streets, where life had hardened them.

"I understand, doctor. We'll get your replacements as soon as we can."

TWENTY-NINE

Buck sat on the plane by himself this time—no politicians or business cronies of Chamberlain. Being alone didn't ease the degree to which he was upset with himself. He couldn't see himself conversing with anyone at that moment. Yet, somehow the idea of having company on the flight, someone with the *potential* for conversation, made him think he wouldn't be kicking himself as much if he had a distraction.

Rather than water, he helped himself to two fingers of Chamberlain's single malt . . . and didn't feel guilty about doing so. He realized that he did so only because he *was* alone on the flight. In fact, since he was alone, he might just finish the bottle. Well, no, he couldn't do that. Word would get back to Chamberlain.

He sat in his chair and stewed. He had made contingencies . . . and staked out the hotel personally. He had backed up Lewis and his gang with a tracker in the kid's backpack. And still, he missed his opportunity.

And yet, as he sat there, he realized he hadn't thoroughly analyzed the situation. Specifically, why Portland? Afton could have arranged to meet his kid brother someplace closer to home. If he knew about the kid's plans to go west to California, why not meet there despite the lockdowns? That would have been far less likely to catch Buck's attention or to arouse his suspicions.

But he chose Portland. Why was he there?

He contemplated Afton's history with the company. He had been an exemplary employee and a key, if not *the* key, player in developing AlterNet. His skills had awarded him with a healthy, upper six-figure income, while his improvements to the system had provided him with several five-figure bonuses. At one point, he had even overheard Chamberlain talking about grooming him for the CEO position for that time when the boss decided to retire.

But he had changed. What was it that happened then? Buck struggled to recall the incident that had occurred shortly before the man lost his superstar status.

Then Buck remembered. The kidnapping. The family turmoil that led to his divorce. Afton's dive into the bottle and almost taking his own life. His getting caught using AlterNet for his personal business. What was it that he'd been looking for?

He picked up his cell and called his office.

"Yo, chief. Didja get 'im?"

"Hey. Pull up Afton's file for me. Find the part about his daughter's kidnapping and where he was caught using AlterNet for personal matters. Send it to me."

"I take it that means no."

Buck didn't want to discuss it, but it wasn't right to take it out on his team. "Roger that. It didn't pan out. Send me the file."

"Bummer. Okay, file . . . is . . . on . . .the way. You should get it momentarily."

Buck's phone dinged. He checked the alert. "Yep. Got it.

Thanks. I won't be back in until morning. You guys holding down the fort okay?"

"We got you covered, Buck. Call me if you need anything else."

Buck took another sip of scotch and opened the file. Afton had been looking for his daughter's kidnapper—specifically a van he had told the police about. The police hadn't found the van or traced an owner. No, wait a minute. Information from AlterNet showed that the detective never bothered to look for it and had received a large sum of money *not* to look for it. Did Afton know that? Had he found the van and somehow traced it to the Portland area? But this line of inquiry raised new questions. Why and who had paid the detective?

Buck kept reading. There was a notation about some kind of adjunct software being linked to AlterNet. The company's attempt to trace and find that software never got past step one. They believed Afton had used his knowledge of AlterNet to hide his new program from it. And then came the big reveal. That was also when Afton learned of Chamberlain's secret life, one with a proclivity for young girls. Very young, but not as young as Afton's daughter. Would he have suspected Chamberlain of being behind the kidnapping?

Buck knew of Chamberlain's pedophilia. He'd always suspected that his highly paid job with CCS was Chamberlain's way of making sure that secret was safe. Buck didn't judge the man for it. Personally, Buck was into prostitutes, the kinkier, the better—things he would never ask his wife to do. How could he judge his boss for *his* preferences?

The visage of J.B. Gradison, Chamberlain's guest on the flight out, came to mind. If his visits not being recorded at CCS were of a personal nature, was this it?

Buck's mind was moving as fast as the jet. No wonder Chamberlain wanted Afton dead and buried. What else did Afton know? Had he tracked the kidnapper? To Portland? Was the only reason he hadn't pulled the pin on the grenade he held over Chamberlain the hope that his daughter was alive? Exposing Chamberlain and the pedophilia ring definitely would lead to their killing all of their victims and witnesses. Keeping his daughter alive under such circumstances was a powerful motivation to stay quiet.

Gradison did mention having two facilities in Oregon. Was one of them in Portland? Thinking back on that conversation, how could a *small* pharmaceutical firm support multiple facilities in California and Oregon? Just what type of "facility" was it? The kind like the farmhouse Chamberlain sometimes visited?

Buck realized he could fumble his way through the maze of investigation this whole thing presented itself to be, or he could take a direct route. He retrieved the business card Gradison had left for him upon deplaning and called the number the man had scribbled on the back.

"J.B. Gradison."

"J.B., this is Buck, Wallace Chamberlain's special projects chief."

"Of course, Buck, to what do I owe the honor of this call?"

Buck did not hold back. "You might not think it an honor after I ask. The situation I'm investigating is a delicate one, and I think you might have some answers for me. What type of service do you provide my boss?"

Silence held reign on the other end. After a long span of dead air, the man replied, "I'm not sure what you mean. Should I be offended at what you might be implying?"

"Offended or not, I'm asking. Look, I know about my boss's sexual preferences and his visits to a certain farmhouse in Maryland. Would I find you at the end of a chain of shell companies tied to that property? If so, I think someone else already has and is prepared to take you down along with Chamberlain. That someone is who I'm looking for, and he was in Portland. He had to be there for a reason. You mentioned having two facilities in Oregon. Is one of them in Portland?"

"Give me a second." The phone clicked to hold. Two long minutes later, Gradison returned. "Okay, sorry. I had to get clearance to tell you . . . from the board. Without getting into specifics, yes. We just recently closed down a holding facility near Mt. Hood. We're building a new one, but it won't be ready for a while."

"Holding facility?"

"That's all you get to know, but I can divulge that it was not a brothel or any place where clients might go."

Buck thought about that for a moment. "Okay, so were any of the personnel at that site located in the D.C. area three years ago?"

"I'd have to double-check, but I think two or three, maybe four, were transferred there from D.C."

"Where are they now?"

"Again, I don't have the records handy, but they would have been transferred to existing centers in California or our new one in Wisconsin."

Buck smelled success. His gut told him he was on the right track. "When you get the chance, please send me the records on those employees. You can send them to this number. It's secure. And sooner would be better . . . if you want me covering your six as well as Chamberlain's."

THIRTY

Aric used every bit of encouragement he could muster to calm Adam down, not that he felt optimistic at the time. What could be worse for a parent? To not know what happened to a missing child or to think that this was their fate? And yet, whether or not Carolyn had been, or was, there, other parents would soon experience that emotional trauma.

The brothers returned to the 76 Station and sought out the clerk they had previously talked with. She was in the process of restocking shelves in the convenience store with chips and snack crackers.

"Hey, did you find it?"

Both men nodded. In somber tones, Aric whispered, "Who has police jurisdiction there? They need to investigate it. Right away." He paused for a couple of seconds. "We would have called for help, but our phones weren't getting a signal there, and we didn't know who to call anyway. Can you call them?"

She stood up and looked at them. "Uh, I guess so. But what do I tell them?"

The Afton brothers looked at each other for a moment. Aric wasn't sure what to divulge, so he hoped Adam would take the lead. He didn't. He still looked shell-shocked from the thoughts that Carolyn might be buried there, so Aric continued.

"The place has been abandoned. Only things left are cages that appear to have held children, not animals. And . . . " He paused and took a deep breath. ". . . there's at least one shallow grave. In the big barn or equipment building, or whatever it was. We saw a hand, a child's hand, sticking out of the dirt under a pile of crates that appear to have been placed on top to hide it."

The look of horror on the woman's face appeared as if it would be etched there for eternity. Tears flowing, she ran behind the counter and snatched the phone from its cradle.

Adam and Aric pointed to the outside. "We'll be out there," Aric lipped to her as they passed by. She nodded in understanding.

The brothers sat down on a bench next to the building and gazed toward the top of Mount Hood. Clouds shrouded the peak while the sun caused the snow below to glisten. It would have been a beautiful place to sit and take a break from work under other circumstances.

A moment later, the clerk exited the building.

"Ends up that place is under the jurisdiction of the park rangers. It's owned by the National Park Service. They'll be here in a few minutes to talk with you."

She returned inside to work, and Aric noticed her talking with the two other employees on duty. They kept looking outside toward the brothers. The woman who had mentioned hearing crazy things about the place repeatedly nodded as if validating the rumors she had heard. For Aric, what they had discovered more than confirmed her comment.

Within minutes, the sound of sirens emerged from the pines—two vehicles from the sound of it. Adam suddenly bolted upright, alert, and ran to their car. Aric followed.

"Adam? What's wrong? The rangers will be here in a minute. We need to talk with them."

Adam shook his head vigorously as he began to do something on his laptop. "No can do, bro. If we do that, our story won't stand for a minute. Then, we look guilty, and they'll hold us. Plus, within minutes of that police report being uploaded to national park servers, AlterNet will catch it and alert Chamberlain and Buckner to our whereabouts. We have to go."

Aric understood but felt divided between doing his civic duty of talking with the authorities and protecting themselves. "What are you doing?" He pointed to the laptop.

"While I can access this place's Wi-Fi, I need to see if I can access their security video and wipe all traces of us from it." His fingers flew rapidly over the keyboard. "Yes. There."

He typed some more, folded his laptop closed, and started the car. No one seemed to notice as they pulled away.

"We can't afford to have my car ID'd. That would give Buckner a head start in finding us."

The sirens closed in as they pulled out from the lot. Aric imagined the clerk's confusion at finding them gone but felt confident that the rangers—well, maybe a lone ranger— would check out the old CCC camp. In the meantime, hi ho, silver, they were off to . . . to where exactly?

Tavernier had placed his specimens in their cryostat and the remaining tissue in formalin before grabbing a quick lunch himself. He then performed the thin slices and began to review them. Now, almost two hours later, he completed that task.

He hadn't expected it to take so long. After all, frozen sections were routinely done while patients remained in surgery. The test was meant to be quick. Yet, when he found no abnormalities in the first few slices, he kept going, expecting something, anything, to change on subsequent slides. Einstein defined insanity as "doing the same thing over and over and expecting different results." Tavernier had crossed that threshold.

Twice. Once with the kidney samples and once with the brain samples.

Edgar walked into the room. "I take it from the look on your face that the tissues look normal on frozen."

Tavernier looked at his assistant. Was he that transparent?

"*Oui*, I reviewed dozens of slices, and they all look normal. I found no evidence of acute kidney inflammation and no intratubular precipitation of xenobiotics or crystals that might promote acute or chronic kidney injury. I do not suspect we will find much else on the paraffin samples."

"Have you looked at the heart tissues?"

"No." Tavernier knew that adrenochrome toxicity had been linked to myocardial damage in rabbits. However, he was less interested in what might have killed the chimp than in why its dopamine levels were so markedly decreased. "My concern is the decrease in dopamine, not what killed the animal."

Edgar nodded. "Then you might find this interesting. I focused on the brain tissue and found lowered levels not only of dopamine there, like we found in the blood samples, but also lower than expected levels of L-tyrosine and L-dopa. I'm running tests on L-phenylalanine levels now."

Tavernier's expectations rose. The primary route of dopamine production was L-phenylalanine to L-tyrosine to L-dopa and then to dopamine. Had the young girl's serum contained something that directly affected one or more of those amino acids? Perhaps something that affected the aromatic amino acid hydroxylases responsible for converting those amino acids.

"We must also check the enzymes—the phenylalanine hydroxylase and tyrosine hydroxylase."

Edgar nodded. "Yes, sir. That will take a bit of testing we don't routinely do. I took the liberty of ordering the reagents we need to check those."

Tavernier smiled. "*Très bon*, Edgar. Good work."

Of course, that was but a first step. Should one or more of those enzymes be affected, the next and main question was why? Likewise, with the amino acids themselves. What was it in the formulation that precipitated those drops?

Tavernier's phone rang in his pocket. He removed a glove to retrieve it.

"Edgar, can you clean up for me? I need to take this."

He left the lab and walked toward his office as he answered the call.

"*Allo*, J.B."

"Alaine, I hope you've had a productive day."

"We have, sir. I don't have anything definitive yet, but I believe we are on the right path." He informed his boss of their progress and of what remained to be done. "The biggest delay might be in the shipping of the reagents we need to finish our tests. The shipping companies have not been very expedient these days, even with overnight express."

"Understood. I'm pleased with the progress so far. I don't want to appear to be pushing you, and that's not really the reason I called. I had an interesting call this afternoon. Did anyone else transfer in with you from Oregon besides Hashim and your assistant?"

That question hit Tavernier like a bolt from a clear blue sky. He had to think for a moment. "Those two, yes. Skelter came from southern California, as did several of his people. The others in the lab came from Texas and the east coast if I recall correctly." He had to think through the people in the center, counting with his fingers to make sure he had the right number. He was missing someone. "Wait, yes. One of Skelter's people was also with us at Mt. Hood. Harrison."

"And did any of those who joined you at Mt. Hood come from Washington?"

"I think so. If I recall correctly, Edgar, Hashim, and Harrison all came from D.C."

"Thank you. That's what my records show as well."

"Why?"

"You need to be on the alert." He detailed his call from Buckner without revealing any names. "Someone might be on to one of you. Our friend followed two men to Portland and thought they were looking for someone who transferred from D.C. The center at Mt. Hood came up in the conversation."

Tavernier's heart raced at that thought. This was not good news. It was not *any* kind of announcement he would want to hear.

THIRTY-ONE

The trip east along U.S. Highway 26 was beautiful—the Mount Hood National Forest, the Warm Springs Reservation, Ochoco National Forests, and the Painted Hills region. Each had its unique features and beauty, and the Painted Hills in the late afternoon were amazing. As for Warm Springs, Aric had never traveled through an Indian reservation before and was disappointed to find it no different from the surrounding areas. Although, in truth, he couldn't identify what he had expected to see and chastised himself for thinking in stereotypes.

He thought the John Day Fossil Beds National Monument would be fascinating, but Adam sped right past its entrance. What was the hurry?

"Why couldn't we stop and check out the fossil beds? That would be interesting."

"Not in the mood."

That was true. Ever since finding those cages and seeing that child's hand sticking out from the dirt, Adam had been a dour and silent brooder. Not that Aric blamed him. He wasn't married and had no kids. He couldn't really understand what might be going through Adam's head right now, but he knew what was going through *his* thoughts at the idea of his young niece experiencing such a fate.

"Besides, they'd be closed, like every other national park facility."

Aric nodded. He had a point. It was a pitiful time to want to sightsee, even if this ended up being their only opportunity to see what this part of the country had to offer. So far, the year 2020 had been full of disappointments . . . except for his joining up with Adam. And even that was heading for a nadir.

"So, you keep driving. Where are we going?"

Adam turned toward him with a questioning look, as if he'd just woken from a trance. Maybe he had. Perhaps the last four-and-a-half-hour drive had been on autopilot.

"What?"

"Where are we headed? Do you have a plan?"

"I, uh . . ."

"Look, Adam, what we saw at the CCC camp disturbed me, too, but we can't think the worst. I have faith that Carolyn is still alive. To be honest, I think God has been reassuring me of that for the past four years. But we can't just drive on and on. We need to figure out how to proceed."

Adam returned his focus to the road. "I . . . I guess I was just heading for Wisconsin and hoping to figure things out on the way."

"Okay, but the lady said Wisconsin *and* California. California is just four hours south of here. Wisconsin is four days east. How do we know we should be heading for cheese land?"

"Well, first off, it's no longer *we*. I don't want to put you in jeopardy any longer. I was going to swing through St. Louis, drop you off, and then head north. I—"

"No way, Jose. I'm in this with you all the way. No way

you're going to pass me off to our folks and a boring summer in lockdown. Besides, you said you had something you needed me to do, something that I'm perfectly suited for."

Adam shook his head. "I do. I mean, I did, until I learned that Buckner is on your tail, too. Everyone blames me for losing Carolyn. I don't want to be blamed for your getting injured . . . or worse."

Aric put his hand on his brother's shoulder. He had never blamed Adam. He had been between the proverbial rock and hard place, with gravel being dumped on him.

"Not everyone, bro. I don't, for sure. I just know we're gonna find her. *We*, not you alone. I want to help."

Adam offered him a weak smile. "Thanks. I . . ."

"I'm trusting God. Maybe it's time that you returned to the fold and started to, as well."

Was that a tear he saw coming from Adam's eye? He wouldn't point it out and embarrass his brother. Then he realized that he had witnessed his brother in a complete meltdown. What was a few tears?

"Maybe," Adam whispered. "I'm having a hard time with this. I pray and see no results. I've been questioning what faith I have left more and more lately."

He surprised Aric by slowing down and turning into a pullout for a place called the Sumpter Valley Railroad Interpretive Site. The sign also said it was part of the Malheur National Forest. Wasn't that near where the President had been kidnapped and held while still a candidate? Aric remembered following those events on the internet at alternate news sites because the mainstream press avoided the story. The man who'd found him had been a detective in St. Louis, but Aric couldn't recall his name.

"I need a break, a distraction," said Adam, and he exited the car.

Aric followed. Despite being early June, there were still smatterings of snow, and the mountain air was brisk in the late afternoon sunshine. The scent of pine made the fresh air stand out. Had Aric ever breathed such clean air?

Adam walked over to the nearest snow, bent over, and picked up a wad of the icy stuff. He didn't hesitate to form it into a ball and throw it at Aric. Aric dashed to another melting drift, armed himself, and returned fire. Soon, it was all-out war as the two laughed and dodged each other's missiles.

"Ouch!" cried Adam as one of Aric's snowballs scored a direct hit on the back of his head. "That's icier than I thought." He tossed the ball in his hand to the side and held up his hands.

"I win!" declared Aric.

"In more ways than one, little bro." Adam walked over to Aric, put his arm around Aric's shoulder, and squeezed. "In more ways than one."

Adam walked over to the car and leaned against the hood. Aric joined him.

"You're right. I need the help, and I'd much rather do this *with* you than without. I can't go on wallowing in guilt. I've spent four years looking for Carolyn, and I won't stop now. I won't ever stop without confirmation that my search would be futile."

Aric read between the lines. Only confirmation of Carolyn's death would be enough, and then they and their family would face such news together. Yet, Aric felt another of those nudges he attributed to the Holy Spirit that they would never have to deal with that.

"I do have a preliminary plan that you can help with. We'll have to make up the rest as we go."

Aric smiled. "So, what can I do?"

"Right now, our biggest threat is Buckner. He won't stop looking for me, for us, and if he finds us, we're toast. My friend was taken out by a sniper from across the street. We're likely to meet the same fate if they find us."

"I would agree about Buckner. So, how do we beat him?"

"That's what I've been thinking about. I know it sounds like Hollywood stuff, but he's a ghost, one of those guys you'll never find in any database. Really. He was Army Special Ops, and our government made sure his past was buried. CCS makes sure his present is buried as well."

Aric thought he saw where this was going without needing Scrooge's dreams. "So, we need to make sure his future isn't."

Adam looked surprised. "Yeah. How'd you . . .? I knew you'd be able to help. We need to pull his white sheet away and display his real corporeal self to the world."

Aric nodded, but one thing nagged at him. "Okay, but with one caveat. The ninth Commandment says we're not to bear false witness against our neighbor. How do we do this without making up stuff about him? That would be bearing false witness."

Aric expected Adam to protest. From a human point of view, the guy deserved whatever he got. In Biblical terms, he would reap what he sowed. But that had to be achieved ethically. Aric still believed in *real* ethics, those based upon

Biblical truths, not the postmodern version where truth and ethics were relative.

However, instead of protesting, Adam smiled and walked around the car to the trunk, which he opened. He pulled out a Manila envelope stuffed to overflowing.

"I have all of this on my laptop, too, but here's his pre-military records, military personnel file, and some things from recent days that someone thought needed to be recorded. I guess they wanted some form of insurance in case he went rogue."

Aric frowned. "You got this how?"

Adam shrugged. "What didja expect? A polite, unredacted response to a FOIA request? I had to hack the Pentagon to get it."

Aric sighed. He had a point. It wasn't like you could request confidential personnel records from the military and expect to get them. Yet, he also didn't think it Kosher that the man's info was expunged from the public records in the first place. The government would hide a mass murderer if the killer did the work they asked him to perform. He and Adam would have to fight fire with fire. As long as the information was valid, Aric would not balk at using it. After all, the Word also said that a man's actions in the dark would be exposed in the light. It was time to shed some light on the activities of the man named Buckner.

October 2020

THIRTY-TWO

Sure, lots of women are late with their first one. Right. The baby will come when the baby is ready. *Don't tell me that,* she thought. *Tell the baby . . . it's time.* Amy paced the front room of their new home, a week past her EDC. Why did they call it an estimated date of *confinement*? The past month had been more confining than anything she'd experienced, including being kidnapped and held in a pervert's harem. They should call it the EDF—estimated date of *freedom.*

Of course, that was just the hormones, or her moaning, or something, talking. Freedom? Whenever did a newborn produce freedom? When they say life changes forever with a child, she now had a fuller understanding of that truth, but they forgot to comment on the body changing forever, too. She would never fit through a door sideways in her current state.

She was ready to meet this kid face-to-face. More than ready.

"Are you still having back pain? What about contractions? I have your go-bag at the front door. Just say the word."

Lynch sat in his overstuffed chair nearby, his feet on the ottoman, coffee in hand. He looked so comfortable and at ease. Was he trying to rile her? She wanted to just slap him upside the head.

The back pain persisted. More false labor? She hoped not.

And then it hit—a cramping pain like she'd never felt. In that instant, she stood in the middle of a small flood on the wood floor near the front door. Her water had just broken.

"Lynch! It's time!"

His eyes bulged at the sight of amniotic fluid on the floor. Amy knew that *he* knew what that meant. Yet, instead of rushing for the door, he ran toward the kitchen. Her husband emerged with the roll of paper towels, from which he began to pull off two and three sheets at a time. Lynch tossed those over the puddle and repeated his effort until the towels had absorbed the fluid.

"Okay, I'll finish that later." He grabbed her bag and rushed out the door.

She stood there, watching his antics and shaking her head. He was halfway to the car in the driveway when she shouted, "I could use a little help here!"

He gave her a thumb up and continued to the car. She tried to waddle forward but found it difficult as another contraction hit. She watched as he opened the door and threw a towel across the seat. After securing the towel, he ran back for her.

She grimaced from the pain, and then it eased. Lynch didn't hesitate. He scooped her—them—up in his arms and scurried to the car, where he helped her into the seat.

They had mapped out the fastest route to the hospital and drove it in several test runs over the previous month.

Now, following another contraction, the fifteen-minute drive seemed to take a year.

"Are you timing the contractions? How long between them?"

What kind of questions were those? Of course she was.

"Yes, I'm timing them. Five min—" Another hit and lasted a bit longer. When it eased, Amy caught her breath and said, "Make that three minutes now."

"Almost there."

She looked at her husband. *Probably wishes he had lights and siren right now,* she thought, although he'd always been a stickler for officers using such for personal reasons. Yet, even without those professional appurtenances, he arrived in record time.

The nursing staff whisked her from the Emergency Room entrance to Labor & Delivery, where, surprisingly, her physician waited for her.

"Dr. Bishop, I'm—" Another contraction caught her.

"Hi. I happened to be here for another delivery when I got your husband's call. So, perfect timing . . . for both of us. Water broke at home, right?"

Amy could only nod her affirmation.

"And how far apart are the contractions?"

Amy tried to control her breathing. She couldn't reply, so she held up three fingers.

"Okay, let's get you to a room."

At Tavernier's request, the four-year-old girl, 20161025F290, had been spared additional extractions . . . and all of the terror involved. Her removal from their schedule had not lowered their production forecasts, thanks to Hashim's success in obtaining new production units. However, her elimination had stopped further problems with dopamine levels in their test chimps, and there had been no additional issues with Parkinson's-like symptoms in YFM Corp.'s clients. To date, Tavernier had been told only of two such clients, although Gradison had withheld their names from him. That was probably best. He didn't want to know.

As he neared the girl's cage, she retreated and cowered in the corner farthest from the door. Tavernier stood and observed her, as he had done on numerous occasions over the past three months. She appeared no different than the others. She ate no differently than the others. Her environment was no different.

Yet, something in her makeup had caused the problem. Hadn't it? Could something in the chimp have triggered the problem? No, one other animal had developed Parkinson's symptoms when injected with her extract. Plus, there were those two clients. It had to be something in her body's chemistry. But what? They had run every test they thought to do on her blood's serum. They had only one additional avenue they could pursue—euthanizing her and performing a necropsy.

Tavernier felt determined to discover the cause of the dopamine issue. The problem might crop up again, and he preferred to understand why, so they could overcome it. They might even be able to capitalize upon it if they understood what was happening.

Skelter walked up behind him, and the girl buried her face in her knees, drawn up tightly to her chest. Although

Tavernier knew what was required to increase adrenochrome levels for extraction, he preferred not to be a party to those events. Still, the girl's reaction to Skelter told him a lot . . . as did the grin on the man's face.

"So, doc, are you ready to put this one back on the schedule?"

Tavernier shook his head. "Not yet. Please do me a favor. This one's birthday is coming up. Could you give her something special that day?"

Skelter took half a step back and stared at him.

"Umm, sorry, but no. You know we don't do that with the units. For a variety of reasons."

Tavernier nodded. Maybe he would be able to slip her something clandestinely.

"Look, doc, if we're not going to use her anymore, we need to dispose of her. If you want to do that necropsy, fine. We can handle it that way. But we also have a hunt coming up soon. The young ones don't usually offer us much of a challenge, but you never know."

Tavernier shook his head more vehemently this time. Something about releasing children on a farm or in a forest and then hunting them like one hunts deer never sat right with him. He had never participated in a hunt and never would.

"No. No hunt. That stress could alter any findings we might get in a necropsy, and I'm still weighing that possibility."

In truth, he didn't understand why he hadn't pulled the trigger on this one. A necropsy might or might not provide him with the answer he sought, but if negative, that in itself would show the whole incident to be an anomaly. Why *was* he keeping this one alive? He wouldn't risk a repeat of the problem by using her blood, so why?

"Doc, you're getting soft with this one. Do you fancy her for yourself?"

Tavernier looked at him, aghast at what he suggested. Never.

"I do gotta admit, though, doc, she does kind of resemble your daughter."

Tavernier felt his heart race. Was this why he hesitated? The girl was about the same age as Grace, and her coloring—skin tone and hair—was similar. Did he see something of his own daughter in 20161025F290 that made him hesitate? Would killing her and performing a necropsy be too much like doing so to Grace? The idea of such made him sweat.

"Well, doc, you need to make a decision soon, or I'll be forced to do it for you. I don't have a budget for feeding and caring for units that don't produce."

"Breathe! You're doing great, Amy!"

Considering its auspicious start, labor had become laborious. Amy was ready for drugs and a C-section to finish the ordeal. Who had talked her into doing this naturally? The monitor beeped that another contraction was beginning . . . as if Amy needed to be told.

"C'mon, sweetie, push!"

"Harder, Amy, the head's coming," said Doctor Bishop. She held her hands as if ready to take a football from the center. "Heeerre we go."

Amy wanted to watch but forced herself to focus on

pushing and breathing. She grunted again as she did her best to get this over with. She did see the nurse hand her doctor an aspirator and heard that distinctive sound of a baby's airway being suctioned clean. A moment later, the pressure was gone, and Amy heard Doctor Bishop announce, "Congratulations, you have a son!"

"Yessss! Way to go, sweetheart." Lynch leaned over and gave her a huge hug and a kiss.

The nurse wiped their son clean as his lungs propelled a healthy cry into the room and brought him to Amy. Tears of joy flowed, and the past few months of misery and discomfort were forgotten . . . mostly. Amy held him against her chest, skin to skin, his pink glow in contrast to her pallor from being cooped up for weeks.

In that instant, Amy understood the love a parent had for her child—the love God must have for those who follow Him.

THIRTY-THREE

Over four more months had passed, and still, no ax had fallen on Wallace's neck. He had come to believe Buck's theory that Afton either had no smoking gun after all or that he held out in the hope of finding his missing daughter and didn't want to jeopardize her life by exposing Chamberlain and the others. Either way, they had been given more time to find him . . . only to be 100% stymied in their efforts.

Yet, however much Wallace wanted to rid himself of that Sword of Damocles hanging over his head, he also had powerful masters to deal with, and they had tasked him with a different project. Bradley Graham's campaign was moving along much better than expected. The man held rallies numbering in the thousands, while Sidon's handlers used COVID to keep him out of the limelight for fear of further exposing his Parkinson's frailties. The board needed some assurances of Graham's losing.

A knock at his door broke his mental meanderings. The hour was late, and his executive assistant had been excused for the day. He expected Buck for a meeting that his assistant did not need to know about. He opened the locked door to find his special projects chief. He made a point, too, of locking the door behind them. No interruptions or spying ears could be tolerated.

"Drink?"

Buck nodded. "Yes, sir, thanks."

Wallace knew the man's spirit of choice and poured him two fingers of Kentucky's finest. He did likewise for himself with his Glenfiddich. They sat in their customary seats across the room from Wallace's desk.

"So, we're now two weeks away from the election. Can I tell the executive board that all is well and ready?"

Buck nodded. "We're close enough that I think we can safely give them that assurance. My people will be meeting with the last few judges tomorrow and the next day. I don't expect any real resistance from them. AlterNet has more than paid for the board's investment in it."

"Good. Good."

While Wallace had hoped to task the system with his own longstanding problem, the software had been directed toward the dozens of judges and politicians in the six swing states, which would make or break the election. Lawsuits and challenges would be forthcoming.

Tens of thousands of "lost" ballots had been preprinted for those states. Operatives had been out buying absentee ballots from seniors in care centers. State election directors, attorneys general, and cooperative governors had made last-minute changes—typically not fully legal ones—in election rules. Ballot stuffing was in progress where early voting occurred, and mail diversions from known conservative districts would trash ballots that would likely go against them. And, in a technological coup, their friends at Communion Software had provided back doors to Ascendant, their electronic voting equipment, so that they could switch Graham votes to Sidon and give the board the guarantee they sought.

However, these efforts to give the election to "Po" Sidon would not go unnoticed, except by their friends in the media. State legislators would be asked to regain their constitutional control over State Electors. All the way to the Supremes, judges would be asked to intervene, grant emergency injunctions, and even overturn certified election results. However, AlterNet had found the "dirt" on each one, giving Wallace and the executive board sway over their decisions.

Yet, they still had free choice in their decisions. The board emphasized that they could not *make* them act one way or another. They could work against the board's wishes and see their lives and families destroyed, or they could refrain from acting at all and continue in their prestigious positions of power. Not much of a choice, but it was still theirs.

"We've had several unhappy campers but no outright rebellious ones. I'm confident they'll play nice. To make sure, we've sent those folks pictures of their loved ones in open, public spaces. You know, kids and grandkids at school. Wives at the grocery. Spouses in the parking lot where they work. Stuff like they see on TV crime shows all the time as reminders that we know where their family members are and could get to them. Whether or not we're serious is up to their imaginations." Buck grinned.

Wallace offered a slight smile. "Well, the board does have *some* scruples. They've taken out opponents and traitors directly, but never family members."

"I don't think it will ever come to that. Fear is a great motivator, just like with the fear of this virus. I'm still amazed at the level of control that's been just handed over out of fear."

Wallace nodded. He, too, had not expected the American public to simply roll over and give up their freedoms. The guys at NIAID who had sponsored and funded the "gain of function" research on a common cold virus had been genius in setting this whole pandemic thing in motion.

"Anything else to report?" asked Wallace.

Buck shook his head. "Not in that department."

Wallace raised his brow. "Oh? Do you have something in a different department?"

Buck nodded. "I think I know where Afton will be heading."

Wallace hadn't expected any advances on this front. AlterNet's resources had been busy.

"Too bad AlterNet isn't quite the bright star of *NCIS: Los Angeles.* Imagine what we could do if we had the tracking ability of that show's Kaleidoscope software on a national level."

Wallace agreed. Buck didn't know everything there was to know about AlterNet. Nor did he *need* to know. They *could* locate vehicles of a given make, model, and color within specific cities and do so quickly—just not quite up to the speed of "real-time." That was something Afton had been working on—the algorithms that would "follow" a vehicle, predict where it might be heading, and prioritize which traffic and security cams to use for the highest probability of picking it up again.

"So, where do you think—"

There was a pounding on the door.

"Mr. Chamberlain, Mr. Buckner, open the door. This is the Metropolitan Police. Mr. Buckner, we have a warrant for your arrest. Open the door, or we'll blow it open in 30 seconds."

The two men looked at each other, aghast. Buckner swore beneath his breath. He reached for his gun, but Wallace stayed his hand.

"They can't know for sure that we're in here. And the door is fortified."

"But they said they have a warrant for my arrest. What the—" Anger etched his face, not concern. "How is that even possible? I'm a ghost. What could they possibly have on me?"

Wallace wasn't sure how to answer that one. The man had a point. Yes, he was responsible for multiple "indiscretions," to put it politely. Any one of them could put him in prison, but how was it possible? Fingerprints, DNA, past history, military record, current identity—all of it had been wiped clean from every known database.

"We know the door is fortified, so we *will* blow it open if necessary. Fifteen seconds!"

"Look, Buck, you know we'll take care of you. I don't want to risk their blowing up my office. Surrender to them, and we'll get it all sorted out. Trust me."

Buck always had trusted him before. Wallace owed him.

Buck retrieved his handgun and slid it across the floor toward the door.

"I'm coming," yelled Wallace.

He walked to the door, released the locking mechanism, and opened it. A Metro Police Emergency Response Team swarmed into the room. The surprise at seeing such a demonstration of force showed clearly on Buck's face. Wallace had no doubt his face appeared the same.

"What's the meaning of this intrusion? I'm General Wallace Chamberlain, and I—"

The officer-in-charge interrupted, "Yes, general, we know who you are. Please stand down and stand aside."

"Again, what's the meaning of this?"

"We have a warrant and were warned that the suspect was armed and very dangerous."

"Of course he's armed. He's one of my security chiefs, and we deal with highly classified material. Your man already picked up his weapon." Wallace stopped long enough to point to the officer who had secured the handgun. "Henry Buckner served with me in Iraq and Afghanistan. He's one of the finest soldiers I know. You're making a—"

Wallace's protests were ignored . . . and he was not a man used to being ignored.

"I demand to speak with your superior officer."

He watched as an officer cuffed Buck and frisked him for additional weapons. It seemed evident that they were aware of Buck's martial arts skills and sought to minimize his use of his hands. How? How could they know?

"General, here's just the man you need to talk with."

A man well-known to Wallace walked into the room. His suit might look informal, but Wallace knew a Canali suit when he saw one. He had been to their boutique in City Center DC on I Street more than once. His own made-to-order suits ran over $4,000 each. U.S. Attorney for the District of Columbia Wayne Cooper cut a formidable figure in his navy blue Canali.

Now Wallace grew concerned. The U.S. Attorney himself had brought the charges against Buck, whatever those charges were. Not an assistant, but the man himself, a man dedicated to uncovering corruption on both sides of the aisle. He was also a man who would not cower to the executive board, as he played for keeps. Rumor had it that he sought the Attorney General position but would accept it only if earned on a level playing field.

Cooper nodded at Wallace. "Wallace, sorry to intrude like this." He then walked up to Buck. "Henry Buckner, you're under arrest for the murder of Sam Renner, as well as additional charges which will be forthcoming."

Buck's rights were read by the Metro Police Special Operations Division Captain, who had accompanied the U.S. Attorney. These men were serious. No underlings had been tasked with *this* arrest.

What could they possibly have on Buck regarding Renner's death? Wallace had attended the man's memorial service, consoled the widow and family, and provided a generous settlement to help them financially. To him, the matter had been settled months ago.

As the officers led him out, Buck looked at Wallace with a gaze that said, "I'm trusting you." For the first time in their association and friendship, Wallace wondered if he was destined to break that trust.

U.S. Attorney Cooper stopped near Wallace as he followed the parade out of the office. "Wallace, I expect you to give us your *full* cooperation on this. If not, expect obstruction charges." With that succinct promise, he left.

Wallace pondered that comment, still bewildered at this turn of events. He followed the troupe through the outer office, where his corporate security team escorted them back to the elevators. His team would make sure everyone left the building. He then rushed back to his desk and placed two calls—the first to their corporate lawyer to get Buck the representation he required and then to Greg Compton. The executive board needed to be aware of this twist and come to Buck's defense.

Five minutes later, he slumped back into his chair, stunned. The board was already aware of the situation . . . and Wallace, with respect to helping Buck, was on his own.

THIRTY-FOUR

J.B. ran his hands over his face before rubbing his temples. The headache coming on was not the result of too much wine or even one of his increasingly common tension headaches. He had been in touch with Chamberlain's man, Buckner, about a problem he was working on for Chamberlain. Just now, J.B. received word that Buckner had been arrested on murder charges.

How was that possible? He had heard rumors of Chamberlain's "wealth-building" plan. Blackmail had its benefits, as did providing certain sexual services to wealthy clients or selling a fountain of youth to other well-connected individuals. Playing in those games had risks. Sometimes, those risks had to be mitigated with a properly planned and executed robbery-gone-wrong, auto accident, suicide, or a simple case of disappearance. In their line of work, death was simply a problem of proper disposal. Had someone gotten sloppy?

While Buckner's arrest was more Chamberlain's problem than his, J.B. saw it as strike two. He didn't want to see another pitch hit the zone with the potential to take him out.

Strike one was *his* problem. Someone in his organization *had* been careless. He, or she, had purchased a flash drive from Amazon, loaded critical organizational data onto it, and subsequently returned it to Amazon without erasing that data. Now, someone in Germany—who had purchased the drive as new, discovered it wasn't, and got curious—had dumped the data onto the web. The six PDF files had personnel records for nearly a dozen of their detainment camps in California, an email and photo regarding a disposal site that was obvious on Google maps, and lists of dozens of their production units with names, dates, their adrenochrome quality grades, and ultimate disposal dates. There was also a list of names of units that would be hunted and in which counties the hunts would take place in forthcoming months.

YFM Corp. was in full damage control mode. He faced the looming prospect of having to close down and move facilities, as well as critical shortfalls in production. This was on top of the problems they encountered with the California wildfires. He also had clients who already had paid handsomely for an upcoming hunt and who might require refunds. That was always a hassle, not just for bookkeeping but also for their image and reputation among that fickle client base.

As he gazed out the window of his private office, the distant haze of those wildfires brought home the reality of the situation. The importance of their new Wisconsin center increased almost exponentially.

His thoughts were interrupted by his cell phone. A glance at the Caller ID revealed Wallace Chamberlain on the other end. Did he genuinely want to take this call? He shook his head, but Chamberlain was too important, too high up on the food chain, to ignore.

"Wallace, nice to hear from you. To what do I owe the honor of your call?"

"Can it, J.B., I'm not in the mood for fake cheeriness. I know you've already gotten wind of what's happened to my man, Buckner."

J.B. shook his head again. Maybe he should have let the call go to voicemail.

"I have. Sorry to hear about that. I'm sure your friends on the board will be able to get that taken care of."

The silence on the other end caught J.B. off guard.

"J.B., as it ends up, the board has washed its hands regarding one Henry Buckner. They made it quite clear that his defense would be up to CCS and me. I'm calling to let you know that I expect your help."

J.B. took a deep breath.

"*My* help? We had nothing to do with whatever he's done."

"True. But Buck's upset, to put it mildly, about this turn of events and has informed me that if I don't get these charges dismissed, he has enough information on me . . . *and you* . . . to get us adjoining cells."

"Me? Info on *me*? What could he possibly have on me?" He paused. "Let me rephrase that. What could he possibly have on me *that the board would allow him to spill?* With a threat like that, he's asking for the Epstein special."

J.B. personally knew the man who had killed Epstein and staged it as a suicide. He was an upper-tier adrenochrome client on whose good side J.B. preferred to stay.

"Perhaps, but that would trigger what he's calling his insurance, a data dump that would put what I hear you're facing seem like pennies in a gold mine."

J.B. wanted to groan. His headache now zoomed toward a new zenith.

"How can I help?"

"Buck was working on a theory. We have a, shall I say, a thorn in our side. He was our top programmer, and he's gone rogue. He had a daughter who was kidnapped three-plus years ago. The incident destroyed him, his marriage, and his family, and I'm convinced that's what turned him. Anyway, she'd be going on five now. Buck succeeded in tracking the guy to Portland and believes the man had traced his daughter there, or at least the kidnapper. He told me he talked with you about it."

J.B.'s eyes widened. He recalled the phone conversation, but then Buckner never contacted him again.

"I remember the phone call. Nothing more came of it."

"Oh? Nothing? Where was that facility he talked with you about? Wasn't Mount Hood by chance, was it?"

Stunned by a realization, J.B. stepped away from the windows and sat down at his desk. He'd been so busy, he hadn't connected the dots.

"It was. I-I was so caught up with work on our new facilities, I never really paid attention to the news then."

The story hadn't lasted long. An anonymous tip had led authorities to an old Civilian Conservation Corps camp—a facility that YFM Corp. had leased under a long string of shell companies—where two mass graves of children had been found subsequently by cadaver dogs. The tip came after animals had unearthed a shallow grave inside one of the equipment buildings, and someone discovered a hand poking out of the dirt. After two weeks of investigative work, the story leaked out to the news and became a lead story throughout the northwest during the last week of June and persisted in the Portland news cycle until the wildfires started in Oregon a week later. Nothing more came of it. YFM Corp. had never been implicated.

"One of your people screwed up big time in their rush to get out of there."

That they had. One of J.B.'s assistants had handled that problem. Another thought hit him. Had his assistant played a role in those fires to take the spotlight off of them?

"Are you implying that this rogue programmer was the one who found the body and alerted the park rangers?"

"That's exactly what I'm saying. I've looked into the formal reports, and whoever it was who was snooping around had a gas station clerk call the police and then left without talking to anyone. The police got no names. The story relayed by the clerk about why they were there turned out to be bogus. The park service almost dismissed the whole thing but sent one ranger just to take a look, and it turned out to be true. If I recall correctly, they ultimately unearthed 32 children."

The man paused, leaving J.B. with a sinking feeling. Was this going to be strike three?

"So, J.B., my question to you is, were there any four-year-old girls there, and if so, where did they come from? And also, if any are still living, where did they go?"

J.B. could offer no details without delving deeper into their records.

"I'll have to look into that. As for anyone still living at the time we closed down the center, a four-year-old would have been sent to our newest center northwest of Madison,

Wisconsin."

Yet, one problem child, a four-year-old girl, came to mind immediately. He would check that unit's records straight away and contact Tavernier.

THIRTY-FIVE

"Hey, bro, take a look."

Aric walked over to the table where Adam had established his "command center." Three monitors and two laptops filled the top except for a small area where they used to eat. Aric took a bite of his homemade taco, set the plate down, and leaned over to scrutinize the closest monitor. As he read the screen, he smiled, and upon completion, he raised his hand for a high-five with his brother. It would appear that their efforts were beginning to pay off. At the least, their most deadly opponent was incapacitated. The screen showed news reports of Buckner's high-profile arrest.

Adam smiled at him. "I knew you could do this, so I could concentrate on finding Carolyn."

Aric had enjoyed the challenge. He had thought often of his comments to Dan months earlier that school hadn't been demanding enough. This task had been. Yet, going to college to become a hacker wasn't exactly what he had in mind.

"Well, you made it easy. You already had all the records. All I did was follow your instructions on how to access the various databases and re-enter the data that had been removed."

"But you solved the time stamp issue on your own. All

that data looks like it's been there since, well, whenever it was supposed to have been added. Even I couldn't prove otherwise."

Aric smiled. That had been a dilemma he had faced early on, and it took him three weeks to figure it out. Each database had been slightly different, but the same solution handled each one with only minor tweaking. Overall, restoring a man's lifetime of records had taken him over two months of full-time work. Of course, that had been interrupted by random moves between states and towns, so the entire effort consumed their summer and early autumn.

The *pièce de résistance* had been served up just a week ago. The men involved in Sam's murder consisted of a trio, of which Buckner appeared clearly to be the leader. Despite their impeccable cleanup efforts, they never found the hidden video cam or its uplink to Adam's cloud server. Apparently, they never discovered Adam's escape route either.

Yet, that failed discovery proved to be both a blessing and a curse for Adam. Power outages had wreaked havoc on the timestamps from that camera's uplink, and the landlord had leased the place to two women upon the expiration of Adam's contract. He and Aric had shared the load of checking camera footage from the apartment. Aric developed a new appreciation for detectives who had to review security camera footage related to a crime. The job was a boring one, which for Aric was complicated by what was often on the video. He couldn't say for sure that the women were a lesbian couple, but they sure paraded around the place *au naturel* a lot. He felt like a voyeur, and to maintain his sense of morality, he fast-forwarded through such footage.

The boredom had paid off with dividends the previous week. They finally found the footage from that night, and it had clearly shown Buckner and his two cohorts entering the apartment within minutes of Sam's murder. That, too, was a bit graphic, but it was necessary to show that he'd been shot and hadn't merely fallen. At one point, the men removed their masks to discuss options after not finding Adam. *That* was what nailed Buckner's coffin. Adam didn't know the other two but knew that a bit of investigation might find them, unless they, too, were ghosts like Buckner had been.

Adam hacked into the U.S. Attorney's private email account and left the evidence there for the man to discover. There would be no routing data in the header. It would be as if the email had been composed on the lawyer's private computer. Adam also left a letter explaining who he was, what the video showed, how he'd come into possession of the video via his personal security system, and that he would remain in hiding because the men were targeting him and still at large.

That was still the case for the two unknown subjects. One out of three was a good start.

"Chamberlain is bound to put two and two together. So will Buckner. Even if they find those two other men, you're, we're, still not in the clear, Adam."

His brother nodded. "I know. Between the two of them, they know dozens of special ops folks who would be happy to take care of their brother-in-arms' problem."

Adam stood up and paced. "What I need is the missing piece of a 3,000-piece puzzle."

Aric knew just what he meant—not only that they had

a missing piece, but also that the pieces were tiny with a puzzle that size. However, that would be second on the list of priorities.

"Okay, so we need to go big as whistleblowers so that we're too public for them to touch. And we need to get Chamberlain out of the way in doing so. But first, we need to find Carolyn. If she's still alive, we need to get her out of harm's way. 'Cause otherwise . . ."

Adam nodded. Aric already knew they were on the same wavelength there. They couldn't go public and risk Carolyn's life as the bad guys cleaned up loose ends.

"Now that Buckner is locked away, I can help you with finding her," said Aric.

Adam sat back down and danced his fingers across the keyboard of one of the laptops. "Sound good. Here's where I am right now." He began to point to data on one of the monitors. "We know she wasn't among the dead found at Mount Hood. The DNA studies have been done on those remains, and nothing matched up with the DNA I have on file as the parent of a missing child. So, I remain optimistic." He leaned back in the chair.

"But that place was a gold mine of data. The lease went through a dozen shell companies. Those companies and the listed directors were all bogus, as expected. But I found many of those same companies listed on a bunch of properties and leases in California. Those listings, in turn, exposed another dozen or so shell companies. And from that collection, I found a place here in Wisconsin with two of those names. But, getting info on what's going on in those places has been impossible so far."

Aric didn't want to ask the next question.

"What about Carolyn, though?"

Adam covered his eyes with a hand and sighed.

"I know. I-I don't know if she's there or not." He leaned forward suddenly. "But I came across this." He pointed to a second screen.

Aric saw six files opened in separate windows. He frowned as he read through some of the info they revealed. It was distressing, to put it mildly. A company that actually kidnapped and detained young kids, terrorizing them to increase adrenalin levels and then harvesting their blood to extract a chemical called adrenochrome. Was that what happened to Carolyn?

He didn't want to contemplate that possibility. Adam continued to fluctuate between faith and discouragement. Aric prayed daily for the strength and words needed to continue building up his brother.

"Disturbing, isn't it?" asked Adam. He seemed to be holding up better than Aric would have anticipated with the data he'd just perused.

"On a more positive note, the owner of that van I saw and traced to Oregon doesn't appear to be an employee of that company—and it has hundreds of employees—or any of the shell companies. I searched and couldn't find a single employee for any of those. However, going on the comment about the owner being transferred and using Wisconsin as a key, I set up my software to watch Madison, Milwaukee, and Chicago. A week ago, I got a hit. The van was picked up on cameras on the Illinois Tollway coming out of Wisconsin, going into Chicago, and heading back into Wisconsin a few hours later."

Upon hearing the good news, Aric sat down next to him.

They were on the right track.

"I focused the system on cameras in Wisconsin and followed it to the camera on I-90 and 94 at County C, which is at Camp Douglas."

A camp? That sounded like the Mount Hood property.

"Camp Douglas? Is that where you found the leased property listed under the shell companies?"

Adam faced him and grinned as he held up his hand for another high-five.

"Yes!"

They were indeed one step closer, and maybe this time, not too late. Even if Carolyn wasn't there, the van owner would be a valuable source of information. Getting him to talk would be a hurdle to cross after finding him.

"So, where is that from here?"

They had found a cabin for rent on a small lake outside of East Troy, Wisconsin. The location had put them somewhat in the middle of a triangle formed by the metro Chicago, Madison, and Milwaukee areas. How in the world Adam found these places was beyond Aric, but his skill put Vrbo and Airbnb™ to shame. It had been their home away from home for the past three weeks—the longest they had stayed in one lodging since joining forces in Portland—and Aric was growing a bit fond of the place.

"It's about two and a half to three hours from here, depending on whether we take back roads or the interstate."

"Then let's pack up and head out. We have plenty of daylight to get there."

Adam shook his head. "I need to look at the area through property records first, and we need to make a detour."

That puzzled Aric. They had been on the straight and narrow path to finding Carolyn or her kidnappers. What could have possibly convince Adam to make a voluntary lane change?

"A detour? We need to find her as soon as possible."

Adam again leaned back in the chair, this time folding his arms across his chest.

"No, a detour first. Look, I want to get Carolyn back more than you do, but I've come to some realizations. After seeing all of this data on child trafficking, I recognize two things. One, she might already be dead, and, two, the trafficking aspect of this is way above our heads. We need expert help on that. But, even if, or when, we find her, there are a few possibilities. In none of them am I her daddy." He choked on those words, and tears welled up in his eyes. "If she's been part of this adrenochrome harvesting scheme, she could be so emotionally damaged she might as well be dead. How will Rachel respond if I bring her a zombie of a kid that requires help we aren't capable of giving? And if I find her alive and well—the best possible scenario—she won't know me. She was one when she was taken, and now she's four, almost five. I'll be a complete stranger."

Aric sensed the despondency and felt the weight being carried by his brother. He had been looking forward to being Uncle Aric again, playing with a niece who could play and interact with him now. Yet, he, too, would be a stranger.

"Okay, so what's the detour? Where are we going to find help up here in cheddar land, someone we can trust?"

That was the crux of the question; who could they trust? Even in St. Louis, where they had grown up and had all sorts of contacts, could they know for sure that whomever they reached out to wasn't somehow connected to this? No. However, in this state, they didn't have even that breadth of contacts.

"Well, there is one person I believe we can trust. He was involved in shutting down a human trafficking ring in St. Louis several years ago. You would have been too young at the time to have paid attention to it. But I think maybe God really has heard my prayers because it so happens he's now a professor and lives less than an hour from here."

Aric closed his eyes and said a silent, *Thank you, Lord.* Even after living together for the past four months, Aric had been unsure that his brother would ever again fully trust in and call on God. Now he wondered if God's hand had been on their journey the entire time. He would trust Him wholly, no matter what has happened to Carolyn.

"Well, then, let's reach out to the guy . . . and let God take it from there."

THIRTY-SIX

Wallace sat stewing at his desk. Three days had passed since Buck's arrest. They had not been days that brought good news to Wallace or his friend. One additional murder charge was issued among dozens of others ranging from fraud to racketeering to money laundering. There was even discussion of charges to be brought amounting to war crimes for actions in Afghanistan. Wallace had been forced to walk a tightrope so thin one could use it as a guitar string. He pursued every avenue possible to defend Buck and yet, had to avoid being implicated himself.

To the defense team's surprise, Buck's complete life history—from elementary school records to military personnel records to his current life's records—had become an open book. Even incidents involving alias names used by Buckner had been added to his records, with the aliases detailed. The apparition that had once been Henry Buckner had taken on flesh and blood.

On his one visit to Buck in jail, Wallace had been upfront with the man. The executive board had abandoned him and left Wallace holding the reins of his defense. Wallace had assured Buck that he would spare no expense in trying to free him, but the reality was that the charges would not be dismissed, and bail would be denied. Should

Buckner ever regain his freedom, Wallace would not want to be in Director Compton's or any other board member's shoes. Buck would take them all out within weeks.

However, at the moment, the man's venom was unleashed elsewhere. To both Wallace and Buckner, only one person had that kind of access and ability to "restore his life"—Adam Afton.

Wallace reflected on the end of their conversation.

"Sir, I appreciate your efforts in my defense, but whatever happens, please do one thing for me. Find Afton *and* his daughter, and send Karl and Gio to avenge me."

Wallace had nodded. "I will make sure of that."

However, Wallace had his own worries. If Afton had been able to bring Buckner back to life, what might he have planned for Wallace? Besides the more recent information Afton had discovered, Wallace's past military record held incidents that could be called into question and black ops where details had been scrubbed. Wallace knew all too well that *nothing* ever got completely deleted from military records. Like a deleted email, there was always a copy somewhere.

Indeed, Wallace had his reasons for seeing the threat named Adam Afton removed. Yet, he had another priority in mind.

He jumped at the knock on his door—a sound reminiscent of the police "raid" a few nights earlier. Were they back for him?

His assistant opened the door and ushered in Karl and Gio. They walked to the center of the room, faced him at his desk, and came to attention.

"Sir," they said in unison.

"Relax. Have a seat."

They each took a chair opposite the desk while taking curious glances about the room. Wallace knew they'd never been to his office before. The prospect of getting called to the boss' office might seem daunting to them, particularly in light of Buck's arrest.

"Okay, guys, I going to lay it out straight. Buck's being thrown under the bus for reasons I don't know. Has he ever mentioned an executive board to you?"

Karl nodded. "It's been mentioned. Why?"

"Because ultimately, they call the shots, and they're the ones doing the throwing. They could have had Buck released the next day but chose not to. Again, I don't know why. I am concerned that I might be next, but that's water not yet under the bridge. Anyway, Buck has a request of you—to avenge him."

The two men looked at each other, questioning.

"Buck wants us to go after this executive board, and you're okay with that?" asked Gio. "I mean, you said it yourself, sir. They call the shots. We'll become targets. I thought we were supposed to keep looking for this Afton guy."

Wallace nodded. "I'll get back to him." He stood up and walked to the window. He took a moment to watch the traffic outside while forming his next statement. He turned back to face them.

"If you strike quickly enough, they won't know what hit them or who. You guys are still ghosts. Afton was able to pull the sheet off Buck and expose him. But, from what I can tell, that has nothing to do with the board's decision. As I see it, they need a shake-up. If we can retire, say, at least four of the nine members, there's a better than 50-50 chance I'll get a seat on the board. Then, I can work from within to help Buck. Otherwise, he's going to be wearing an orange jumpsuit for quite some time."

"And Afton?" asked Karl.

"We still don't know where he is, but we have an idea where he's headed. Buck and I talked about this." They hadn't, but Wallace knew where these men's allegiances lay. "You two can help best by dealing with the board first. Hopefully, by then, we'll know for sure that Afton is heading to where we think he's going, and I can get you there by jet within hours."

At this point, the two men again glanced at each other, shrugged, and nodded.

"Okay, we'll do it for Buck. But if we're to hit them hard and fast, we need to know where they are and where they'll be."

Wallace smiled. Even members of the executive board were not immune from being probed by AlterNet. "Understood. Here's a list of the members, where they live, work, and places they frequent. The data also includes maps and other intel you might need, like their personal security details. It's my understanding that all of them plan on being home or here in Washington for the election in twelve days. You can choose your targets and methods based on expediency. Report back to me once the mission is completed."

Karl took the flash drive being offered by Wallace. Then, the two men arose, shook Wallace's hand, and left. Wallace grinned. If this worked, by election day, he would become a member of the executive board. Perhaps Buck's fate held a silver lining after all.

As for Afton, he had another plan. He placed a call to Robert Jennings on his personal cell phone. This was not a call to go through his company's phone system. The man answered on the second ring.

"Wallace, can I call you back? Not good timing."

"Oh?" Wallace discerned from the tone of his voice that whatever was happening there was of consequence.

Jennings whispered, "Graham has sicced his dogs on us. The FBI is here now, pulling our computers and more to find any evidence we've been funding the 'defund the police' movement and Antifa."

While Wallace was sympathetic to the cause and Lex Fortis Consolidated's efforts to automate policing, Jennings' saying it that way did seem ironic.

"Just a minute."

Wallace heard voices in the background, one of which was Jennings' protests against taking his private computer. More voices, then quiet. A moment later, the man returned to the phone.

"They're gone now. . . the . . ." The following expletives lent truth to the image of blushing sailors. "This is just another witch hunt. They're not going to find anything illegal on those hard drives."

Wallace waited for him to add, "We're not that stupid," but the admission did not come.

"Robert, I have a task for your RCPAD-5." Jennings was not a client of YFM Corp and likely was unfamiliar with adrenochrome, so Wallace went on to explain that a fellow businessman's research facility in central Wisconsin needed additional protection. Their budget was too tight to afford more personnel, and Wallace had mentioned RCPAD-5. "Would you consider putting RCPAD-5 to the test there? Maybe at a reduced price, or even gratis? Perhaps in return for new marketing materials. I'll even add my personal endorsement if it works well."

The man's mood changed in an instant. "Would you? An endorsement by Lt. Gen. (Ret.) Wallace Chamberlain could be a big boost for us. A reduced price I could approve. For a freebie, I'd need to run it past our board. When would you need the RCPADs?"

"ASAP, I'm afraid. Lab personnel have been getting threats from activists, and they can't afford any vandalism or damages to their labs. They use animals for testing, and you know how those protests can go." Jennings didn't need to know the whole truth. "They're looking for perimeter protection and monitoring."

"How big is this facility, acreage-wise?"

Wallace and Jennings worked out the details and decided three RCPADs would do the job, two on duty while one recharges. Jennings balked at offering lethally armed units, so Taser® and stun modules would have to suffice.

"Wallace, I'll go ahead and get them delivered. We'll work out the cost later, but I think I can get the board to agree. We'll have to be allowed the opportunity to video them on duty, of course."

"I don't see that as a problem as long as the lab's identity and location are kept confidential." Wallace knew he was speaking out of turn on J.B.'s behalf but did not expect the man to disagree.

With their discussion concluded, Wallace stood from his desk and walked to the window. Rush hour was over, and the traffic below his office was light. Without the usual crush of tourism, D.C. had seemed desolate over the summer. With the election, however, he suspected that would soon change.

J.B. reviewed the records retrieved by an assistant regarding the production units at the Mount Hood facility. All total, six females of the age of four had been at Mount Hood. Two had been buried there upon disposal. A discreet check of the DNA recovered by authorities there, however, did not turn up either of those two.

He dialed the extension of the man he had tasked with handling the Mount Hood fiasco.

"Yes, sir."

"Howard, I'm looking at the records you forwarded to me about the Mount Hood situation. The media reported two mass graves and 32 bodies, but the two four-year-olds on the list that were disposed of there were not among those bodies."

"Yes, sir. The authorities discovered only two of the five mass graves there. There were a total of 117 disposals along the slopes of the mountain, and I hope they don't find the others. From what I can gather, I think they've stopped looking."

J.B. fully agreed with that. To find more bodies would cause an uproar that the authorities would not be able to ignore.

"Were any of the four-year-old females taken in the D.C. area in 2016?"

There was a brief pause on the other end.

"I know that three of them came from the east coast, and if I recall correctly, the only collection team we had at that time on the east coast was in the D.C., Maryland, northern Virginia area. So, yes, sir, I'd have to say three of them for sure. If you give me half an hour, I can double-check all of them and get back to you."

"Sounds good, but first, where are those three now?"

He heard the tapping of fingers on a keyboard.

"One was among the two disposed of at Mount Hood. One was shipped to Texas in 2018. And the third was transferred to Wisconsin."

J.B. nodded.

"Thanks, Howard. Double-check and let me know."

J.B. again scanned the info that appeared on his screen. Howard's summary agreed with the data he had in front of him. Or did it? As he studied the collection reports for 2016, there appeared to be four one-year-old girls collected on the east coast, not three. Those records' format was that of a paper form that had been later scanned into the system, and one of the tallies appeared partially erased. An error? Were there three, or were there four females taken?

THIRTY-SEVEN

Adam had satisfied his curiosity and performed his due diligence on the properties in and around Camp Douglas. The facility in question had once been owned by the National Guard, but its current ownership was enshrouded by misty shell corporations. Two of those entities were among the corporations he had discovered through the Mount Hood camp, so he felt confident he was on the right track.

However, his search had led to another discovery. There were multiple listings for the dozen or so corporations he had found, and a pattern had evolved. Each involved the use of old, decommissioned military bases. Many, if not all, of these centers had extensive underground facilities as protection from a possible enemy attack. Yet, those underground structures had been alluded to, not confirmed. However, despite a lengthy search, he could find no plans or other documentation about those buildings. They had been removed from the records. Plus, whoever did the deletions had made no effort to hide their clumsy efforts.

Such was the case for the Camp Douglas property as well. To Adam, that confirmed his suspicion that this was the place.

"So, I understand your thinking about this place," said

Aric. "Makes sense to me, but isn't it just circumstantial? I've watched enough cop shows to know the police would need evidence to support a warrant to enter the property and perform a search."

Adam frowned and nodded. "I know. It's a dilemma I've been working on. I'm hoping the guy we're going to see can help me."

They were driving east along Wisconsin Highway 20, heading toward a place called Mount Pleasant. Adam had contacted the man through the college, offered him nebulous info about his identity, and tantalized his curiosity. He knew enough about the man to feel perfectly safe in revealing themselves to him.

"Here it is." Aric pointed to a mailbox at the end of a long driveway.

A house was not visible from the road, and the drive entered a copse of trees.

"There, up to the left," said Aric as he again pointed, this time to a partially hidden old farmhouse.

However, Adam turned right at a fork and continued further into the woods before breaking out along a farm field. Ahead and to their right was a contemporary home in a style influenced by Frank Lloyd Wright, although of recent construction. The driveway made a sweeping curve to the right, forming a U-turn that led to the front of the home. Two other cars were parked on the blacktop apron.

"Wow, nice and secluded. And what a house."

The single-level home appeared to be constructed of concrete with angular corners, large plate-glass windows overlooking two ponds, and landscaping of native grasses and wildflowers that showed the usual withering of the season. The flat roof added to its modern look, while selected walls were dressed with natural stone that made it look like part of the landscape. Adam suspected it was very low maintenance, the type of home he envisioned for the future.

Together the two walked up to the front door, and as Aric reached for the bell, it opened, and a tired-looking man of about forty appeared.

"Professor Cully?"

"Ah, my somewhat mysterious guests. Adam?" He pointed to Adam.

"Um, yes, sir. And this is my brother Aric, with an 'A.' Are we here at a bad time, professor?"

The man chuckled. "Please call me Lynch. I'm still not accustomed to this 'professor' stuff. Come in." He backed away to allow them entry. "As for good timing versus bad timing, we just had our first child six days ago. Not sure when exactly would be a good time. We haven't gotten much sleep."

A second, older man appeared at the entrance of what seemed to be the main living room. Professor Cully turned to him.

"Mike, these are the young men I told you about who wish to present me with a mystery. Adam, and Aric with an 'A.' Their last name is also part of the mystery. Guys, this is a dear friend of ours from St. Louis, Mike Southworth. He and his wife Mary drove up to meet their adopted grandson, so to speak. Mary is in the other room helping my wife, Amy, with our little guy, Joshua."

The three shook hands and exchanged small talk about St. Louis. They learned that Mike was a retired army colonel who lived in Ferguson, MO, while his wife was a retired nurse. Amy, too, was a nurse. The professor led them to another room where the large windows overlooked pines and another small pond.

"Can I offer you a drink? We have a variety of Coke products, bottled iced tea, flavored mineral waters, or just plain water, filtered."

The young men expressed their choices and sat down together on a leather sofa facing two matching chairs. Bookcases at the end of the room overflowed, but Adam couldn't see any titles. They looked like texts and non-fiction as opposed to novels, but he wasn't sure. However, Aric made no effort to hide his inspecting the books on the end table near him. They appeared to be Christian titles, along with two versions of the Bible. That should encourage Aric that Adam's choice to seek help from Professor Lynch Cully was a sound move.

The professor returned with drinks, glasses, and ice. He set the tray down on the coffee table, grabbed his own glass, and sat down in one of the two chairs.

"So, how can I help you?"

Adam and Aric looked at each other, and Aric flicked his eyes toward the older man, questioning. Adam faced the colonel.

"Um, no disrespect, sir, but we thought we'd be discussing this alone with just the professor. It's highly confidential, and—"

Professor Cully interrupted. "Actually, Adam, I asked him to join us. Mike's a retired Army colonel with incredible insights and experience. I've trusted him with my life and will continue to do so if events should come to that again. I even trusted him once with the life of the King and Queen of England and their family."

Adam saw Aric's eyes bug out. They both knew *that* story since it had dominated the St. Louis news cycle for weeks.

"This is . . ." Aric couldn't complete his sentence.

Mike laughed. "Yes, my wife and I hosted the king and his family at our home in Ferguson." He paused. "Look, I'm happy to leave if you wish."

Adam shook his head. "No, no. If you're *that* guy, I . . . Sorry, that didn't come out quite like I meant it. I mean, if the professor, uh, sorry, Lynch, trusted you with that task, I'm glad to get your help, too." Adam felt as tongue-tied as he thought he sounded.

The older men laughed. "He's *that* guy all right," said Lynch. "So, I'll ask again, how can I help you?"

Adam had rehearsed his spiel for the past few days and started right from the beginning—the kidnapping of his daughter. He detailed his search and the discovery of Wallace Chamberlain's involvement in pedophilia and blackmail for political and personal purposes, Sam Renner's discovery of Chamberlain's involvement in fixing the upcoming election, and Sam's subsequent murder and Adam's escape. He told of how he had contacted Aric, arranged to meet in Portland, and their grisly discovery at Mount Hood.

As he paused to take a breath, Lynch spoke. "I guess you know I ran a special task force for President Graham. That's why you're here, right?"

Adam nodded.

"Well, the President and I had Chamberlain under

surveillance at one time, but we could never get anything solid on him. I'm impressed with your computer skills, that you were able to get that info. I assume you have documentation and proof."

Adam nodded. "I do." Adam felt the professor's eyes studying him. He worked to avoid squirming under the intense scrutiny.

"So, how is it you're still alive? Chamberlain and his overlords play for keeps. He's got a team of ex-special ops men doing his dirty work for him. I'm figuring they're the ones who killed your friend."

Adam gulped. He hadn't wanted to bring up Buckner. What they had done to him wasn't precisely up-and-up legal.

"They are." He sighed. He might as well go all in. "That group has been led by a man named Henry Buckner. Aric had dealings with him in Portland, where he tried to use Aric as bait to get to me." He went on to detail how the man was a ghost, but that he'd hacked the Pentagon, found Buckner's confidential records, and used that data to restore Buckner to the land of the living. He then told of their finding his security video from the apartment and using it to get Buckner arrested and arraigned on murder charges.

The colonel and Lynch started laughing. "Good for you," said the colonel.

"Serves the sucker right. Where were you when I headed up that task force? I do have to say, though, it's a good thing I'm not still an active-duty police officer or on the federal payroll. What you've done—the hacking and all— could get you jail time. Don't worry. Your secret is safe with us. We're more interested in justice these days than doing things strictly by the book, a book that's been rigged."

"Thank you." Adam saw Aric visibly relax. "Aric and I realize Buckner's buddies are probably gunning for us, but we have an advantage—they don't know where we are and don't know where we're going. Plus, I put a block in Chamberlain's AlterNet software that deletes anything it picks up that might come close to relating to us. They'll never find my car, even if they knew what to look for, and we've been using cash for all expenditures. I deleted our facial recognition profiles from their system, too."

"So, just where *are* you headed? And I'm still not hearing anything about how I can help."

Adam launched into a description of what they'd found out from the Mount Hood facility and how it had led them to a place called Camp Douglas, northwest of Madison. He described what he believed was taking place in the facilities and talked about the German data dump.

"Do you think your daughter's there?" asked the colonel.

Adam shook his head. "I honestly don't know. I've accepted the realization that even if I find her alive and well, she won't know who I am. And I hate to think of the alternatives."

Lynch had closed his eyes and seemed lost in thought. Upon opening them, he said, "I'm aware of that data from Germany. Are you saying you believe one of those detainment centers exists here in Wisconsin?"

"I am, and that's where I need your help. I can't go around the law like we did with Buckner if we want to take that place down. It will require warrants and law enforcement, and they won't act on what they'll just call a hunch. How do we do this the right way?"

"Well, you didn't exactly go around the law with Buckner. You provided evidence from a security system *you* owned. You were in the right to provide that to law enforcement. It's the hacking aspects of what you did that could get you in trouble, even planting it in the U.S. Attorney's private account as you did."

Adam nodded. "I understand that. But I don't have that kind of evidence for this place."

Lynch didn't offer him an immediate response.

The colonel, however, spoke up. "No, you don't, but you know, the authorities get anonymous tips all the time. They would just need a tip that was compelling enough to get them to act."

Lynch smiled. "What you need to do is get *me* that compelling evidence. We don't know who to trust in the local and state authorities, and I haven't lived here long enough to make those connections. I do, however, have the connections we need with the FBI and federal marshals. I'd offer to help physically, but my wife would kill me if I took off right now."

The colonel nodded. "That she would, and my wife would help hide the body."

Lynch looked at a nearby wall clock. "Hey, it's getting late. Would you two want to stay for dinner? Nothing fancy. I'm still exploring local pizza joints to find the best one."

THIRTY-EIGHT

"What? I suppose you want me to get her a cake with candles, too. Tavernier, you're losing it."

Skelter crossed his arms and stared at him, but Tavernier held his ground. 20161025F290's birthday was but a few days away, and he was determined to do something radical and kind for her. He still was unsure as to why this girl mattered. The corporation had used thousands of children and discarded them when their usefulness was over. Before that, well, pedophilia and child slave labor had been alive and well for millennia. That was the fate of tens of thousands of children who went missing in the U.S. alone.

So, why did this unit, this girl, matter? Yes, there was a resemblance to Grace. He had acknowledged that much. Something other than that intrigued him, however. She presented an enigma to him. Why had her blood caused so much trouble?

He felt determined to figure out that puzzle. He had decided that to solve the problem, the girl needed to live. And he had decided on a course of action—a story of sorts—to placate their warden.

"For normal children, a cake would be nice, but she wouldn't know what that was or its significance."

Skelter shook his head. "Not going to happen, doctor.

For one, the other units would see it and expect similar treatment. We can't set such a precedent."

"I understand, Brian. I do. But I wish to try something radical. I want to treat her differently for a week or so. That means being nice in ways she'll understand—a warm blanket, more food, and foods that will be like treats for her. Perhaps we can move her to an isolated cage so the others don't see it. I want to see if her body and blood change without the continuously elevated cortisol levels. There is a range of normal blood values in the outside world that we don't typically see here because of the stress the units live under. Once her lab values normalize, then we'll stress her again and see what happens to her serum values."

The detention center warden stared at him but no longer appeared angry. The man seemed to contemplate the concept.

"Who knows, the idea might produce a higher quality adrenochrome."

This time, Skelter nodded. "There is some validity to what you say. Terror that comes on unexpectedly should result in a higher adrenalin response." He paused as if calculating an odds ratio. "Do you really think we might get a better product?"

Tavernier smiled. He knew his idea would work. If Skelter could be convinced of that, the girl would get something of a reprieve. That might be all he'd be able to accomplish, but he'd give it his best.

"I can't predict that with assurance. To be truthful, that unit is a puzzle to me, and I need to solve it. I hope this idea gives me the answer. To see a higher quality product would be a secondary benefit, but it's a plausible outcome."

Skelter nodded. "Okay, we'll give it a try. But, doctor . . ." He paused, apparently for emphasis. ". . . don't delay this too long. 20161014F290 either starts producing soon or else."

Tavernier nodded. "*Trés bien*. Thank you."

Aric joined Lynch and the colonel in the kitchen to refresh his drink. Food from a local family pizzeria—less than five minutes away—would be ready shortly. The colonel had volunteered to go pick it up.

"Sir, thanks for helping my brother. Losing his daughter has nearly destroyed his life. He wants closure, one way or the other."

Lynch smiled. "Actually, as we jokingly put it, my helping out is God's fault." The two men laughed. "I don't know if you believe in this kind of thing or not, but back in June when we were celebrating my getting my Ph.D., Mike felt impressed by God that I would find myself involved in something unexpected and presenting as a mystery. That's exactly what your brother did. He presented this as a mystery, and I recognized God's hand in it right away. God's directing this whole thing."

Aric perked up. He would have guessed that Lynch was a believer by the books he had seen in the other room. This confirmed it. Maybe he could answer some of Aric's questions. He knew he could always find books on the topic and talk with his pastors at home. But when would that be?

"I do believe such things. Adam, not as much, but I accept Christ as my Lord and Savior. He did, too, once . . . before the kidnapping. I, uh . . ." He furrowed his brow and frowned.

"Something wrong?"

"I, well, I feel I've let God down. I failed at . . . I don't know. My faith was challenged on my way to Portland, and I didn't know how to counter the guy's argument to back up my faith with words."

Lynch nodded. "Been there, understand that. This guy here . . ." He poked Mike on the shoulder. ". . . has been my mentor, my spiritual father. He led me to the Lord years ago and has been a faithful friend ever since. He'd be the first to tell you that you're not alone in feeling like that, by any means, and that sometimes faith is shown best by our actions, not by words alone." He paused and glanced at the clock on the nearby stove. "Pizza should be ready. Why don't you go with him to pick it up and pump him for answers?"

Aric looked at the colonel expectedly.

"Sure. Let's go. I hope I have some answers for you."

No sooner had they settled into the colonel's car, Aric began to describe his dilemma. He briefly described who Pete was and his role in the whole Portland thing. He then presented Pete's challenge: that the Bible had to be make-believe because it told of creation being accomplished in six days, and that couldn't be right if the earth was billions of years old. Aric spoke of Pete's comments that man had evolved from apes and that chimpanzees shared 98.5% of man's DNA as proof of evolution.

He also mentioned Pete's argument that a God Who is love wouldn't leave the world riddled with evil, hate, and injustice. Aric had to admit to himself that after what they'd discovered near Mt. Hood, that argument had stuck in his craw. The children whose bodies were uncovered there were innocents.

"Wow, he hit you with some big ones, didn't he? Let me answer the easy one first. Chimps and apes. When researchers tested the DNA of chimps, it was in the early days of DNA sequencing. They had a lot of gaps in their DNA sequences. So, what did they do? Like so many scientists who are convinced about evolution, they used the human genome as their map because, after all, man evolved from apes, right? Like using the cover of a jigsaw puzzle to complete the puzzle. Well, they were wrong. Later research revealed a lot of human DNA contaminating their results, and when something was missing, they assumed it to match our human DNA. Then, two independent sets of researchers in 2016 and 2018 redid that study with modern technology. They used two different approaches, yet their results differed by only two one-hundredths of a percent, confirming that chimps only share about 84.5% of human DNA. That pretty much blew the humans-evolved-from-apes argument out of the water."

Aric had always assumed scientists to be objective. Between this revelation and what he had witnessed with the COVID pandemic, he had learned the hard lesson that integrity in science was almost as rare as honesty in politics.

"How come we haven't seen or heard about that study? You'd think that would make the news."

The colonel shrugged. "When was the last time you read or heard anything in the mainstream media that supported God's Word?"

He had a point.

The colonel continued. "That guy, Pete, was right about one thing. The creation story and deep time theories about the age of the earth and universe are contradictory. If deep time theories are true, then the whole premise of the Bible is wrong. According to the Bible, creation was 'very good,' as God put it, and death did not exist. Death came into the world through Adam's sin. Christ came to earth to redeem man and creation from the death caused by that original sin. That's the most basic premise of the Bible. But if deep time is correct, death has been part of the universe for billions of years, and there is no point to a redeeming savior because there was no original sin requiring redemption." He paused as he pulled into the parking lot fronting the pizza joint. "Think about that as I get our pies."

Aric soaked it in. He wished the trip to the pizzeria was much longer—about an hour longer. He had too many questions to ask during such a short trip.

As soon as the colonel handed him the pizza boxes to hold on the way back to the house, he asked, "So, how do we know the earth *isn't* that old?"

"Well, the simplest answer is through our faith that God's Word is true, but I recognize that most people won't accept that as a valid answer. One of my favorite quotes about the Big Bang Theory is, 'First there was nothing, and then it exploded.' Deep time believers are quick to talk about the Big Bang and the first primordial soup of chemicals from which life emerged. But have you ever noticed how they never address where the elements came from to create the universe and that primordial soup?" He paused. "Are you familiar with the laws of thermodynamics?"

Aric nodded. "Sure. The first law states that energy cannot be created or destroyed but must be conserved by changing from one form to another. The second law talks about entropy, which is a state of disorder, randomness, or uncertainty. And the third law says that a system's entropy approaches a constant value as it nears absolute zero."

The colonel smiled. "Very good, young grasshopper."

"Huh?"

"Sorry, that movie was way before your time. So, where did these laws come from? Did they, too, just appear out of the random mess of a big bang?"

Aric shrugged, but the man had a point. How could something like that just develop? A law of physics would have to have been valid from the beginning, or it couldn't be justified as a law.

"Anyway, if these are indeed laws, they had to exist at the time of said Big Bang, which would seem to go against all three. After all, if the Big Bang is true, it created an incredible amount of energy out of nothing, and the formation of the universe goes against the concept of entropy."

The colonel glanced at Aric to see his reaction. Aric could only nod as he processed it all.

"Okay, so let's look at chemistry, oxidation in particular. Oxidation destroys most chemicals. It breaks up proteins, causes rust in iron, and is generally a destructive process. Our atmosphere, even at just 21% oxygen, is an oxidative environment. Amino acids, lipids, and other compounds required to make up a cell simply cannot form in an oxidative environment without being protected. So, how do you create that first cell from components that are destroyed before they can come together to form that first protective cell wall?"

Aric saw where this logic led. These processes all went

against the most fundamental laws of physics and chemistry. Someone would need great faith to believe these theories, and yet they criticize believers for *their* faith.

"The odds against a single protein forming randomly, much less something as complex as DNA, is astronomical. A protein is made up of amino acids, but the synthesis of amino acids in nature requires various protein enzymes. How does that work? You can't have proteins without amino acids, but you can't have amino acids without proteins. It's the classic chicken or the egg dilemma."

Aric shook his head in wonder. Why hadn't issues like this been presented during his science classes? Instead, the Big Bang, deep time, and evolutionary theory were presented not as the theories they were but as facts.

"A skyscraper is simpler than DNA in structure. Why didn't skyscrapers simply evolve over time? The same assumptions used to justify the evolution of animals could be made about buildings." He shifted in his seat. "So, let me ask you another question. Why do we still have mountains?"

"Um, because tectonic plates push the earth's mantle up to form them?" Aric had no idea where this was leading.

"That's true, but erosion from wind and water outpaces such buildups. Current science shows that mountains erode at a rate of 40 feet in a million years. If the earth is billions of years old, there shouldn't be any mountains left. What about dinosaur remains? Did you know that over 250 samples of soft tissues, like cartilage and ligaments, even skin, have been recovered from skeletal remains? Today's science tells us such tissues can't last but a few thousand years at best, not millions of years."

They arrived back at the house, but the colonel did not

jump out of the car.

"Aric, a lot of science supports the Bible's creation story. We have mitochondrial DNA tracing all of mankind back to a single mother. Deep-well core samples show a uniform layer of sedimentary rock across the globe that's consistent with a global flood. And Mount Saint Helen's eruption in 1980 created a canyon with rock layers just like the Grand Canyon in mere weeks, not millennia. Faith in God is not incompatible with science, or vice versa. He created science, too, to allow us to explore and understand His creation."

The colonel climbed out of the car, and Aric followed with the pizzas. How could he tactfully invite themselves to stay the night? He had so much much to ask and hoped to continue these lessons sometime soon.

THIRTY-NINE

"Cool. Can I fly it?"

Adam looked at his brother as they drove away from the hobby store outside of Milwaukee. At the colonel's indirect suggestion, he had located a store that specialized in drones. The colonel hadn't come right out and suggested a drone, but he had made a point of telling a story about using drones for military reconnaissance. His point became clear by reading between the lines.

After discussions with the store staff, he had settled on a quadrotor, mini drone with a 30-minute flight time, 4K HD video, and a transmission range of up to four kilometers. He had hoped to find something smaller than its 9.5 x 11-inch silhouette, but the smaller devices were less stable to fly, had lower quality cameras, and shorter limits both in time and distance. They had no idea what kind of range they would require at their destination.

Aric settled back in his seat for the two-hour drive to Camp Douglas. Adam noticed that he'd pulled a book out of his pack for the trip.

"What's the book?"

Aric held it up for him to see. Adam had heard the author's name before but knew little more about him. His brother seemed to settle in to read.

"So, am I to be the chauffeur while you read?"

He regretted the tone in which he'd said it as soon as it came out of his mouth. But, in truth, he didn't want to drive in silence. Not this day.

Aric put the book in his lap and stared at his older brother. "Sorry, did I do something?"

Adam shook his head. "No. I-I'm the one who's sorry. I shouldn't have snapped at you." He took a deep breath. "What's the book about?"

"It's on Christian apologetics. Colonel Mike gave it to me, so I can answer guys like Pete in the future."

Adam sighed quietly. Not exactly a topic he wanted to discuss, but anything would be better than silence.

"I started to read it last night. Got to the part where he talks of mankind's four basic questions on the meaning of life. Origins, or how did we get here? Morality, how do we know what's right and what's wrong? Meaning, or what's our purpose for being here? And, destiny, what happens after life? It's weighty stuff."

"Sounds like it. Well, go ahead and read if you want to."

He noticed Aric still staring. His right index finger tapped nervously on the wheel.

"You're tapping your finger again. You only do that when something's bothering you. What's going on?"

Adam sighed audibly this time. "What's today?"

"Saturday, October twenty . . . oh. Man, I should have remembered. I'm sorry."

"Not your fault. I can never remember Mom's or Dad's birthdays. How could I expect you to remember Carolyn's? It's not like we've celebrated it these last few years."

"Yeah, but still . . ."

"It's okay, really. I'm just being morose. She'll be five tomorrow."

"Just think how cool it'll be to find her on her birthday. That's what we're going to do, right? Think positive."

Adam found his brother's unbridled optimism supportive, but he would be fooling himself to think they'd find her so quickly. Right? After all, they couldn't simply walk in the front door and ask for a tour, and flying a drone would not get them interior video. But who knows? Maybe they'd get lucky, to use a term Aric would debate. For him, there was no such thing as luck or coincidence for followers of Christ.

Tavernier's curiosity got the better of him. He didn't typically bother himself about the center's security because that was Skelter's domain. However, J.B. had called both of them individually about the new additions to their protection detail. Tavernier valued the precautions offered by the corporation. He had once worked at a lab where animal testing was involved and had found himself a target for PETA. That had not been pleasant.

However, these guardians were different. Previously, he could have a discussion or an after-work beer with the guards. These new defenders were straight off some sci-fi movie set. The entire workforce gathered on the snow-framed parking lot to watch the technicians offload, assemble, and power up their new robocops.

Edgar stood next to him, shaking his head. "Never thought I'd see this in *my* lifetime."

Tavernier chuckled. *Neither did I*, he thought.

"Are they gonna be safe? I mean, if I have to come to the lab after dinner some evening to finish a protocol, are these things going to shoot me or something?"

"No, no. They are armed only with Tasers®, but make sure you update and wear your employee ID. A small transponder is being added to our cards to let them know you belong here."

Edgar nodded. "You bet. It's only going to take one of us getting tased to make sure everyone remembers." He laughed. "I just hope it's not me."

Tavernier smiled. His assistant was known for forgetting his ID and borrowing other employees' cards to access locked doors.

These robots were called RCPADs, Robo-Cop Police Action Drones, according to Gradison. Tavernier noted that each sported a different colored racing stripe, for lack of a better term. That was to identify the different units quickly from a distance. Other than that, they were identical. To him, they looked more like updated Daleks from *Dr. Who*, minus the toilet plunger arms. And yet, they were equipped with Tasers®, pepper spray, advanced sensors—to include limited facial recognition for aiming the spray—and the ability to move at up to 25 miles per hour and turn or stop as agilely as a person on the run. With armor plating that could stop a .50-caliber round and an overall weight nearing 350 pounds, Tavernier would not like seeing one of these things bearing down on him, whether in the dark or the light of day.

"So, where are these things going to be again?"

Tavernier looked back at Edgar. "From what I was told, they will patrol the perimeter along the blacktop security drive around the building." That had answered his curiosity about why the service road had been plowed a day earlier. "This version is not designed for off-road travel. They will know where each other is at any given time, so they do not patrol close to each other, and a variety of sensors are being installed around the property to alert them to potential intruders."

"Wow. I'm really, really going to have to remember my ID."

"Sir, the RCPADs have arrived and have now been successfully implemented, but tell me again why we need these.

J.B. shook his head. He'd explained their need to Warden Skelter in terms other than the real reason, that his facility faced the potential of an actual threat. The man was a bit of the bluff and bluster type—lots of big talk but no real experience to back up his rants. He *was* a good administrator and had made some excellent contributions through changes he'd made in the Wisconsin detention center. Yet, J.B. couldn't trust him under a real threat.

"It's a manpower issue. We're testing these units for another company, and they're going to use the opportunity to record some video of the units in action in a real-life situation. Be assured, they've promised not to reveal anything about the facility itself, and they know nothing about what goes on there. But if they work well, we might expand the program to other centers. Surely, you can see that they'll save money in the long run."

He was appealing to the manager's instincts to cut costs

while improving operations at the same time.

"Well, these things are big, heavy, and fast. I just hope they don't injure one of our own here. That would negate any savings they might offer."

J.B. closed his eyes and sighed. So much for his appeal.

"As I said, it's a test, and it costs us nothing except some support expenses while they're there."

He heard a subtle grunt on the other end of the call. "You're the boss. We'll make a go of it one way or another. I'll call with an update in a day or two after they get some of the kinks worked out."

Were there problems with the installation? wondered J.B. "Kinks? Are there problems with the units?"

"Sir, there are *always* problems with these kinds of setups."

FORTY

As Adam exited the interstate at Camp Douglas, he noted a sense of nervous expectation. Could Aric be right? Would they locate Carolyn on her birthday? He made a conscious effort to cut off such thoughts. He couldn't afford to get his hopes up.

Aric had been studying the map app on his phone. "Not much in the way of restaurants here, but it looks like there's a small sandwich carry-out place along the route we need to go."

Adam followed his directions, which required several turns after leaving the highway. Only one route allowed them to cross the railroad that ran between I-94 and the town. Sure enough, the small stand sat a block southwest across the tracks. The freshly painted, concrete block building sat at an angle on the corner lot, its pickup window facing the intersection. Most of the rest of the town, like much of small-town America, had seen brighter days.

Adam picked up a cheeseburger and fries, while Aric ordered the beef and cheddar on a pretzel roll. Soft drinks were a buck, with refills.

"This beef and cheddar's delicious. How's the burger?"

Adam nodded, his mouth full. They sat in the car to eat as Aric pointed out their upcoming route on his phone.

"We pick up Bluff Street just a block that way, and it turns into Camp Hill Road. We follow that to the end and turn right onto Schucht Road. There's a farm lane that comes off that road, right here . . ." Aric pointed to the spot on the map. ". . . If we can use that lane, we can get to less than a quarter-mile from the property, behind it. Its access drive comes off Justice Road over here and winds up into the woods to the buildings."

Justice Road? Adam hoped to bring some justice for those being held there. At the same time, he had a fear that this was one big snipe hunt, that they'd come this far to find nothing. What if all his research had been for naught? He tried to chase those thoughts from his mind, but they persisted. What if whatever company now leasing the old military buildings was on the perfect up-and-up? What if there were no children there at all? He relied on *Aric's* faith to bolster his confidence.

"That's perfect, provided we can access that lane. How far?"

"Only three-point-six miles from here."

Adam nodded. He planned to do aerial surveillance of the property first with the drone. He didn't expect to gather any incriminating evidence on their first attempt, but he hoped to be able to spot a weakness in whatever security the place had. They would spend the night a few miles north, outside Tomah, where half a dozen or more motels existed, along with a much better selection of eateries.

He finished his burger, washed it down with the remainder of his drink, and looked at Aric. "Ready?"

Aric shook his head. "One minute." He dashed from the car and disappeared around the corner of the building. Two minutes later, he reappeared carrying two soft-serve ice cream cones. Upon entering the car, he extended one to Adam.

He shook his head. "Actually, I'm full, so, no thanks. You should have asked first." Besides, with snow on the ground from an early-season, mid-October snowfall, Adam would have preferred hot chocolate.

Aric shrugged . . . and devoured the first one. Adam laughed as he pulled away from the stand and drove toward their first turn. By the time they hit Camp Hill Road, his little brother had finished off the second cone.

The drive was beautiful between snow-covered trees and fields. The road twisted, rose, and dipped much like a roller coaster, but a dozen minutes later, they came across the target farm lane. Although there was no fence, posts on both sides of the drive were connected by a chain stretched between them. Adam pulled into the lane as far as he could to get off the country road. The last thing they needed was someone speeding around the nearby curve and not seeing them in time to stop.

Before he could say anything to Aric, his brother jumped from the car and ran to inspect the chain. He tugged at one end to find it secured, but as he approached the other end, he turned back toward the car and gave Adam a thumb up. Seconds later, the chain lay on the gravel, and Aric waved him past. In his mirror, he watched Aric reattach the chain and run to the car.

"No lock. Just hanging on a hook. Let's go."

Adam slowly drove the vehicle down the snowy, gravel drive, past fields—that appeared to have been plowed shortly before the snow—on one side and white dusted, wooded hillsides on the other. At least one other vehicle, a tractor by the size of the tire tracks, had been down the lane since the snow. That helped hide their car's tire tracks. As they came to the end of one field, the next plot would exchange sides of the vehicle with the trees. Adam guessed they had traveled about a mile when the lane stopped at a small pond formed by an earthen dam that stretched between two hills. Only the beginnings of an icy cover could be seen on the water.

They were as close to the facility as they could come. By all estimates, it was nestled into the trees on the hill about three football fields to their north. And the day had turned out to be perfect for their task—only a slight breeze with bright blue skies. Adam would have liked a warmer temperature, but the snow worked in their favor. The drone's white body would blend into the frosty mantles draping the trees.

He donned a knit cap and gloves after preparing the drone inside the car. Aric, too, readied himself for the cold and followed Adam to a spot in the sun, which would act as their takeoff and landing zone. He first tested the drone over the adjacent field and became accustomed to its controls with gloved hands. The camera offered a hi-res view that would be captured on a high-capacity SSD card plugged into the device's body.

He prepared to launch the aircraft toward their destination when Aric placed a hand on his arm to stop him.

"I was thinking. The place might not have windows to spy through, and getting it inside without being spotted and destroyed is unlikely. What would it take to use this thing to tap into their Wi-Fi? From there, we might be able to hack into security cameras."

In his hurried anxiety, Adam had forgotten a critical step. The drone could not detect a Wi-Fi system, but Adam had something that could.

"Whoa, thanks. Almost forgot that. I'm a step ahead of you." Adam returned to the driver's seat and retrieved a cell phone and duct tape. "I set this phone up to spoof the burner phone in my pocket. What it sees and hears, we'll see and hear in real-time on my burner. It will also let me detect their network." He taped it to the body of the drone. "I don't know if we'll be able to hack their system, but at least it will give me information to help me try."

With that accomplished, Adam manned his control unit, and soon the drone rose over the trees. A few minutes later, the buildings came into view. Adam hovered over the facility at a distance where he hoped no one could spot it, yet the camera's zoom capabilities would give him a closer view to enable him to decide on a next step.

"What's going on?" asked Aric.

What indeed? There were a dozen or more people assembled on the parking lot in front of the building. A small box truck sat at one end of the lot, and other people were gathered there. They appeared to be working on something.

"I'll get a little closer."

Aric gasped. "What in the world are those things?"

Adam used the camouflage of nearby snowy trees to get even closer. However, he needed to stay far enough away that no one would pick up on the noise of the drone's motors, despite being as quiet as they were.

"What's our time?"

Aric had been tasked with tracking their flight time on

his phone. "You only have five or six more minutes on site."

They watched in mild awe as three robots came together. As technology geeks, they would have liked to watch longer, but their time was running low. Before lifting away, they saw one of three robots take off along the facility's perimeter road.

"Can you zoom in on the body of that thing before you go?"

"I'll try. It's faster than you'd expect. I don't know if the drone can keep up."

Adam followed as best he could. Fortunately, the road it traveled brought the drone along its path back to them as well. He risked closing in on it, got a close-up photo, and guided the drone back to their landing pad.

With the drone secured, the brothers focused on the still shot they had taken of the robot.

"Wow, that thing's impressive. It looks like it's armored, and those things on its sides look like Tasers® for sure. The head has both wide-angle and regular cameras on it. I sure hope it didn't catch the drone on video."

Adam had to agree; those things were not something he wanted to wrestle with. And if someone spotted the drone on its video feed, their efforts at being stealthy might be in vain.

"Any idea how fast that thing was moving?"

"Well, the drone can travel about ten meters per second, so that's what?" Adam stopped to calculate the speed.

"36,000 meters in an hour, so about 22 miles per hour."

Adam nodded. "That's right. Just a bit over that without wind. We have a slight breeze, but that's coming in from the side of its flight path. So, yeah, 20 to 22 miles per hour, and that robot was faster."

Aric shook his head. "No outrunning it, that's for sure."

"Not on pavement anyway."

Not that he had any plans on trying to infiltrate the facility. Real guards were likely to be armed with more than Tasers®. Yet, rather than feeling defeated, Adam felt assured by the presence of the robots.

"You know, in a way, I'm happy to see them."

"What?"

Adam nodded. "Yeah. Why would a place in the middle of nowhere Wisconsin, owned by a shell company and surrounded by tall security fencing, need robotic guards capable of disabling intruders?"

Aric smiled. "You're right. Only if they have something they feel needs beefed-up security. This *must* be the place."

With that, Adam replaced the battery on the drone and flew back to the building to test its Wi-Fi network.

FORTY-ONE

Wallace paced in his study at home, a glass of scotch in hand. He had slept little since Buck's arrest, as much from wondering when the ax might fall on him as from J.B.'s comment about Buck earning an Epstein special. Word had gone out among a circle of influencers that a certain assassin employed by the executive board had completed that task. That "rumor" had accomplished its goal. Leaks from within the board and its upper echelons had stopped.

However, a smaller circle among those in the know were aware that Epstein had been smuggled out of prison and his autopsy photos staged for the press and authorities. In Wallace's opinion, Buck *had* earned the same treatment.

Wallace's difficulty in accomplishing Buck's "jailbreak" lay in the fact that the board had not sanctioned it. That made the logistics more complex and the required bribes much, much higher. Nobody in his right mind would go against the board, but Wallace had learned long ago that people could lose their minds at the right price.

His clandestine effort to release Buck combined with his goal of reshaping the executive board produced a level of anxiety he was unaccustomed to. All it would take was one minor slip-up, and that certain assassin would be knocking on *his* coffin lid soon.

The stress produced a craving for release, but a farmhouse trip was out of the question. For one, Wallace needed to be available should he succeed. Second, the farmhouse could be under surveillance. If Afton had produced sufficient evidence against Buck, he could use the farmhouse and its occupants to do the same against him. It was a potential risk that Wallace sought to avoid.

His personal cell phone, sitting on his desk, vibrated, rattling on the polished mahogany top next to his bottle of single-malt. Only a handful of people had that number, and he doubted it would be a member of the board. The Caller ID revealed it to be Karl, Buck's sniper.

"Yes."

"Sir, I'm sad to report that Director Compton has had a nasty auto accident. He didn't make it. Also, I'm told that Director Harrington accidentally ate some shellfish and went into anaphylactic shock. He made it to the hospital, but a delay with the ambulance might have resulted in severe cognitive damage."

"I am so sorry to hear that. My wife, Marla, and I will reach out to their wives right away to see how we can help them. Thank you for letting me know."

He smiled at the ploy. After all, he was in his own home, although for all Karl knew, he could have been someplace public, thus making the ruse necessary. Still, even at home, walls sometimes had ears, and he would take no chances. Compton and Harrington made it two down, two to go. Now, if only word would arrive about Buck. Then he might sleep that night.

He finished the Glenfiddich and was about to pour himself a second glass when the same phone rang. This time the Caller ID said "Unknown." He debated answering it but gave in to his curiosity. Buck could have given the number to the man who had freed him.

"Yes."

"Good evening. I don't know who this is, but your attempt to free Henry Buckner has failed, and both he and your operative are dead. You will hear about it in the morning news."

Wallace's knees buckled, and he caught himself on his desk. He managed to land in his desk chair rather than fall to the floor. Quickly he retrieved the phone and turned it off to avoid it being traced. His heart raced. He hastened to pour another glass of scotch and downed it in one gulp. This was not good news, for obvious reasons. The less apparent reason was that he recognized the voice of the man calling him—U.S. Attorney Wayne Cooper.

He felt as if the man was circling him like a shark moving in for the kill. Worse yet, the executive board would learn of the attempt to free Buck, and they would know who was behind it and that he'd failed. In truth, they might already know.

Would they suspect that he, too, was behind the events involving two of their own that day? Only if Karl or Gio had gotten sloppy in their work. Right? He had to convince himself of that, or he might never sleep again, always looking over his shoulder for a bullet with his name on it.

FORTY-TWO

"How's it coming?"

Aric had been reading the book given to him by the colonel, biding his time while Adam worked on a device to get them the evidence they hoped would be inside the building. For his part, Aric had been helpful when he could but mostly stayed out of the way.

"Almost ready to test."

Three days had already passed since their visit to Camp Douglas. Their additional time surveilling the property had possibly paid off. They had yet to know for sure.

In the meantime, they had returned to the cabin near East Troy, where they had more privacy and seclusion. One day had been spent trying to locate a physical unit of the wireless camera scanner Adam wanted. The second day was spent waiting for its overnight delivery, and day three saw Adam working on modifying it to his needs.

At first, Aric had felt a bit of surprise when Adam told him what he'd ordered. The scanner could tap into a security camera system's Wi-Fi and show them everything the cameras saw. That such a system existed seemed an affront to personal privacy. That one could order it right off Amazon was . . . Well, it didn't jive with Aric's sense of propriety, but he acknowledged its usefulness in their situation.

"So, tell me again how this is going to work?"

Adam eased his chair back from the table where the scanner, a cell phone, and the drone sat.

"Okay, you saw for yourself that our recon mission isolated their Wi-Fi network, but I had no way to gain access by brute force."

Aric nodded. He'd seen his brother's brute force software break into sites using an algorithm that cycled and cycled through possible combinations of letters, numbers, and symbols to find the password. He couldn't use that via the phone attached to the drone, although the phone had detected their network.

"Sure, but you found a flaw. Those robots communicate through the network without any sort of protection."

"Right. And I hope it stays that way until we get back. They could rectify that shortcoming in minutes." He paused. "So, we needed a way to intercept that video feed. Police departments use a system called 'Stingray' that allows them to intercept cell phone communications. They can collect everything a cell phone does, voice calls, text messages, data exchanges, everything. There have been rumors on the dark web that it does more than that, but the use of the system is so protected by non-disclosure agreements that no one knows exactly what it does or how."

"But that thing is different?" Aric pointed to the scanner that his brother had paid a pretty penny to obtain.

"*That* thing is called a CD Pro Scan Wireless Camera Hunter Scanner Detector. It will allow us to intercept the robots' wireless video transmissions in real-time. The problem is two-fold, its range and output. The video feed has to be within 300 feet, so this thing has to go onto the building's roof. And it has an audio-video output meant to feed into a TV or monitor. That's not useful for monitoring something hundreds of yards away. So, I'm modifying it to feed into the phone that's spoofed to the other burner phone. We can watch and record as much as we need, limited only by battery life."

Aric was impressed. They had discovered that the building had a ramp leading down to a lower level, garage door-like access point. The robots appeared to gain entry to the building there, perhaps to recharge—at least, that was their best guess. They had seen no other charging station along the outside of the building. Their hopes lay in finding something incriminating on that level.

"Another hour, maybe two, and I should be ready." Adam pulled up close to the table and continued his work.

Aric went back to his reading. He had been pondering the meaning of life, one of the four major questions. If atheists were right and there was no God, then we—not just humans but all life—were just random, freak accidents of natural selection, collections of atoms destined for nothingness at the end of our short lives. We live, and we die. Period. Aric extended that logic further. In that scenario, what did it matter whether we treated each other kindly, sought significant advances in science, or tried to better man's condition? Everything was meaningless if all we did was live and die, dust returning to dust.

But Aric's faith told him that God existed and that He created us in His image. That alone—being His image-bearers—gave us value and meaning. That fact gave man dignity, which in turn gave us reason to treat each other with respect, as equals, not as merely some means to an end.

That also gave us the foundations for Western morality and ethics.

In a simpler sense, God created us for fellowship with Him. He walked with Adam and Eve in the garden before man's original sin created a barrier between man and God.

Aric was lost in his reading when Adam spoke up, "It's finished. Let's go see if it works."

Aric put his bookmark in place, hopped up from the chair, and grabbed his coat. He held high hope that his brother's tinkering was spot on and that they'd get the evidence they needed. If kids were being held in that place, for whatever reason, they deserved to be treated with dignity, too. Morality—Biblical morality, that is—was on their side, and God would honor that.

The last three nights had been no better than those of the previous week. Wallace had hoped that the message of Buck's death had been like that of Epstein's suicide—a false flag. Yet, he had failed to materialize—or was that resurrect—afterward. When Buck's wife had called and asked him to join her to identify and confirm that the body was his, the truth began to sink in. The full force of reality hit as they confirmed that the deceased was indeed Henry Buckner.

Wallace was too tired to fight for Buck's honor. The man had served with distinction through three tours in Afghanistan and two in Iraq. His Special Ops comrades considered him a legend. The man had earned two Purple Hearts, a Bronze Star, and ultimately, a Silver Star awarded to him personally by Wallace since it could only be presented by a three-star commander-in-theater. And yet, the circumstances of his arrest and subsequent attempt at freedom overshadowed his accomplishments. He would not be allowed interment in Arlington nor military honors wherever his body ended up.

Wallace watched Buck's wife and children in their grief as his body finally found rest in a small private cemetery in rural Virginia, close to his childhood home. They only knew him as a war hero, husband, and father. Wallace *had* fought for and won one thing—sparing them the truth of his arrest and other activities. Yes, that would have come out in a trial, but now, they could be shielded from that embarrassment and shame.

The same might not happen for him. Who would fight for him?

"Ellie, he was a great man, a true hero. I think I'll miss him almost as much as you." He offered an extended hug to the widow and shook hands with the children. As they departed, he said, "If I can do anything for you, please let me know." He meant that. He also hoped he'd be around to honor that promise.

Wallace's driver opened his door for him as he neared his car.

"Sir, a call came through on your phone while you were graveside. I believe it went to your voicemail."

He acknowledged the information with a nod and climbed into his seat. "Thanks, Sam."

He closed the glass partition between the driver's seat and back compartment. Sam was as discreet as they came, but some things required total privacy. He retrieved his phone and checked for messages. The missed call had come from Karl.

However, another missed call showed up on his call log—Robert Jennings. He decided to make that call first.

"Robert, sorry I missed your call. I've been to a funeral. How can I help you?"

"You already have, Wallace, you already have. In more ways than one. We rolled out three of our RCPADs at that lab in Wisconsin. So far, the deployment has gone well. You never told me what they did there or about adrenochrome. You've been holding out on me. I thought we were friends."

Wallace noted the distinct disdain in the man's voice. Acquaintances surely, but not friends. "Wasn't my decision to make. I don't control who knows or who gets it. How did you find out?"

"Well, that's one of the reasons I called. I know that you're aware of Gregory Compton's death and the incident that disabled Sean Harrington. I've been selected to fill one of those voids. Thank you for your vote of confidence."

Robert didn't have to spell it out. All of the directors were taking adrenochrome. Naturally, he would learn of it upon rising to the executive board. But what vote of confidence? Wallace couldn't recall ever mentioning Jennings as a possible board member, should a vacancy ever occur.

"Actually, it was your recommendation of my company and our robots that brought me to the board's attention. And on behalf of the board, I was asked to tell you that you'd be hearing from them soon, very soon."

That sounded more encouraging. Wallace smiled. His plan was moving along as hoped for, other than Buck's unexpected death. He could see himself and Jennings working more closely together, along with the others.

"Well, congratulations, Robert. That's quite commendable. They must like what they see in you, as well as the potential of your company. I know I did."

"Thank you, Wallace. And again, it won't be long for you."

The man signed off, but something in the way he said that last phrase struck Wallace as odd. Just what did he mean by that?

He put those thoughts aside and enjoyed the Virginia scenery as they moved along the interstate heading back to D.C. After a short time, he knew it was time to call Karl. If he and Gio had succeeded, Wallace held zero doubt about what the call from the board's chairman would be. He dialed, but a different voice answered.

"Karl?"

The voice seemed out of breath.

"No, sir, it's Gio." There was more panting. "Sir, it was like they knew we was coming. Karl got sniped before he could even . . ."

More panting. The man was running. *Running from what?* was the thought that ran through Wallace's brain.

"Gio, what's going on? Are you running from someone?"

"Sir . . .<pant>. . . I'm running <pant> for my—"

The man's voice went still. Dead air. A premonition for Wallace. He knew in that instant what Jennings had meant.

Less than a hundred yards further down the highway, small explosions rocked the car, and it began to swerve. Sam did a great job controlling the vehicle. As he did so, he yanked open the partition.

"Rear two tires just blew out, sir."

The driver tried to maneuver onto the shoulder, but having been in the middle lane, he couldn't get through the right lane before the rims of the wheels disintegrated, and the car came to rest on its rear axle. The last thing Wallace saw was the look of sheer terror on Sam's face in the rearview mirror. The last thing he heard was the squealing of air brakes preceding the grinding of metal on metal as an eighteen-wheeler drove into and through them at nearly full speed. The last thought he had was, *Clintoned*.

FORTY-THREE

"Are you nervous? I'm nervous," said Aric as they drove back to Camp Douglas.

Adam considered that question. Anxious? Excited? Apprehensive? Depressed? His emotions had run through the gamut. What would they find there? Might they really find Carolyn, finally? Would they get caught? What if Carolyn wasn't there? Had all of this time and expense boiled down to a waste of both?

He tried not to dwell on the latter thoughts because those led to thinking that she was dead and gone forever. He wasn't prepared to accept that possibility, and yet, that likelihood held the highest probability of all.

"I-I'm not sure how to answer that. I'm feeling a lot of different emotions today."

Aric stared at him. "Yeah, I guess I can understand that." He paused. "Look, I know that you're still not convinced that God's behind us, that whatever we accomplish today will be for something good, for His glory, but I am."

Adam nodded. "You've been pretty stoked up from reading that book. Maybe . . ."

He didn't know why he was about to say it, but his curiosity had been stirred up by his young brother's enthusiasm, confidence that Adam sure didn't possess. Aric had a boldness that Adam couldn't understand. A fearlessness. Even death was of no concern to him. Why was that?

"… maybe I'll borrow that book and read it, too."

"You'll find it challenging. It talks about morality and destiny and all sorts of things the world doesn't get, and most people, to be honest, don't *want* to understand it. The world no longer believes in absolute morals and truth. It's called postmodernism. Most people want *their* definition of morality and truth to be right, but in the end, it's God's definition that wins, so to speak. Not that there was ever really a competition."

Aric stopped but appeared to want to say more.

"Go on. I can tell you've got more on your mind."

"Your eternal destiny isn't determined by how good or bad you are, but solely on God's grace, the redemption He gives us through Christ. It's not 'all roads lead to heaven' like so many people teach today. That contradicts Christ's own words. He alone is the way, the truth, and the life. Only by accepting Jesus and repenting of our sins will we become part of God's eternal kingdom. And repentance doesn't mean becoming perfect. We all still fall far short of Christ's perfection. But it does mean trying our best to model our lives after Him, striving to become more like him."

Adam reflected on the last preacher he'd heard briefly on TV while channel surfing. Indeed, the man had used the phrase "all paths lead to God." He talked of a God who was all love and forgiving, that no matter what we did, He would accept us. What Aric just said contradicted all of that.

"But I've heard preachers say that God is love and accepts all of us."

Aric nodded. "God *is* love, but that concept is one of the most widely misconceived teachings about Him in today's church. The book talks of that, too. The Bible has twice as much to say about God's judgment and wrath as it does about His love. You see, God is also holy and sovereign, and those in sin cannot stand before Him. Every one of us deserves His judgment and wrath because we all sin in one way or another. As I said, it's only through Christ's redemption that those of us who follow Him are saved from that wrath."

Adam chewed on that as he drove. He noted that doing so seemed to calm his emotions. At the least, thinking about Aric's comments kept the other thoughts out of his mind.

A short while later, they exited the interstate, drove the winding road into the farmland southeast of the town, and found the same farm lane. As before, the chain proved not to be a real barrier. Minutes later, they arrived at the now-frozen pond and unloaded the drone and other equipment.

"Well, it seemed to work okay with our tests yesterday. So, it's now or never."

Aric gave him a thumb up. "It's gonna work. Have faith."

Faith was something Adam sorely needed, and not just at that moment. At least Adam was honest enough with himself to admit that.

The drone lifted off into the air and soared over the trees. The video scanner's extra weight did not seem to hinder its flight, although Adam had determined he would need to be more conservative concerning its battery limits. He planned to land it on the roof of the building and power the drone down. The scanner and phone had their own batteries and would last all afternoon without concern. He hoped that their task would not require that long.

Once the drone sat in place, they returned to the vehicle for warmth. Adam's modifications allowed him to use the phone to communicate with the scanner to perform essential operations. Within minutes they hit the jackpot.

"Wow. It's working. Look at those images."

Adam smiled for the first time that week. "Are you kidding me? It's working much better than we expected. Not only are the robots linked via their Wi-Fi network, so are all of their other security cameras."

With minor adjustments to frequencies, he ran through a series of camera feeds showing the front and back entries, laboratories and a hallway connecting them, and outdoor video links. As he found a productive frequency, he noted it and what part of the facility the camera appeared to cover. He found the correct frequencies for the robots outside. From those, he calculated that of the third. He concluded that its lack of images was due to the camera being off while the unit recharged.

"What about the lower level?"

Adam frowned. Either the level had no cameras, or they were connected differently, perhaps by cable. He continued to scan until he had worked through the spectrum of possibilities.

"Nothing. I can't find anything on a lower level."

Aric shook his head. "That means one of two things. Either there's nothing there they feel requires cameras for security, or there's something there they *really* don't want someone accidentally discovering."

Adam grunted. His brother was right, although how would someone uncover such video "by accident?" His money lay on a separate system, one they could hide from outside inspectors. As a lab, they undoubtedly had such visits from governmental regulators who would expect a security system.

He returned to the frequency of the first robot. It appeared to be on the far side of the building. What he wanted to do was catch the third unit when it powered up.

"Hey, go back to the feed that covered the rear door, the one on the lower level. That'll let us see when one of those robot things is heading inside for recharging."

Of course. Thank you, little brother, Adam thought. That change in their tactic was rewarded just ten minutes later as the red robot moved toward the lower entry. Adam switched to that unit's video feed, and they watched as the door lifted and the robot entered.

"Good Lord, help us," cried Aric.

Tears welled up in Adam's eyes. He almost forgot to begin recording. Cage after cage held a child, sometimes two. They looked well-nourished but listless. Hopelessness and despair covered their faces. As the robot turned into its charging station, Adam switched to the frequency he had calculated for the third sentry. After a minor tweak, that camera's view came across the phone's screen. There, straight ahead, was a cage with a small girl. Her dispassionate gaze followed the mechanical beast as it moved toward her and then turned toward the outer door.

Frantic, Adam rummaged through his coat pocket and pulled out a sheet of paper. He held it up for Aric to see.

Tears to match his brother's began to flow down his cheeks. "Thank you, Lord," he whispered.

Adam could only nod. The girl in the cage was as close

a match as he could imagine to the computer-generated, age-accelerated image of Carolyn on the paper.

FORTY-FOUR

Tensions ran high among the "troops" gathered on the northeast side of I-94 at Volk Field, the Wisconsin Air National Guard base, across from Camp Douglas. Adam and Aric stood with Lynch Cully nearby, watching the preparations. Even then, no one was allowed to speak of the raid's target out of concern that the team was being electronically eavesdropped on. The collection of over two dozen FBI agents and US Marshals, plus child welfare experts, spoke to the serious nature of the endeavor.

"Why are we doing this today, Lynch?" asked Aric. "Tomorrow's election day."

"That's precisely why. People's attention is on the election, and we hope the same is true of the people working here. We don't want anything to spook them."

"But don't we *want* attention drawn to this? According to that data dump in Germany, there are a dozen or more such centers in California alone. If we're going to close them down, too, we need as much heat on them as possible, don't we?"

Lynch shrugged. "You have a point, but manpower and time to coordinate efforts are required. If you want the agencies to run coordinated raids on several centers at once, we're looking at a month or longer from now. Do you want to wait that long?"

Aric watched Adam shake his head with vigor. Carolyn was in that building and needed rescuing, now not later. Waiting longer was not an option. Both were grateful that Lynch had convinced the President to authorize this operation on short notice. A presidential order had been required to get the federal agencies involved to act as quickly as they did. Lynch had said earlier that four days probably won the award for the fastest federally coordinated police action in the history of the country.

Four cars from the local sheriff and state police joined them, and after a quick consultation, the team leader signaled that it was time to move. The men and women of the task force climbed into their vehicles and began to move ahead. Aric felt a cold sweat of apprehension join the tachycardia of anticipation as they walked toward Lynch's car.

"Remember, stick with me. We are *not* part of this crew. We're to stand apart and observe only. And, Adam, this is important. You are *not* to approach the young girl without the approval of the child welfare team. Got that? If not, we'll be forced to leave the scene."

Adam nodded and climbed into the passenger seat of Lynch's car. Aric claimed the backseat. He watched Adam tapping his finger again. His brother might acknowledge the no-contact rule, but Aric knew he didn't like it. Adam had already expressed his reservations about Carolyn's acceptance of him, of what used to be his family.

Lynch turned toward Adam. "By the way, you both clean up nicely. I didn't recognize either of you at first."

"Uh, thanks. I doubt Carolyn will recognize me after

almost four years, but for sure she wouldn't if I still had the long hair and beard."

Aric had been the one to suggest they both get haircuts and shave. News of Wallace Chamberlain's accidental death on an interstate in Virginia had reached them two days earlier. With both Buckner and Chamberlain dead, they felt cleared and confident to come out of hiding. That included a tearful, yet excited, phone call to their parents. With Thanksgiving just a few weeks away, plans for a grand family gathering began to take shape come lockdowns or high water.

Aric recognized the homes and farms along Camp Hill Road, but their path would not take them past the farm lane entrance. Instead, they turned in the opposite direction onto Schucht Road to pick up Justice Road from the south. Eight minutes later, the caravan sped up the lab's private drive and breached its tall gate to rush into the parking lot. No robots appeared to be in the parking lot, which meant they were on patrol along the service drive. The second and third cars took up positions blocking that road on each side of the building, effectively keeping the robots at bay.

Agents poured out of the cars and rushed toward the building. A lone, armed guard emerged from the front doors, took one look at the invading force, laid down his weapon, and knelt with his fingers interlaced on top of his head. The officers quickly entered the building and secured it. Soon, a parade of employees, many in white coats, their wrists cuffed behind their backs, shuffled out the front doors under armed escort.

Aric wanted to record the event but had been warned off. At the first sign of his cell phone coming out, it would be confiscated. Earlier, Adam had mentioned that he, too, wanted to record the event. Both wished they had left the drone in position on the roof with the scanner cycling through the frequencies they had captured. Now, as Aric reflected on that conversation, he wondered where the drone was. He hadn't seen it in Adam's car that morning.

Another half an hour passed before teary-eyed child welfare workers began to leave the building with children in tow. Aric had seen virtually what they now saw in person. He understood the tears. Anger would soon follow. For him, he had felt a wave of righteous outrage over the inhumanity he had witnessed.

The twelfth child to see freedom was Carolyn being carried by an agent, wrapped in a blanket. Adam pointed as soon as he saw her.

"That's her, Lynch."

He showed the computer printout to him. Lynch looked at the paper and back at the girl. He offered a subtle shrug that said, "Maybe."

"Stay here." Lynch walked up to the team leader, and the two spoke for a moment. The commander waved the head social welfare worker over, and the three talked. Then Lynch waved for Adam to join them. Aric followed, hoping he wouldn't be shooed away.

"We're going to let you approach the girl, but you're not to touch her. You can say hi, mention her name, maybe introduce your brother as her uncle. We want to see if there is any sign of recognition at all. But, again, no physical contact, and the authorities will require DNA confirmation of your paternity before any further contact."

Both young men nodded. Lynch led the way to the

worker watching over the girl. The worker looked to her boss, who nodded approval.

"Hi, Carolyn. Do . . ." Adam's voice cracked with emotion. "Do you remember me? This is Aric, Uncle Aric." He pointed to Aric. "Do we look familiar?"

The girl's blank stare caused Aric's heart to sink. He could only imagine how his brother felt at that moment.

FORTY-FIVE

The authorities in Wisconsin had made things quite clear. The children retrieved from the detention center were severely damaged emotionally, not to mention developmentally delayed. Many of the younger ones had not yet learned to talk. A few were barely potty-trained. Even after confirming parental rights through genetic testing, it might take months before the children could move to family settings.

Lynch had convinced Adam that sticking around would serve no purpose and that he'd have no access to his daughter for some time, even if their relationship would be confirmed. Lynch promised to stay on top of things and to keep Adam informed. He also vowed to expedite the DNA testing, using his contacts within the forensics community to do so. The FBI labs could take months to do the same thing.

At Aric's insistence, they left before dawn and drove home to St. Louis, surprising their parents and sisters. Their mom screamed in joy at seeing them at the door. Aric half expected a verbal lashing from his dad and knew he deserved one, but it never came.

His dad did, however, take him aside a bit later.

"You should know that Dan came over in early June. He

explained what happened and that he was pretty sure you had connected with Adam. I'm still not sure how and why all that transpired, but I've always had faith in your abilities and intellect."

Aric debated how much to tell them. Still, they deserved to know, even if not all of the gory details were given.

"Dad, Adam was in trouble. His old boss was as corrupt and evil as they come, and Adam stumbled upon what he was doing. He was targeted by the man and his henchmen. He needed someone he could fully trust to help."

His father nodded and smiled. "Well, I'm glad that someone was you."

He put his arm around his son's shoulders and squeezed. Aric smiled at his dad's standard version of a manly hug.

"Both men are now dead, so we think we're safe." He hesitated to say anything further but went on. "But there's more to it, Dad. Adam found out about his boss because he was using a powerful computer program he helped design to find Carolyn. Please don't say anything to Mom, but we might have found her. DNA tests are pending. I don't want to get Mom's hopes up, and the tests come back negative."

His dad nodded, but Aric noted tears in his father's eyes. Aric couldn't remember the last time he'd seen his dad cry, if at all. The man sniffed and quickly wiped his eyes as he whispered, "We can only pray."

After a hastily prepared lunch, Aric came up to his folks. "Have you already voted?"

They nodded. "We have," replied his mom.

"Well, I haven't, and it's my first big election. Can I borrow a car?" His dad reached into his pocket and pulled out his keys. Aric took them and said, "Thanks. Oh, and I think I need to stop by and see Dan. If that's okay?"

"Sure thing. Tell him 'hi' from us."

At his designated precinct, Aric stood, masked and not quite six feet apart, for over an hour before being allowed inside to vote. A sense of pride filled him as he completed and entered his ballot for President Graham. And yet, a sense of dismay also encompassed him. The Lord's words that Sidon would steal the election had not been lost on him.

Aric had no idea how that would come to be but knew that the next few weeks were going to be "interesting," as Lynch had told him. Aric had shared his prophetic word with Lynch and the colonel because he knew they were friends with the President, and he felt they needed to be prepared. They had been skeptical, as Aric had anticipated. Yes, the next few weeks would be "interesting" . . . and challenging.

On his way home, Aric stopped at the Lewis home. Mrs. Lewis opened the door and grinned at seeing him. "Well, well, well, the prodigal son returns. I think he's upstairs."

She moved to the base of the stairs and yelled up to the second floor. "Dan, Aric's here!"

"Woohoo! Send him up!"

She nodded her head up the stairs. "You know the way. Glad you're back. He's missed you."

Aric was halfway up the steps when she said, "Thank you, Aric. I don't know what you did, but he's going to church with me now."

Aric hadn't made it three steps down the hall when Dan came rushing from his room and squeezed him with a brotherly hug. Aric felt a bit awkward, not from the hug but from feeling unworthy of the friendship. He had, after all, drugged his friend and left him amid the Antifa rabble.

Dan dumped the stuff occupying his chair onto the floor and offered it to Aric. He then sat on the bed.

"Man, I am so glad to see you. I figured you hooked up with your brother, but then, when weeks went by, I started to really worry."

Aric hesitated but said, "Dan, I need to apologize to you."

Dan shook his head. "No way, man. You needed to do what you needed to do. Pete was sitting on you like a, like a . . . uh, I don't know. I can't think of the right analogy. Anyway, what you did was brilliant. Like, I wish I'd thought of it."

"But I drugged you and left you there to fend for yourself."

"And it got you free. You gotta know, we woke later with that mad dude pounding on the door. Pete wasn't even aware you'd skipped until he looked around and you weren't in the room. Oh man, was that dude angry. Pete and his gang were instantly cut off. No funds for the rooms, no free food, nothing. Not even gas money for the trip back to Denver. I had my car back and kinda meandered my way home. Got to see some of the sights we had hoped to see together, but most of it was still closed, thanks to this stupid virus thing. I gotta say, there's truth in that old saying about having a story to tell your grandkids. This one was a doozy."

Aric felt relief that his friend held no grudge. "Well, that angry dude, as you call him, is dead now, along with his boss. So, Adam's in the clear."

"No way, man. Tell me everything."

Aric proceeded to give his friend a detailed account of

their escapades, beginning with watching naked women on closed-circuit video. Well, that's where he wanted to start, knowing Dan's sometimes prurient interests. But his mom had mentioned his return to church, so he withheld those details. He didn't want to contribute to any backsliding.

FORTY-SIX

When Aric had told him months earlier that God had warned him about events to come and that the sign validating that message was that "Po" Sidon would steal the election, Adam let it go in one ear and out the other. It was crazy Christian stuff at the time. However, their discussions and Aric's unwavering faith had taken effect on him. Maybe not so crazy after all.

Now, eight days after the election, lawsuits were flying, politicians were falling on their political swords, the media was more propagandist than ever, and the country was divided like never before. Adam had always considered himself middle-of-the-road when it came to politics. The movement to disown President Graham and everything he had done to rebuild the country amazed Adam. A conservative friend had once told him that he'd left the Republican Party long ago because it was little different from the Democrats. He called them two cheeks on the same global arse.

Nowhere was that more evident than in the way many in the Republican Party now disowned an independent president's conservative accomplishments—accomplishments they once embraced when they served their purpose. People whose eyes had been opened by the corruption and fraud so evident in the past week's events—whether Republican or Democrat—were eager to find a new political home. President Graham's American Party began to swell in numbers.

And yet, none of that hit Adam with the impact of Aric's prophetic word. Unless the courts intervened, which they hadn't so far, that word was coming true. Part of Adam realized that the courts *wouldn't* take a stand and that Sidon would successfully steal the election because God actually *was* involved in this whole thing.

Adam reflected on this as he drove back to Wisconsin. Aric had insisted on joining him to offer moral support but was currently asleep in the passenger seat.

Lynch had called to inform him that the DNA test results were due back soon. They were to be provided to the FBI, which had taken the lead in this case. This was not news that Adam wanted to be delivered via phone, so Lynch agreed to meet him at the agency's offices in Madison's northwest corner when they became available. Adam had booked a motel room next to those offices so he could be available on short notice.

He noticed Aric waking up with a stretch of his arms. "Are we there yet?" He laughed.

"Rockford's just ahead, so maybe an hour and a half to go. Hungry?"

"Yeah, but I can wait that long. We should get there in case they call."

The drive took about 15 minutes longer than he'd estimated, but they had arrived, checked in, and were now sitting down in a barbecue joint next door to the FBI offices. Both were hungry, and few words were spoken. About halfway through his pulled pork sandwich, Adam's phone rang.

"Hey, Lynch. We're here."

"That's great. I'm about an hour out. Special-Agent-in-Charge Wiese called this morning to say the results were in. That's sooner than I expected."

"Me, too, but I'm ready. Like I said, we're literally next door to the building."

"I'll call them, set up a time, and get back with you. Don't rush eating."

That's exactly what Adam felt like doing. He forced himself to slow down and enjoy the food, even if it lacked something. What was it about barbecue places in the north? He had yet to find an eatery north of the 40th parallel that had the knack for making good southern Q. He made a mental note to head to Pappy's or Sugarfire, or both, upon returning to St. Louis.

A few minutes later, Lynch called back to tell them he would be in the lobby at three p.m. Adam checked his phone for the current time.

"So, what are we going to do for the next 80 minutes?" asked Aric.

Good question, thought Adam. He did whatever he could to fill up the time and take his mind off what might be coming. Finishing lunch and gassing up the car chopped about twenty minutes off. They returned to the motel, where Adam took a shower and cleaned up. He wanted to look good should they be allowed to see Carolyn. He tried to fill the rest of the void by watching Newsmax on his phone, but he couldn't focus on anything other than meeting his daughter.

At three p.m., they met Lynch in the lobby, and by three-ten, they sat in a conference room waiting for a Special-Agent-in-Charge Chip Wiese. Several minutes passed before the agent's secretary stepped in and offered everyone a drink. She had no takers. For one, Adam already felt his bladder calling between his sweet tea at lunch and the anticipation of this meeting.

After a few more minutes, the agent entered the room, and introductions were made.

"Lynch, I don't know if you remember me. We were on a drug task force together in St. Louis, maybe sixteen years ago. That was before I got promoted and transferred here."

Lynch scrutinized the man's face. "You do look familiar, but I apologize for not recalling details. We have a newborn, and I'm so sleep-deprived I might not even recognize my own mother."

They all chuckled.

"So, Agent Wiese, what are you allowed to tell us about this operation?"

The man shrugged. "Not much, I'm afraid. You understand the drill. Since you all already know about that data dump in Germany, I can affirm that this is related. We arrested 21 individuals on a variety of charges, but that's about all I can say."

"And the children?" asked Adam.

The agent looked at him, and sadness consumed the man's face as he shook his head. "Worst thing I've seen in my career. I have an ER doctor friend who has told me more than once that there are cases he wishes he could forget. Now I understand. I can't share how many kids we rescued, but they ranged in age from four to thirteen. I can't share anything more, but you saw the conditions inside, so . . ."

Adam took a deep breath. How do you go about forgetting something like that? How would someone ever forgive something like that? He had an inkling of what God must feel like as He watched mankind destroy itself. And yet, as Aric kept driving home, He *did* provide redemption to those willing to accept it.

"And that brings us to why you're here," said Agent Wiese. "Lynch, once again, I thank you for helping to expedite this. Our labs are so backed up, it could take months, not weeks, to get an answer." He turned his attention to Adam. The look on his face preceded his words. "Mr. Afton, I'm not sure just how to phrase it. Under the circumstances, this is probably a good thing, but that little girl is *not* your daughter. There is no genetic match. I'm sorry you drove so far just to get this news."

Adam sank back into the chair. Not Carolyn? He had been so sure. Aric seemed so confident that they'd find her, and he sure appeared to be tuned into God. Wasn't he?

He blinked back the tears that fought their way to the surface. Yes, maybe it was a good thing that the girl wasn't his. Yet, at the same time, he didn't want to accept that Carolyn was gone for good.

"Uh, thank you, Agent Wiese. Is there, uh, is there a restroom close by?" He didn't know if it was just his bladder or if he was about to vomit, but he needed a bathroom quickly.

"Outside this office, take the hall to the left, and it's on the left."

Adam jumped up and rushed from the conference room.

Aric and Lynch stood as Adam left the room. The agent followed suit. He and Lynch made small talk while Aric stepped into the hallway. Another agent stood outside the bathroom, apparently to escort Adam back to the office when done. They had been told they needed an escort at all times within the offices. Aric waved at the agent, who simply nodded back.

Just before the doors to the restrooms, Aric found a water cooler next to a drinking fountain. That seemed redundant until he realized the fountains were turned off due to COVID-19. He stopped and grabbed a small cup to take a drink, and as he did so, another office door opened. A female agent led a handcuffed woman from the office and toward the elevators while another woman led a young girl behind them. Aric recognized that woman as one of the child welfare officers he had seen at the center. He could not see the girl's face.

At that instant, the girl broke free from the woman and ran up to Aric.

She poked him in the belly. "Hey, mister, do I know you?"

The woman rushed up and took the girl's hand to direct her along their original path. "Sorry about that."

Aric stood there, stunned. The girl appeared to be a closer match to Adam's printout than the girl who had been rescued. He ran back to the conference room, which Lynch and Agent Wiese were now exiting.

He pointed to the elevators. "Lynch, Lynch, that's her. That's Carolyn."

At that point, the elevator doors closed behind the

women and the girl.

Adam exited the restroom to find the younger agent who had escorted them to the conference room waiting for him. He had indeed relieved both bladder and gut and felt better, physically at least. Why had he let his hopes get up? He should have known better. Carolyn was gone.

After a quick drink from the nearby cooler, he glanced up and saw an animated Aric talking with Lynch. Aric kept pointing to the elevators. Special Agent-in-Charge Wiese was nowhere to be seen. As he approached, Lynch said something to Aric, and his brother quieted down in an instant.

"What's up?" Adam asked.

"Oh, nothing really," replied Lynch. "Look, I, uh, I have something else to discuss with Agent Wiese. Why don't you let your escort take you down to the lobby, and I'll meet you there in, say, ten minutes."

The escort started to protest when Lynch held up credentials for Homeland Security.

"I'll be fine, Agent James. I don't require an escort here, and I'll be in your SAC's office if anyone comes looking for me."

"Yes, sir."

Adam felt a moment of confusion. Hadn't Lynch told them he was no longer an officer of the law when he'd said he'd overlook his hacking infractions? Yet, he had just flashed the credentials of a law enforcement officer. Then Adam recalled that Lynch had phrased his statement as not being on active duty or the federal payroll. What? How? He decided not to ask and rock the boat, but he gave Lynch a look. Who was this guy?

He and Aric followed the agent back to the lobby and waited. True to his word, Lynch appeared about ten minutes later.

Aric had been acting antsy the whole time they waited and finally said, "Look, Adam, I don't want to get your—"

Adam interrupted. "Lynch, I want to thank you for all you've done, but at this point, I've had enough. I give up. I don't think I can do this anymore. Carolyn's gone, and I need to come to terms with that."

Aric raised his brow. "Adam, I think you need to—"

"C'mon, Aric. I just want to get out of here. What I really want is a stiff drink, but that almost killed me once. Lynch, again, thank you."

With that, he turned and marched out the door. Outside, he turned south toward the motel, which was but three blocks away. Aric could find his way there on his own.

FORTY-SEVEN

Two weeks had passed since that day in the FBI offices when Adam had learned the young girl was not his daughter. Aric had taken Lynch's advice not to push anything. To raise Adam's expectations yet again and then see that hope dashed would be more damaging than to let him deal with the loss he had already half anticipated.

Aric watched as his mother and sisters started preparations for their large, "forbidden" family gathering on Thanksgiving, just two days away. He, for one, could barely wait for the day. The year had been such a strange—and in many ways bad—one for so many people that social media saw lots of people commenting on how the holidays would not be the same. All Aric could think was, *they believe their year was strange. They should've walked in my shoes.*

He stood on the sidewalk about two blocks from home, watching the family's dog, Rufus, do his business when his cell rang. CallerID revealed that it was Lynch.

"Hey, Lynch."

"Hi, Aric. Are you alone?"

"Umm, yeah, unless you count Rufus, our dog. I'm taking him on a walk."

"You and Adam need to get back up here ASAP."

Aric's eyes widened, and his spirit launched into the

stratosphere. "It's her?" He could see no other reason for Lynch to say that.

"Yes! It's Carolyn! The DNA proves it, and she even remembers the name."

Aric started to dance on the sidewalk until he saw a neighbor give him a strange look.

"One of the men arrested, their chief scientist, and his wife were unable to have children. After Carolyn was kidnapped, he saw her arrive at the detention center where he worked at the time. He was smitten by her and took her to be theirs. The wife had no idea what he was involved in or where the girl came from but admitted that there was no formal adoption and that she had suspected the girl was stolen. But she was so happy to have a child, she refused to confront her husband about the truth."

Aric began to dance again. This time Rufus joined in.

"And the best news. Carolyn, she's called Grace now, is in excellent health, is emotionally well-developed, and is beyond the expected milestones for a five-year-old. With the DNA confirmation, the child welfare folks are willing to release her to her father, to Adam, if . . . I repeat, *if* she appears willing to go."

Aric wanted to shout praises to God but hesitated because of the neighbors. And then he gave in and began shouting, "Hallelujah! Thank you, Father! Thank you, Jesus! Thank you, Holy Spirit! Praise God!"

He heard Lynch laughing on the other end and then, "Amen to that!"

An idea came to Aric. It seemed devious at first, but the more he contemplated it, the more he liked it. Yet, if he was somehow able to convince Adam he was telling the truth, they likely wouldn't arrive in Wisconsin. Adam would be so anxious, he'd run off the road.

"Lynch, if I tell Adam now, he won't believe me. I've been watching him mope around the house for the past two weeks. He needs to hear it straight from the child welfare folks and, well, from Carolyn. To be honest, I want to call her Grace, too. What a wonderful name." He proceeded to plot his scheme with Lynch.

As he arrived home, it took all he had not to spill the beans, but this would be a Thanksgiving for the books all right. He slipped into his room and went to his knees in a prayer of thanksgiving. As he later prepared for dinner, Adam approached him.

"Hey, look, I know it's right before Thanksgiving, but I got a call from Special Agent-in-Charge Wiese. They need us back in Madison, like, tomorrow. Something's come up with the admissibility of the video we sent them, and it needs to be cleared up right away, before the long holiday weekend."

Aric wanted to roll his eyes. Lynch was playing this to the hilt, but at least it sounded convincing enough to get Adam there.

"Yeah, I got the same call ten minutes ago. I'll be ready to go whenever you want to leave."

"Super early if that's okay. Then, with some luck, we can drive back tomorrow afternoon and not miss Thanksgiving. It'll be a long day."

"For sure. But Mom will shoot us both if we're not back in time."

Adam nodded and turned to head into the kitchen. As soon as Adam could no longer see him, Aric pumped his fist once in the air as he whispered, "Yes!"

FORTY-EIGHT

The drive north was a quiet one. Aric realized they'd made this trip weekly for the past three weeks. The car should have the route on autopilot by now. Adam seemed complacent, more so than Aric expected. The trip was something that needed to be done, so they were doing it. That's all. For Aric, he could barely contain himself. He knew that within hours, Christmas would arrive before Thanksgiving, and not just via store displays. The trip home would be like riding on Santa's sleigh with the reindeer on ultra-potency steroids, bearing an incredible gift to the family. He fully expected to be doing the driving. Adam would not be up to it.

Having left the house at o-dark-thirty, they arrived in Madison by mid-morning. Aric had provided Lynch with updates on their trip via text, so as they entered the FBI office lobby, Lynch was waiting.

"Lynch, I didn't expect you to be here."

"Yeah, well, I needed to be here for this one."

Lynch was not alone, however. Amy had joined him, along with Josh. The brothers had not yet met the Cully's infant son, as he had slept through their entire visit a month earlier. Amy extended hugs to both of them as they greeted her. To Aric, she also offered a wink of an eye. He forced himself not to grin.

The group was led immediately to the SAC's conference room. It looked no different than before, and yet, Aric sensed a difference in the atmosphere.

Special-Agent-in-Charge Wiese entered the room. "Thanks for coming on short notice. I think this is going to be a different kind of meeting than we're accustomed to here."

With that, two agents approached the door, one carrying a small cake with a sole candle on it. Behind them, Aric spotted the caseworker he had seen before, along with Carolyn, now Grace. The four entered the room.

"Mr. Afton, let me introduce you to your daughter. She's known as Grace now. Grace, like we talked about, this is your real daddy."

The little girl walked directly to Adam and wrapped her arms around his legs. Adam began to shake, and tears welled up in his eyes, which he wanted to wipe away. Instead, his arms reached down to his daughter as he knelt and engulfed her in them. Aric was gratified when she did not pull away. It was a good sign.

Grace got to blow out the candle, and cake was served to all in the room. Grace devoured hers.

"Mmmmmm, that was good. Can I have more?"

How could anyone say no? She finished another piece as Adam just sat and stared at her. Aric wondered what was going through his mind at that moment.

For Adam, the drive to Madison was nothing more than a task he needed to do. The trip was quieter than expected.

Usually, Aric wanted to talk unless he had a book to read. This time he seemed to spend half the trip texting someone. He suspected it was Dan. They had spent a lot of time together chasing girls, seeing old friends, chasing girls, playing basketball, and chasing girls.

Upon arrival, Adam was surprised to find Lynch and Amy, and their son, waiting in the lobby. He had been under the impression that he and Aric were needed to clarify their testimonies. Why was Lynch here? That was the first indication he should have suspected something else was going on, but it breezed right over him.

Not until he saw two agents, a cake, and a child welfare caseworker did he begin to wonder. He hadn't seen the little girl at first. And then he did.

Agent Wiese's words skipped right past him. He knew from that first glance that they had found Carolyn. He had no words. His body trembled from the emotions within, and tears began to flow. And when he knelt and felt her hug, he thought he heard angels singing.

Watching her eat cake was amazing. Listening to her talk was awesome. Seeing her smile enchanted him. She had once had him wrapped around her little finger. Now she was wrapped around his heart in a way he had never known. He never wanted to let her go again. Of course, that wouldn't go over well once she reached her teen years, but . . .

He felt a tap on his shoulder. He looked up to see Aric.

"Look at the time."

Adam didn't want to see the time. He didn't want to leave his daughter.

The caseworker leaned down next to Grace and asked, "Grace, your father would like to take you home, but if you're not ready to do that, we understand. We can work up to that if you like."

"Do I have to see my other daddy?"

Agent Wiese answered that one. "No."

She gave a defiant look and said, "Good. He took me from a bad place, but he still worked in a bad place. Sometimes I got scared he would take me back there."

All of the agents looked at each other.

And then, with an innocence he didn't expect, she looked at the woman and asked, "Does Uncle Aric get to come, too?"

The woman looked at Aric, who appeared to have melted in delight, and replied, "Of course he does."

"Okay, I'm ready. Let's go home."

She stated the words as if all was settled, no more questions. She hopped down to the floor, grabbed Adam's hand, and pulled him toward the door.

Lynch said, "Guess that's settled."

Adam followed his gaze to the caseworker, who nodded. "Yes, it is."

Aric did take the driver's seat for the ride home. The agency had provided them with the appropriate car seat and assisted Adam with its installation. Despite his incredible intellect, he seemed clumsy and unfocused when attempting to place it in the car. Aric knew where his mind was.

He didn't mind acting as the chauffeur either. His brother had insisted on riding in the back with Grace. Aric's only request was that he be included in the conversation. Soon, he, too, knew her favorite color, the best toy she'd ever had, what food she liked and what she didn't. They discovered that she was already reading at what, to Aric, seemed to be a first-grade reading level.

And much to their delight, she was equally fluent in French and English. In turn, she expressed her surprise when she first spoke in French to them, and they answered her. Aric found his niece to be an awesome kid. Quietly, he thanked God for the couple's having cared so well for her, even if keeping her as their own was wrong.

They sang songs. They joked. Adam made funny faces and had her giggling. Anyone who wasn't aware of their story would think they were a family who had never been apart. God's grace had extended to Grace.

Finally, she fell asleep.

Aric looked at Adam through the rearview mirror. "I told you we'd find her. God did not let us down." Adam closed his eyes, but his lips moved slightly. Was he praying? Aric hoped so.

When his brother reopened his eyes, Adam looked at Aric and scooted forward in his seat. "Why do I have a feeling you had a role in today's events?"

Aric grinned. "Whatever would make you think that?" He laughed and then gave his brother the whole story, from how he saw Grace for the first time to how he conspired with Lynch to surprise him. They had withheld the information out of concern for him because Grace's return to him was contingent first on DNA confirmation and then on her agreeing to go.

When he finished the story, he said, "I think it's time to let our family know they need to set another place at tomorrow's table and provide another bed for tonight."

Adam smiled and nodded. He retrieved his phone and made the call, placing it on speaker so Aric could hear as well.

"Dad, hey, we're on our way home. We just passed Normal and Bloomington, so we're about two and a half hours away. Is Mom there? Put me on speaker."

"Hi. We're both here. How'd your day go?"

"Incredible. Mom, you need to get another bed ready for tonight and set another seat for dinner tomorrow. We're bringing someone else home with us?"

"Oh?" He could hear the questions in her voice. She would be frantic to make a good impression on a guest.

"Yeah, I think you'll like her. She's incredible. That's why our day was incredible. Mom, Dad, prepare to be reintroduced to your granddaughter. She goes by the name of Grace now."

Silence filled the air until the unmistakable sound of breaking glass was heard. Then their mom shrieked.

"You found her? Carolyn? I mean, Grace. Are you sure?" They could hear the excitement in their mother's voice.

Their father's voice came next. "Sit down, dear, before you fall and hurt yourself. She dropped the bowl she was holding before she started a wild jig. Son, you have no idea how happy we are."

Aric thought, *Oh, we know. We know.*

They talked a brief while longer before disconnecting. Adam sat back, and soon, he, too, fell asleep.

A short while later, they approached a rest stop, and Aric pulled off. He needed a short break and a quick walk outside to prevent his falling asleep at the wheel. As soon as he stopped, Grace awoke, which in turn caused Adam to awaken.

"I need to go potty."

A look of concern stretched across Adam's face. "Um, can you go potty by yourself? I, uh, can't go into the women's bathroom with you, but I can take you with me into the men's."

She shook her head and offered him a stern look. "Daddy, I can do it myself now. I'm five."

Adam shrugged, and they exited the car. It would pain him to let her out of his sight, but Aric knew that his brother would stand guard outside the door to the women's restroom.

In their absence, Aric knew he had one more task to perform. He grabbed his phone and dialed a number he hadn't used in years.

FORTY-NINE

The previous evening's reunion was a joyous one. Adam's mom had been beside herself in glee. She recruited Adam's sisters to go out and buy some clothes for Grace. She made a run to the grocery to buy more kid-friendly foods than Adam had seen in any one place. His sisters fought over whose room Grace could have, which he thought odd since only his youngest sister still called the place home.

Yet, despite the happiness of the situation, the morning seemed different. The television was void of Thanksgiving Day parades. Traditional college rivalry football games had been canceled, played early before empty stadiums, or delayed. The year 2020 still overshadowed the day, despite the extraordinary homecoming.

The mood seemed to normalize as their Thanksgiving feast appeared in the dining room. The family gathered as it always had, and each member of the family was expected to express what they were thankful for. Grace's return won hands down.

But when it came time for Aric to declare his thanks, he said, "Lord, thank you for giving Adam the perseverance to never give up looking for Grace and for helping him succeed."

A chorus of "amens" followed.

The food was delicious, as always. Everyone overate, as always. Their father followed his pumpkin pie with a nap. Again, as always. But unlike other Thanksgivings, their afternoon activities were interrupted by the ringing of the doorbell.

Aric yelled, "I'll get it!"

Adam was playing a board game with Grace and Mabel in the family room when he heard Aric call, "Adam, it's for you."

He arose, curious as to who would be calling on him at his parent's house on Thanksgiving Day. Grace rose to follow him. He almost told her to stay put but thought, why not? Adam liked that she wanted to be with him. He hoped she felt secure around him. As they turned the corner and faced the front door, he stopped. Grace stopped next to him and clung to his leg.

Aric closed the door behind their guests. He then stepped away and left the foyer.

There stood Rachel with tears running down her cheeks. Arthur stood next to her.

Adam knelt next to Grace and said, "Grace, that's your mom and brother. Why don't you go say 'hi.' "

Rachel knelt as well and opened her arms toward her daughter. The girl seemed hesitant at first but walked up to Rachel and allowed herself to be hugged. After a moment, she eagerly returned the hug. Rachel then used one arm to include Arthur in a group hug.

Adam stood. "I never stopped looking, Rachel. Never. And now she's back. And I'm back, clean and sober."

Rachel stood and took a tentative step toward him. Adam reciprocated hesitantly, taking only one step. She had, after all, left him and moved out, leaving him to wallow in guilt. The next moves were up to her, and those moves would determine their future. He knew what he wanted. Did she?

She then walked up to him and wrapped her arms around him. "Thank you. Thank you so much," she whispered in his ear as he surrounded her with his arms. Seconds later, both kids joined them.

Out of the corner of his eye, he saw Aric peering around the corner, grinning. He gave Adam a thumb up, to which Adam mouthed, "Thank you" before closing his eyes and taking in the goodness of family and the grace of God.

AFTERWORD

So, what's real and what isn't in this book? As should be clear, much within the story was inspired by actual events from 2020, such as the Portland riots. Yet, those of you who've read my previous books know that I spend a lot of time researching my books and incorporating real incidents, technology, and such into my stories. This book is no different.

But, let me digress for a moment. This series was inspired by two things. First, my research into the Bible's Book of Daniel and Christ's Olivet Discourse made me realize that the world isn't ready for the judgment of God that is coming. The Western *church* isn't even prepared. I wrote my book *Still Here! Surviving the End Times* as a study of those Biblical prophesies, hoping it would help prepare those who read it. It was titled *Still Here!* in counterpoint to the insanely popular *Left Behind Series* from the 1990s, which in my opinion, was based on errant theology that leaves people expecting to be raptured away before the "bad stuff" hits the fan. As I read the first few stories of that series (I quit on book four), I realized someone needed to write a better series based on John's apocalyptic visions (the Book of Revelation). At the time, I hadn't yet started writing, and I never would have envisioned that someday that task might fall on me.

The second inspiration came from comments on my books and writing by my editor. Pat has been in the business for a long time and has edited some very big names in literature. So, when he complimented me on my abilities, I was quite flattered. However, it was comments he made about Christian fiction that struck home the most. I have to agree with his assessment of Christian fiction in that most of it is bland, has stereotypical characters and formulaic plots, and is afraid to take on issues within our culture. He's read a lot of it over the years and called it mediocre at best. I agree. He also stated that he was a self-proclaimed agnostic who would love to see me tackle Christian apologetics in one or more of my books because he thought I could make it interesting. Wow. That was quite the challenge, and I decided to take him up on it.

So, where does one start when writing an apocalyptic series? It serves well to begin where we are, today, in the current time and culture. The visions of John show us things that have been occurring for the past two millennia—wars and rumors of war, famine, earthquakes, pestilence, etc.— and yet accelerate as the time for Christ's return draws near. Are we now seeing that acceleration? I believe so. For example, the number of strong earthquakes—those we now measure over 6.0 on the Richter Scale (1935)—has increased logarithmically over the past hundred years. [True, the seismograph wasn't developed until the 1920s, but folks have been recording earthquakes for much longer, and big ones were rare.]

The Bible says these End Times will come "like a thief in the night" for most people, who "have eyes but can't see and ears but can't hear." By starting at our current point in history, I can present a story that shows this taking place. The Bible also says that God's people, His church, will *not* be caught by surprise. I can show that, too.

The *Left Behind Series* started with the sudden

disappearance of millions of people in a fictional rapture—the removal of the church from the planet. The beginning of my series needed to be more real to life . . . and to the Bible. That required a suspense story that I could set in today's world. To be honest, at first, although I had certain goals for this book, I had no idea what the story would be to set the stage for this series.

And then God brought to my attention another injustice being perpetrated today—a corporation that kidnaps and detains kids to harvest a chemical from their blood thought to extend life. Yes, the data dump in Germany used in the story is real and even more disturbing than I felt I should portray in my book. Adrenochrome is real, also, although I found nothing in the medical literature to support the idea that it could somehow extend life, that it's expensive to produce, or that it must be harvested from blood. A web search on adrenochrome is interesting and will highlight the "conspiracy theories" surrounding it. And yet, the information in that data dump seems too credible to ignore. Perhaps there's something other than adrenochrome actually being harvested from children. Who knows? If the data dump is a hoax, someone spent a ton of time creating it. Those six PDF files will be made available through my website. If you're interested, you can decide for yourself. Either way, I think it made for a good premise for a suspense story.

Adam's computer software in the story is also real, although I gave it a different name. The military funded the creation of a major software program—ShadowNet—for use in its PsyOps (Psychological Operations) in the Middle East. It was used to create profiles on people and tribal groups in Afghanistan to help the U.S. sway public opinion and the elections against the Taliban. Despite being funded by us, the American taxpayers, the civilian contractors somehow retained their copyrights and ownership of the program. Today, it is being used in major PsyOps against various people, including, I suspect, us, the American public.

One such PsyOps today is the COVID pandemic, although I can't say that ShadowNet has been used here. Still, the so-called pandemic has all the hallmarks of a classic PsyOps program, primarily using fear to control a population. And I call it a "so-called" pandemic because the numbers being used to label it as such are built upon invalid testing and false positives. Yes, for some people, it can be a deadly disease. So can influenza, and COVID's real fatality rate is no different than that of influenza. The truth about COVID, its test and death numbers, fatality rate, and successful, inexpensive therapies for it are all being suppressed by the media and government—additional hallmarks of a PsyOps program. [If you want more on the need for masks and on testing, I have a PDF on my website titled "One Doctor's Take on Masks." It's a 60-page medical literature review on the use of masks and on COVID testing that I wrote in the summer of 2020 after reviewing over 120 medical studies.]

Today, the ShadowNet program, or whatever it's called today, can also track and find vehicles, locate people, and do all of the tasks you would see performed by the Kaleidoscope program used in the TV series, *NCIS: Los Angeles.* It's not as fictional as you would believe. In a recent online interview, that TV program's producer addressed the Kaleidoscope program and how they were asked not to reveal further details about the software on which it was based. The software owners did not want the public to ever consider what kind of surveillance possibilities existed, even if presented in a *fictional* TV program. Big Brother is alive and well.

Also, the RCPADs mentioned in the story . . . partially true, although not called by that name. Such robotic security and police units are under development, although I found nothing about their being deployed anywhere yet. At the height of the "Defund the Police" protests, there were rumors that the companies building these units were behind the protests. Sounds plausible, but I have no proof of such.

Finally, in the story, Aric receives a word from God about a significant upcoming earthquake, fulfilling the sixth seal judgment in Revelation. And the sign validating this word from God was that the ex-vice president would "steal the election." This word and its sign were given to a member of our church. Don't believe that God still speaks to us prophetically? If God is the same yesterday, today, and forever, why would He change now? In my book, *Still Here! Surviving the End Times*, I tell of a dream I had in December 2017 about an impending worldwide economic collapse, famine, and pestilence. We saw all three in 2020, although the famine aspects hit primarily eastern Africa, India, Southeast Asia, and China. God has spoken to me like this only rarely in the past, but so far, these words of knowledge, as the Bible calls them, have been 100% accurate. Whether this is a physical earthquake or a spiritual one, get ready.

If you're not familiar with the Book of Revelation, you might be wondering just what this sixth seal judgment is. In the books of Mathew and Mark, Jesus talks with his disciples about what's to come. This has become known as the Olivet Discourse. In the Book of Revelation, God's earliest judgments on mankind are called the Seven Seal Judgments, where Christ breaks open seven seals on a scroll, and each one launches a set of judgments on man—nations conquering nations, war and death, famine, and pestilence. The first four, which many are familiar with as the Four Horsemen of the Apocalypse, correlate well with what He described in the Olivet Discourse. Those things have been happening since the first century. Christ called them "birth pangs" of what would begin to take place after His resurrection. The fifth seal gives us a glimpse of the altar and temple of God in heaven.

However, the sixth seal describes a massive earthquake accompanied by the sun blackening and the moon turning the color of blood. The quake is powerful enough that mountains and islands are removed from their places. The response of mankind is also envisioned. You can only imagine the chaos and fear that will take place at this time.

There are many interpretations of these scriptures. Some believe the cataclysms described are purely symbolic and not to be taken literally. Some believe them to be future events. Some look to Revelation as holding clues to what might happen. Typically, those in the latter camp also believe in a literal Antichrist and search for a man who will play that role. The Bible never actually mentions such a global leader but speaks of a spirit of antichrist. I believe that humanism fulfills that description.

I also believe that we are in that future, what many call the End Times. The Bible talks about the "latter days," and those days began with the crucifixion and resurrection of

Christ. I'm also convinced that Revelation is a picture book, not a codebook with hidden meaning. As such, the picture I see in the sixth seal is one of a massive earthquake and great volcanic activity (which could surely result from such a quake). The spewing of ash into the atmosphere could certainly darken the sun and make the moon appear red. Are we working up to such a scenario?

As stated earlier, major earthquakes have been occurring with increasing frequency. The following graph shows the number of major quakes between 1900 and 2013:

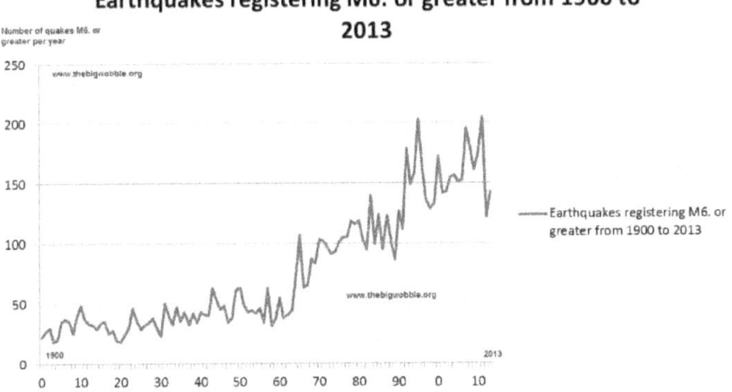

Since 2000, there have been 3,210 major quakes (those of M6 or greater), for an average of 157 major earthquakes per year. In 2020, there were 121 such quakes, the second lowest annual number since 2000. I'm writing this on March 21st, and as of yesterday, March 20, 2021, there have already been 43 major quakes, 15 of which have occurred just in the month of March so far. That's the second highest number of quakes ever recorded in the first 76 days of a year.

The agencies that track volcanic activity say that up to 20 volcanoes are active across the globe on a typical day. On January 15, 2021, 26 volcanoes along the Pacific Ring of Fire were active simultaneously. In the week of January 24th, there were 45 active volcanoes, and in the week of February 15th, 42 volcanoes were active. Warnings were issued to several areas that emergency evacuations might be imminent. On March 20, 2021, Iceland's Fagradalsfjall volcano on Reykjanes peninsula erupted after nearly 1,000 years of being dormant. Between February 24th and the eruption, over 20,000 minor earthquakes were recorded in that region alone. Are the "birth pangs" evolving into early labor?

I admit I could be wrong. Many theologians believe the visions of John in Revelation are purely spiritual and symbolic, not physical. I don't claim to sit in the Biblical "office" of a prophet, and I don't claim to be an expert on the Book of Revelation—although I'm spending a lot of time studying it right now. So, what if this earthquake is purely symbolic? What's it symbolic of and how would that play out physically on earth? Will it occur before the return of Christ or on the day of His return? Personally, I believe that if the world has been seeing physical manifestations of the first four judgments—with war, killing, famine, pestilence, inflation and the lack of peace—why shouldn't the sixth seal also be physical? Symbolic or physical (literal)—and it could be both—the church is still here going through it all with everyone else. That's the track I'm taking with this series.

So, prepare yourself. Examine yourself and your relationship with Christ. Don't get caught on the wrong side for eternity.

All in all, I hope you enjoyed the story and found aspects of it thought-provoking. Stay tuned for installment two.

ABOUT THE AUTHOR

Braxton can't lay claim to wanting to be a writer all his life, although his mother and seventh grade English teacher were convinced he had what it would take. A bachelor's degree in Bio-Medical Engineering led to medical school and a residency in Emergency Medicine. He served for a decade in the U.S. Army Medical Corps with tours such as the Chief, Emergency Medical Services at Fort Campbell, KY, and as a research Flight Surgeon at Fort Rucker, AL. Who had time to write?

By the 1990s, as a civilian, his professional and family life had settled down, somewhat, and his mother once again took up her mantra, "Write a book. You're a good writer." In 1997, a Valentine's Day writing contest convinced him that maybe he could write fiction. He spent the next fifteen years learning the craft of writing.

Now, twenty-plus years after that first hesitant start, he has sixteen novels published, as well as non-fiction books and a children's book, and can't find enough time to write. As a Christian, he writes "true-life" Christian fiction (suspense and thrillers) that many call "cutting edge," as he's not afraid to take on such issues as human trafficking, racism, and more. His characters are real-life as well, with all the flaws and blemishes real people have. As such, his books are never likely to gain acceptance by the Christian Bookseller Association. But then, he never intended to tell stories just to the choir.

Books by Braxton DeGarmo:

Still Here Series:

The End Begins – 1
The Shaking – 2
The Beasts – 3
The Trumpets – 4
The Mark - 5

Non-Fiction Study Guides:

Still Here! Surviving the End Times
Still Here! The Apocalypse is Now
Still Here! Countdown Revelation

MedAir Series:

Looks that Deceive – 1
Rescued and Remembered – 2
The Silenced Shooter – 3
Wrongfully Removed – 4
A Zealot's Destiny – 5
Kidnapped Nation - 6
The Khmer Connection - 7
Resurrected Trouble - 8

Seamus O'Connor Thrillers:

The Militant Genome
Ten Seconds 'Til

Other Books:

Indebted

Children's Books:

The Toucan Who Can Can-can

www.ingramcontent.com/pod-product-compliance
Lightning Source LLC
Chambersburg PA
CBHW070825190726
48292CB00006B/2115